Soul Mate

COPYRIGHT © 2010 Ronald Lewis Weaver

QuestFiction.com
RonaldLewisWeaver.com

All Rights Reserved.

Published by
QuestFiction Entertainment, LLC

ISBN: 978-0-615-35746-1

SOUL MATE
a novel by
Ronald Lewis Weaver

Not since *Bridges of Madison County* have I been so involved in someone else's very private life. For an even more impossible forbidden love you <u>must</u> read *Soul Mate*. You won't put it down.

—*Betty White*

Before I read *Soul Mate*, if you'd told me I'd be rooting for a relationship between a teacher and her student, I'd have said, "You're crazy." But these are great characters and a great story. Not only did I root for them, I was inspired by them. This novel engaged me as much as the four *Twilight* books I'd just finished. And the love scenes—Wow!

—*Katherine Kelly Lang*

Soul Mate turns upside down our usual beliefs about a romance between a teacher and a student. Great characters of depth and passion locked in a seemingly hopeless relationship facing impossible obstacles. Throw in an outrageous, teenage psychic to guide our hero through a maze of riddles, along with a puritanical principal who suspects the worst, and you have all the ingredients for a great story that compels you to keep the pages turning to a surprising ending.

—*Ronn Moss*

A journey of unforgettable intensity, woven with wisdom and passion that ignites the soul leaving it hot and sweet and more alive than humanly bearable. Don't read this book; devour it!

—*Lesley-Anne Down*

I've either seen or acted in a lot of romantic stories in my career and, believe me, *Soul Mate* is unique. Tender, erotic, mystical, globally conscious, with a sense of purpose, Ron Weaver makes it work like gangbusters. A page turner.

—*Jack Wagner*

I've read *Soul Mate* five times. That should tell you something. It's been a mind-blowing experience every time and always leaves me wanting more. Can't wait to see the movie!

—*Lesli Kay*

A wonderful summer read. It's the ultimate plane or summer beach book. Fast-paced with really interesting characters. The hero, Lance, is the guy you'd like to be stranded on a desert island with. This is subject matter reflected in today's headlines. It's important, and should be taken seriously. Perfectly delightful.

—*Susan Flannery*

Soul Mate is one of those novels that gets under your skin. You keep turning the page to scratch the itch. I was smiling when I got to the last page, finally soothed and satisfied. Great characters. Loved the unraveling of a love that shouldn't <u>be</u> (by society's standards), but <u>is</u> because a powerful destiny is in charge.

—*Joseph Mascolo*

ABOUT THE AUTHOR: Ronald Lewis Weaver is Senior Producer for *The Bold and the Beautiful*, the world's most-watched daily drama, seen in more than 100 countries by 37 million people a day. Let's just say he knows how to tell a story.

Soul Mate

a novel

Ronald Lewis Weaver

QuestFiction
Los Angeles

ACKNOWLEDGEMENTS

The late William J. Bell, legendary soap opera creator, and his wife, Lee Phillip Bell, brought Ridge Forrester to life as a central character of *The Bold and the Beautiful.* As senior producer of the series, I decided to try my hand at writing the diaries of Ridge at age seventeen, thinking our fans might be entertained by such offerings on the B&B website. I never got very far with Ridge's diary because about two pages in, other characters began to surface, Ridge disappeared, and Lance Van Arden took on a life of his own. Soul Mate is the result. Other than setting the story in Beverly Hills and the fashion business, there's no longer a B&B connection, except for the great opportunity I've had to observe how Bill Bell, and later his son, Bradley, came up with endlessly riveting stories for more than two decades. I am forever indebted to them for helping me hone my story-telling instincts.

My life partner, Franko Villeda, inspired the character of Marco. His prescience, encouragement and faith in me merits my heartfelt thanks. Witnessing Franko's mystical and magickal wonders for more than 25 years has given me an other-worldly body of experience that informs my life and my work. Given the difference in our ages and the three dreams he'd had years before we met, seeing me in the clothes I was wearing when we did meet, certainly explains the personal relevance of Lance and Claudia's story.

As I began to share my early drafts with friends and colleagues, my friend, Jack Smith, was the first *real writer* to read my early chapters. I was honored by his praise and advice.

Lesli Kay read at least five drafts and I thank her for being one of my biggest fans. Thanks also to the other B&B cast members who read the final draft and supported me with wonderful promotional quotes offering their enthusiastic opinions about the book: Lesley-Anne Down, Susan Flannery, Katherine Kelly Lang, Joseph Mascolo, Ronn Moss, Jack Wagner and Betty White.

Great thanks to Sandra Siegal who played hooky from her office to finish reading Soul Mate and instantly put me in touch with Literary Manager, Ken Atchity, who told me I was a great story teller, then informed me that I needed to cut 20% from the book. How lucky I was to work with someone whose formative years teaching classic literature and creative writing resulted in copious notes that were always spot on. I am greatly indebted to Ken for teaching me what a passive sentence is along with some other rules I'd never managed to absorb.

Thanks also to Carol Weaver for the first and last proofreadings, Michael Breddan for some pithy quotes and early collaboration on other writing projects, and Ann Willmott for her valuable feedback and online expertise.

Most of all, thanks to my dear, departed mom, Dorothy Weaver, and my 101-year-old dad, Bill Weaver, for the good genes, and for believing in me no matter the odd and unorthodox paths my unfolding life took.

Chapter 1

Pieces from the vast wall of light began to come loose and flutter around him. He felt like the snowman in the glass ball his mother gave him when he was five. Lance had never been this far in the dream before and he liked it. The luminous particles tingled when they touched his skin and it felt good. He sensed he was smiling and heard himself utter a joyful, childlike laugh joining a choir of awesome voices that seemed to emanate from everywhere and nowhere. He knew that his laugh, which had been a part of him, would now be a part of this chorus of brilliance forever. *This is absolutely sweet,* he thought. He wanted more.

So he got more. The tiny pieces of light, like happy butterflies, suddenly began to move, following some secret code that made them act in unison like those flocks of birds or schools of fish that turn on a dime. The bright butterflies separated into two flying masses, their individual forms now blending together to form two gigantic globes of light that began to rotate, creating an opening in the center of each. Inside the left globe there was a statue of a young man, very much like Michelangelo's David. In the right globe, there was a statue of a young woman, very much like the Venus di Milo—only with arms.

Lance remembered reading somewhere that a block of marble contained the essence of the figure that the artist must bring to life. As he wondered how that could be, the young man began to move, seeming to enjoy the flexing of his muscles as he started to feel them for the first time. The young woman also began to move, enjoying her naked flesh as her hands explored the sensuous roundness of her body.

Both man and woman became aware of each other. Their first looks showed a cautious surprise. Upon exploring each other with their eyes, their faces became radiant with joyous smiles. Then Lance saw in their eyes that their separation was troubling to them. They extended their hands toward each other. As their fingers touched, the intensity of the globes turned from a golden glow to white hot and they began to move toward each other. As the globes merged, man and woman embraced in an exquisite tableau of adoration and the white hot light enclosed them fully as Lance felt himself straining to continue seeing them well beyond their time of being seen.

Now Lance knew it was time to wake up, which he did—with a monstrous erection.

"Holy shit!" he whispered to himself. "I have to write this down." He reached for the laptop he kept on his nightstand for just such purpose. Lance had discovered that he was good at finding words to express the raucous and restless feelings that pervaded both the waking and the dreaming parts of his eighteen years of existence. Although he'd written some rather good short stories that he'd shared with his parents and a couple of friends he trusted, he kept the memory stick that contained the most lurid of his erotic musings locked in the wall safe in his room to which only he had the combination.

Most of what Lance wrote was his secret, but he knew when he got this dream written it would be a natural for posting on his blog. Since most of his dreams were extravagant and erotic, he had developed a following. Last week he'd gotten 4,132 hits and dozens of replies, mostly complimentary. Most of those who posted super-long rambling replies were keen to give him their interpretations of his dreams. Mostly their replies were amusing and a bit wacko, but some were right on.

TheSuperDreamer was his URL. His profile photo showed him from behind dressed only in a pair of Speedos, flying over a cloud bank in a cape with *TheSuperDreamer.com* stitched on the back. One of his buddies in the photo department at his parents' company shot and Photoshopped it for him. Lance swore him to secrecy. This dream would definitely get his followers riled up.

He was gaining many blog friends as word spread about SuperDreamer. *If I do this for a few more years, he thought, I'll have a gigantic number of fans who'll buy my first novel.*

Lance Van Arden was only eighteen, but the brilliance of his talent and the privileged and celebrity-studded milieu in which his family moved, along with his zest to experience life to its fullest, positioned him for an amazing ride.

Chapter 2

The Van Ardens of Beverly Hills were mythic creatures to Claudia de la Rosa who taught English to their son, Lance. They were icons of impeccable taste. Their elegant demeanor, and vast design firm known simply as Van Arden, dressed America in its image. Their **VA** emblazoned upon everything from shirts to sheets hammered their style upon the nation's psyche.

The iconic Van Arden name seemed almost god-like, pouring forth a constant stream of brilliance and beauty into the world. Like their design house, Edward and Roberta Van Arden also poured forth one elegant and brilliant child after another into the world.

Their firstborn, Lance, was impossibly handsome. Some said he had erotically penetrating eyes at birth. He was 18 when he arrived at Claudia's class. All heads turned and all jaws dropped when he walked into the room, including Claudia's. It wasn't just that he was beautiful. He coupled beauty with appealing ease and a wry, self-deprecating sense of humor that disarmed boys and enchanted girls.

Claudia did not know then that such physical beauty when mixed with a probing mind, a broad talent with words, and an insatiable need to experience life to its fullest would be intoxicating.

Chapter 3

On Claudia's first day in Beverly Hills she zipped down Rodeo Drive in the red Mazda Miata her father had given her when she got her masters thinking, "I have arrived." Her tape deck was set on *repeat* for complete immersion in the seductive strains of The Mammas and Pappas, "California Dreamin." It summed up her romantic notion that a little dark-haired, dark-skinned girl whose parents spoke Spanish at home—a quiet little girl who could never seem to find a comfortable niche in the coldness that was Harbor Point, Michigan—had escaped to America's true heartland, that place where the image-makers created what they wanted America to want to be. That glamorous place with possibilities of making it, with cars that cost more than your parents' house, and with the hint of vaguely dangerous pleasures for those brave enough to explore them. Yes, Claudia de la Rosa was here to stay.

Today she'd blown ten times her lunch money budget for a chance to eat with Liam Neeson, Cate Blanchett and Morgan Freeman. Well, she didn't exactly eat with them, but her table for one by the kitchen door at The Four Seasons Café gave her a wonderful view of power lunching. Between bites of smoked salmon, toast points and capers, she scanned the room for familiar faces. That frizzy-haired guy with the horn-rimmed glasses stroking the hand of the blonde wearing an almost-see-through top must be someone big, she thought. Everyone who came in either waved a hearty greeting or stopped to chat. The chats only lasted for seconds. Most seemed to end with "let's do lunch." Claudia was amused by the ritual of it. What a wonderful cliché, she thought. And she was a fly on the wall.

She wondered where the guy and the blond would go after lunch. Maybe a suite upstairs. He would surprise her, she thought, with expensive champagne and the diamond necklace she had oooed and ahhed over in Cartier's window.

Claudia knew how it would unfold. He would take the necklace from her as if it were a fragile flower. The blonde would turn expectantly for the ultimate caress of the brilliant gem on her neck. His hands would engage the clasp as he turned her to face him again. He would stroke the diamonds lightly with just one finger. The finger would not touch her flesh, but the sensation as he pressed the stones against her skin would quicken her breath. He'd respond with lips that encompassed the dazzling stones and her luminescent flesh. His arm encircled her waist, her back arched presenting the flaming diamond pendant for his searching kiss.

"What are you lookin' at, bitch?"

Claudia was jolted back to the table by the kitchen of The Four Seasons Café.

The blonde and the man whom she'd just imagined nuzzling her chest were looking at her, along with everyone else in the restaurant.

"I hate people who stare," she spat. The man touched her hand and said, "Don't worry about it. She's just a tourist."

As if sucked into a time capsule, Claudia became the little dark-haired, dark-skinned outcast who desperately wanted to crawl under the table. In that moment the dream that brought her to sunny Southern California, that drove her to graduate magna cum laude, that fueled an insatiable desire to be a famous writer—all that was reduced to, "she's just a tourist." Still an outsider. Still and forever, she thought.

Chapter 4

Claudia's father, Leonardo de la Rosa, was a proud man. The first Mexican-American to settle in Harbor Point, Michigan, he had bused tables at the China Feast when he was 22, saved his money and sent for Claudia's mother, Esmeralda. By the time Claudia was in grade school they owned the best Mexican restaurant in town. If it hadn't been the only Mexican restaurant in town it would still have been the best.

After Claudia was born her aunts and uncles, nieces and nephews, cousins and grandparents all trickled into town to visit. Most of them stayed. If you're going to own a Mexican restaurant you need to have people to cook, serve and clean. Who better than family? The air was clean, the sandy beaches of Lake Michigan were minutes away, and with a steady job at Cocina de la Rosa you could buy a clean, new, tri-level with three bedrooms and a big lot for under $30,000. Within a year the de la Rosa tribe bought most of the lots in the Lakeview subdivision. Little Mexico the locals called it. The townspeople were mostly tolerant of these newcomers with habits unlike their own. Leonardo was known and respected, a member of the local Lions club and a generous contributor of tangy munchies to the summer Strawberry Festival. But stories circulated quickly from clucking tongues when a backyard quinceñera got unconscionably noisy with blaring mariachis emanating from hi-fi speakers dragged outside, or a group of cousins got into a fight with local bullies in the schoolyard and used strong words like *pendejo* or *chingado* that no one understood but that everyone knew were definitely not complimentary.

So the growing-up rules in the de la Rosa clan had to take into account who they were and where they were. They all wanted to be respected. Mostly they were, as long as they played by the time-honored mores of Middle America. Claudia never quite got the hang of it. In grade school they called her Señorita Stupid because of the blank, uncomprehending look she got on her face when she didn't get their lame jokes—often made at her expense.

In junior high she hated the way the girls giggled and gossiped. She hated the way the boys made farting noises with their armpits. In high school she vowed she would become a cheerleader and did. When she found out that her father had sternly demanded her admission to the inner sanctum of the pom-pom she understood the polite banter laced with sarcasm that once again turned her into Señorita Stupid. The dreamed-of camaraderie was not to be.

She lost herself deeper in a world she had discovered that was far better and far more exciting than the one she was in. She discovered universes flowing from endless pages of Dickenson, Thoreau, Wolfe, Tolstoy and Lorca. She was thrilled by lush and bawdy images drawn on her mind's eye by Henry Miller. She was mesmerized by the erotic meanderings of Anais Nin. She read and re-read the sonnets and plays of Shakespeare. She kept locked and hidden diaries pouring out a teenager's observations on the lunacy of life, written, of course, in the style of whichever writer was currently monopolizing her attentions. *This*, she thought, *is what will keep me safe and sane until my words will one day equal theirs.*

Now the rituals of growing up in a small town didn't bother her quite so much. She went through the motions and knew one day she would escape. A few girlfriends took her under their wing like an injured bird. Maybe not trying so hard was part of it.

Boys she didn't get at all. She once heard them whispering about a "hot tamale" and was stunned to realize they were talking about her. She had absolutely no idea why this gangly girl who covered her nearly non-existent breasts with baggy denim shirts could, in any way, be moderately attractive, much less hot.

In her junior year another odd-ball named William Potter, III began showing up wherever she went. He was sweetly uncomfortable in her presence and always tried to hide behind something whenever she would stumble upon him. She was amused and a little flattered. One day as he followed her she slipped behind a post.

"Boo!" she shouted, jumping into his path.

"Holy shit!" he exclaimed. "I'm sorry, I'm sorry, I'm sorry."

"About what?" she teased.

"About... I mean, you know, about..." He almost said, 'about following you.' But that would have let her know that he was following her.

"About following me?" she said with an impish smile.

"Well...ummm...I guess..." was all he could muster.

"You want to ask me out or something?"

His jaw dropped and she found it charming.

They had a lot in common. And they discovered they liked to kiss. They would sneak off behind the garage to hold each other with lips pressed together—closed. After a few weeks of this and wondering what all the fuss was about, she decided to take matters into her own hands. William Potter, III was wide-eyed as she swiftly unzipped his fly and, indeed, took matters into her own hands. In an instant he let out a monstrous groan. Something moist and sticky hit her in the chin and she screamed like the victim in a horror film. Suddenly the neighborhood was alive with nervous mothers gathering their children in protective grasps and fathers running out screen doors with baseball bats.

After a sprint into the woods and a clandestine trip to the laundry room, Claudia crawled shakily into her bed and thought to herself, Never again. Never, never, ever again.

Of course she did it again. Not as disastrously, but not with the grand passion pictured by the great romantic writers either. At least, not yet.

Chapter 5

Enter Lance Van Arden. After the initial shock of Lance's entrance into her classroom, Claudia found herself observing that, although she was a 26-year-old English teacher who was eight years older than this young stud, she was momentarily smitten by him. He did remind her a bit of Derek Malone, the handsome boy in her senior class who stood her up once and didn't even remember he'd asked her out. She passed off her initial rush as an aberrational flashback to Derek and called the class to order.

During the usual first day mechanics of laying the groundwork for the semester and putting names with faces, she found herself glancing at Lance occasionally and wondering to herself why she kept doing this. She needed his approval—a look to let her know she was handling the class well. Odd she thought. But not as odd as the moment at the end of class after all the others had left when he approached her desk with a disarming smile and said, "Miss de la Rosa, I'm Lance Van Arden and my mother asked me to give you this." He handed her an envelope with "Miss Claudia de la Rosa" written on it so exquisitely that it looked engraved. With an amused smile he said, "Open it."

She'd never received a formal invitation to dinner at eight with parents of a student. And this student's parents were the reigning king and queen of the fashion industry.

"I know it's short notice," Lance said, "but my mother seems to have this idea that my writing talent needs special attention and she wants to see what you're made of."

"You make it sound like a tribunal," Claudia said.

"Kind of," he teased. "You up for it?"

"Can I say no?"

"No."

There was a smile on his face and a glint in his eye that spoke volumes of something between them. He was charming her and she liked it.

"Well then," she said, "dinner at eight."

"Don't worry. I'll make sure you have a great time."

Somehow, she was sure he would.

Claudia approached the massive iron gate at precisely 8 p.m. She had waited out the 10 minutes early she had arrived by parking on the turnout below the house. Ten minutes spent adjusting her hair, re-applying her lipstick and trying to think what she would say when this formidable woman she was about to meet answered the door. Then she remembered that Roberta Van Arden would probably not be the one to answer the door. They'd have a Jeeves or an Arthur for that wouldn't they? She smiled at the thought. She was prepared to have an adventure.

Upon announcing herself on the intercom, the giant, cast iron shield parted. She parked her little red Miata in the motor court next to a Bentley and a Ferrari roadster. Even her Miata seemed classy parked here. The front door swung open as she approached. A uniformed maid smiled. "*Buenos noches,*" she said. I am Maria Lopez. Mr. and Mrs. Van Arden would like you to join them on the terrace. This way, *por favor.*"

Maria, Claudia thought. Of course. This is Southern California. Probably not many Jeeves or Arthurs here.

They walked through awesome spaces where every detail spoke of impeccable taste and perfection. The inlaid marble floor led Claudia's eye to an alcove with a massive stone Buddha who sat blissfully welcoming her approach.

She smiled as she remembered reading about Chinese emperors who had collected such astonishing works of art as symbols of their power. So too the Van Ardens, she thought. Maria walked slightly ahead of her, almost as if she knew not to get in the way of the eye candy that presented itself with each step and each turn.

"This belongs in *Architectural Digest,*" mused Claudia.

"*Sí*," said Maria. "*Otobre*, 2002."

"*Claro*", Claudia responded. "*Que perfecto*. You must love it here."

"Mostly," said Maria with a slight smile that implied stories she could tell but wouldn't.

By the time they reached the shaded veranda overlooking the world, Claudia was overwhelmed by Ming vases, jade carvings, Picassos, Cézannes and Rodins. She was stunned to discover that the lifelike statues posed by a massive Henry Moore sculpture were the real, live, martini-drinking king and queen of this castle, Edward and Roberta Van Arden.

Maria announced, "Mr. and Mrs. Van Arden, your guest is here."

"Miss de la Rosa," Roberta gushed .

"Please call me Claudia. Miss de la Rosa sounds like…" She smiled as she finished the sentence, "…a schoolteacher."

"And a fine one we've been told," said Edward with a genuine smile. "But Claudia it is, so long as we're Roberta and Edward."

Roberta touched her arm. "We're so happy you could join us. I know it was short notice."

"Yes, no, I mean it's ok," stumbled Claudia. "I'm sorry, it's just…" She glanced at the Henry Moore towering overhead and gestured toward the grand house and the twinkling city.

Roberta finished her sentence "Overwhelming? It's alright to be overwhelmed. That's the point. We create beautiful things for a living and can't help ourselves any more."

Edward said, "And we don't want to. When Lance was born we lived in a studio apartment with a view of O'Toole's Bar."

"I could change Lance's diaper by the light of its red neon sign."

"Geez, mom," exclaimed Lance as he approached. "Does my teacher really need to hear the old diapers-by-the-light-of-O'Toole's-neon story?"

So there it was, the Van Arden way of saying, *Don't be intimidated by all this. We used to be poor too.* They certainly weren't poor anymore and they proved it with elegance, charm, spectacular cuisine and a lovely Brunesco of rare vintage.

At dinner there were stories of hard times, risks taken and rewards earned—Van Arden stories as well as de la Rosa stories.

They talked literature and music and movies. They talked about the creative process. Claudia gushed about a book called *The Artist's Way* by Julia Cameron that had opened her eyes and asked if anyone knew of it.

Edward exploded with delight. "Know of it? It saved our business."

Claudia had touched a nerve of kinship with Edward that resonated in a way that few others whom she had told about the book had felt.

"It was about 10 years ago. Remember, Robbie? I was totally blocked. I came up with a slew of designs exactly like I had done for the last two seasons and I was panicked."

"The fashion press is merciless if you don't keep topping yourself," Roberta said. "I thought we were going to go under."

"My accountant, of all people, suggested I read *The Artist's Way*. I started doing the exercises and, lo and behold, I ended up with a collection that made headlines. And I've been doing my morning pages and all the other stuff in that book ever since." He beamed at Claudia and wryly repeated her question, "Do I know *The Artist's Way*?!"

Claudia was pleased to be so in synch with the master of fashion. She felt like bragging a little. "That book got me to write my very first published short story. It's an autographed copy. I stood on line for half an hour when she had a book signing."

Edward was touched. "Then it must be one of your most-prized possessions."

"Actually, it is." Claudia felt so connected to Edward that she considered offering it to him as a gift. However, the little Observer who stands a bit apart and whispers into a writer's ear said, *probably not a good idea to give it away for a fancy dinner and a little too much wine.*

On some level Claudia was certain that Roberta was measuring her. Edward enjoyed charming Claudia and she found herself more fully engaged in conversation than she could ever remember. And through it all, her little Observer kept telling her there was something going on here.

As luscious desserts and coffee were consumed and aperitifs sipped, the Observer noted that Lance had in an odd way become her anchor during the evening. He laughed easily at her stories, rolled his eyes at his parents' most outrageous tales and, through it all, she felt he was somehow telling her, "something's coming and it will be ok."

As the coffee mellowed the spirits she noticed that Lance's younger sister and brother were missing. She'd found a treasure trove of information about the famous Van Ardens on the web. "You have two other children, right?" asked Claudia.

"Michael is at a basketball game," Roberta said, "and Jennifer is at a sleepover."

The Observer in Claudia thought, *Choreographed by mom.*

As the evening reached that inevitable concluding phase, Roberta nodded to Maria who returned with a silver tray upon which there was a large envelope.

Claudia looked around the table. Everyone had a knowing smile. Lance said, "I think you have an assignment."

"Claudia," Roberta said, "we've had a thoroughly delightful evening with you. I'm very pleased that it is you who will be teaching English to Lance this semester. I think he's exceptionally talented with words and I want him to have the absolute best guidance. He is a writer. What you have in your hand is a short story he wrote that our friend Woody Hartman thinks shows incredible promise.

"Of Hartman Publications?" Claudia asked.

"The very same,"

Lance rolled his eyes, shook his head and buried it in his hands.

Edward said, "I thought Lance might be a designer—chip off the old block. But I can't deny he has a way with words. And his mother wants him to have the best teachers he can get. That's where you come in."

"And what mother wants, mother gets," Lance said with a wry grin. "Dad says there are two rules to remember when discussing something with mom. Rule number one, Mom is always right. Rule number two, consult rule number one."

The laughter around the table was tinged with the inevitability of it all.

"With that not altogether erroneous assessment," Roberta said, "consider yourself assigned."

Claudia responded, "It would be my pleasure. As a matter of fact I'll be giving my students a writing assignment tomorrow—a private diary to explore their feelings and hone their writing skills."

"Private?" asked Roberta.

"Private," Claudia responded firmly. "I've noticed that when writing assignments are shared with the class, students hold back. They don't push the envelope because they don't want to be judged by their peers."

Edward, who had sat back smiling at Roberta's masterful manipulations, came to life. "No risk, no gain. I'm in total agreement. The most creative work is done by people out there on a limb, making mistakes, learning the rules so they can risk breaking them to create something unique. And having the privacy to do so without naysayers looking over their shoulder."

"Exactly," Claudia said. "That's the space I'm trying to create for my class."

"Be careful," Roberta warned. "Just remember these are teenagers. You may be opening Pandora's box."

Edward said, "That's the whole point isn't it? The creative excitement of the unknown! There's no better high than that."

"Yes!" Claudia exclaimed. This man understood.

The Observer on Claudia's shoulder noticed that Roberta suddenly sat up regally straight and, as if putting a period on a sentence, said, "That may be all well and good, but the final product of the creative mind is put out there for the world to judge. I very much look forward to reading Lance's diary. In its finished form, of course. How else can we judge whether Miss de la Rosa is the perfect mentor she seems to be?"

Edward leaned in to Lance and said, "Son, it is up to you to decide whether anyone reads your diary and whether Miss de la Rosa is good for you or not." And with an affectionate, but pointed look toward Roberta, "Sweetheart, sometimes it's necessary to loosen the reins and let the colt run free in the meadow."

Claudia realized she'd just witnessed a battle of the titans. She wasn't sure who had won. It seemed a standoff. *This is why they are so successful,* she thought. *He lets her manipulate their world with an iron hand and she lets him wallow in the ether to snatch beauty and give it form. And they both pull each other back from the brink when necessary.*

As Lance walked Claudia to her car she remembered that Roberta had assured her it was alright to be overwhelmed. This time it was by dozens of flickering lanterns lining the pathway to the motor court mixed with the vast carpet of city lights miles below them.

She put her hand on Lance's arm to stop him. "Wait. It's hard for me to even imagine living like this. And you do. Every day! Let me look."

Soft music from the outdoor speakers surrounded them. An ardent Maria Callas sang "Casta Diva" as they stood together for awhile looking out at the vast city, alive with light and life. Lance turned to Claudia and said simply, "Thank you."

"For what?"

"For reminding me about what I have. I walk by this every day and I never really appreciate it like you are right now. You've made it new for me. See, you've taught me something already—without homework."

He led her to a stone bench under a lush arbor of star jasmine. Taking off his suede jacket he draped it over her shoulders. They sat shoulder-to-shoulder savoring the fragrance, the city lights and the great diva's passionate prayer for the return of lost love.

Claudia felt the warmth of the jacket fresh with the heat from his body and felt a calm that was unfamiliar. Tears welled in her eyes. The moment was pure bliss. She hoped he wouldn't look at her. The emotion was too strong and too revealing. What was happening to her? This was the closest she'd ever come to that feeling of romance she'd always dreamed of. It seemed so odd to be sharing this moment with an 18-year-old boy. It should be a moment shared with a lover. What must Lance be thinking, she wondered, breaking the spell. Almost as if he heard her question, he said, "I like you."

"What?"

"Please don't think I'm coming on to you or anything. I don't mean it that way. I just like the way you were tonight—are tonight. The way you're enjoying this, the way you make me see things differently."

Claudia felt herself pulling back. "Honestly I've never had an experience quite like tonight."

"I told you it would be ok, right?"

"Yes you did. And it was."

She suddenly remembered that she was sitting with her student and the ramifications of the evening began to panic her. She'd drunk a lot of wine and shared some very personal thoughts with charming and sophisticated people who enjoyed her company. All of this witnessed by a student she barely knew. He said he liked the way she was but had her behavior been inappropriate? Had she…?

Lance interrupted her thoughts as if he'd been reading her mind. "Listen," he said. "It would probably be embarrassing if I told anyone in school about tonight so I won't. I promise."

"Yes," she said simply. She wanted to say, *If only you were 10 years older?*

Chapter 6

Claudia arrived at school early the next morning. She'd been awake since four, the whirlwind of last night re-playing itself like a dream. As the first period students began to drift in she found herself looking up in anticipation. Laughing playfully, Lance came in with two of the girls. For a moment Claudia forgot Lance's promise and wondered if he was telling them about last night. *That's paranoid*, she thought. And a moment of jealousy? *How ridiculous. Get a hold of yourself.* She watched as he settled into his seat, looked up and flashed his 'It's ok' smile.

As the class unfolded, Claudia began to see the classic patterns—the class clowns, the button-down geeks, the asshole jocks. They all seemed magnified in this cauldron of wealth and power—especially the bitch-goddess cheerleader types. Momentary flashback! Claudia knew she'd have to make a special effort not to be too hard on them.

The first days were the hardest. They either learned to respect you then or you were lost.

"Who in this class has ever kept a diary?" she asked, scanning the apple polishers who always seemed to sit in the front row. All of the front row hands popped up with scattered results from the rest.

From the back row Dutch Cheatham, star quarterback and would-be class clown piped up. "I keep one." He paused for effect after a chorus of 'Yeah, rights.' "I do. In my bathroom. Makes good toilet paper." Guys chortled, girls groaned.

Upon noting Claudia's dismay, Lance said, "Then you must buy them by the gross."

Dutch drew himself up to full quarterback bulk, "Screw you, Van Arden."

Lance looked at Dutch for a moment, poised for a sharp rejoinder. The rest of the class waited for a delicious put down. They loved watching Dutch's buttons get pushed. Lance just smiled and shrugged as if to say, 'This is too easy.' Starting a war on Claudia's turf right now was a bad idea, he thought. He turned to her, smiled and said, "Sorry."

Claudia continued. "For those of you who've kept a diary, why did you, or do you, do it? What do you get from it?"

Two front row hands shot up. "Yes, Deirdre."

"Sometimes when things are sort of bad-like, you know, it's like having someone to talk to. To say the things you can't say to anybody else."

"Secrets!" said Jennifer from the back row with a delicious grin.

"Secrets and things you'd like to say to somebody's face but can't," Deirdre said.

"Like what?" leered Jennifer to the delight of the room.

"Like none of your business," Deirdre teased.

"Well," Claudia said, "that is the one big attraction to a diary, isn't it? You get to talk about your feelings and say some things you might not want to say out loud, right? This semester you're each going to explore yourselves through your writing. You're all going to keep a diary."

There were a few groans, a couple of 'oh shits', and a handful of giggles. Dutch, along with about half of the guys and a couple of the girls looked downright distressed at the idea.

"No way," Dutch said. "Last year, Mr. Smith made us write essays about things we know about like football. Flunk me if you want, but there's no way I'm gonna write about 'feelings'." He said feelings like he was cleaning dog doo out of a thick-soled sneaker.

Claudia engaged him with a smile. "If you had to write one sentence right now in a diary, something about this class, what would you say?"

Dutch paled and shrank back into his seat.

"Come on," coaxed the class.

"Just one sentence. Try it," Claudia urged.

Dutch summoned up his courage and said, "Today Miss de la Rosa told us we had to do a diary and I...I...almost shit my pants!"

The class erupted into wild applause. Dutch's initial paranoia gave way to a broad smile as he realized that he'd just found out he could, in fact, keep a diary.

Claudia said, "Dutch, I'm proud of you. You were direct and honest and if you keep it up you will get an A in this class."

That might have been the first time anyone had given Dutch a vote of confidence for other than making touchdown passes. After the initial euphoria of the moment Dutch's face clouded and he said, "Yeah, but I ain't gonna write honest stuff like that and read it to the class. No way."

"No you're not," Claudia said. "No one will have to read their diary entries to the class. They'll be totally private. Except for me. I'll read them and either discuss them with you in private or write private notes to you with my comments. You'll be graded on how well you express yourselves. Some of the great writers kept diaries that were ultimately published, but that were written initially for themselves—to explore their feelings and express how they felt about their lives and the world around them. People like Anais Nin and Virginia Wolf. And Anne Frank, a little girl who didn't even know she was a great writer. They're all on your reading list. I'll tell no one what you write. I hope that will give you the freedom to say whatever you like about anything and anyone you like."

A mysterious conspiracy had filled the room and infected everyone in it.

"For tomorrow, I'd like you to start with a paragraph or two, double-spaced, telling me what you would like to learn—what your objective is in keeping a diary." Some blank stares. Start with that and just write anything that comes to mind. Have fun with it.

A handwritten note was attached under Lance's assignment sheet:

Lance: Please tell your mother I had a wonderful time at dinner. She can rest assured that I have great expectations for you.

I liked the short story she "assigned" me to read. I hope you bring some of the same literary quality to your diary.

C. de la Rosa

20

P.S. And thanks for making me feel comfortable enjoying your family and your beautiful home. I had a great time.

Appropriately formal, Claudia had thought as she wrote it last night. No hint of the overwhelming sense of warmth she'd felt that was caused by Lance's illuminating presence on the stone bench overlooking Shangri-la.

Claudia was pleasantly tired as she made herself a tuna salad sandwich and revisited the memories of the day. She was glad Lance had not escalated the dust-up with Dutch. He had helped her once more and she was happy about that. She read a little Joseph Conrad, pondering lines that seemed to have some relevance to the day. "Woe to the man whose heart has not learned while young to hope, to love—and to put its trust in life."

Claudia pulled the covers back and snuggled under the silk comforter remembering how well she'd bonded with her classes, Lance's in particular, and certain that she had embarked upon a marvelous adventure. Smiling, she reached for her diary.

Chapter 7

Dutch stumbled into class the next morning grumbling that he'd been up most of the night doing his homework. He handed Claudia one paragraph about how he couldn't think of anything to write and it pissed him off big time. Claudia patiently convinced him that he'd made a very good start and asked him to write two paragraphs for tomorrow.

Lance handed in his pages sealed in a manila envelope with "Miss de la Rosa" printed in a fine hand.

"Whoa!" Deirdre said, "You sealed yours in an envelope?"

What she didn't know, nor did Lance really, was that he had some things on his mind that he was burning to express and they were definitely private things.

Claudia got home from school that day with a fifty page stack to read. She popped a leftover casserole into the oven and sat down to thumb through these tentative stabs at self-examination, eager to see if there was something that popped out at her. Lance's sealed envelope was at the bottom of the stack. She noticed that the pace of her thumbing quickened as she grew closer to it. She smiled as she realized she wasn't interested in anything except that manila envelope. She drew it out, held it in her hands for a moment admiring the dramatic flourish in the script that spelled her name, and then sliced it open to find a note and some neatly typed pages. The note said:

Miss de la Rosa: My objective in keeping a journal is to get in touch with my feelings a lot better so I can write better lyrics to the songs I'm composing for my band. My songs, so far, seem to have a lot to do with love and sex and personal stuff like that. I hope that's ok. You said be honest. Please let me know if I go too far or off the deep end. Here goes!

Claudia read the title: DIARY OF A TEENAGER WITH RAGING HORMONES by Lance Van Arden.

Uh, oh! she thought. *What have I gotten myself into?* But it was a bold and intriguing way to start and she'd always been easily seduced by great expectations of wonderful titles and stunning first lines. Lance had both:

DIARY OF A TEENAGER WITH RAGING HORMONES
By LANCE VAN ARDEN

Last Sunday I turned 18 and my dad told me I have raging hormones.

I guess this is something your parents say when they're too embarrassed to even think about your discovery of a feeling so awesome it burns you up like a Roman candle.

When I told my dad something was happening to me I didn't completely understand but really liked a lot—maybe too much—he said it's "just raging hormones. You'll get over it."

I hope not!

But, then again, maybe it's better if I do. It did get me into major trouble on Sunday. On this birthday my mom threw a big surprise party for me. You know how when you're a kid your mom's surprise parties are ok, but it's like the aunts and uncles and cousins and the kids from down the block are there because how could they say 'no' to your mother? Well, I guess 18 was a magic number for my mother this year. She invited only my friends.

When the tenth person to arrive turned out to be Jerry Marchand, it clicked. He's the drummer in my band and he gave himself the "stage name" Plunger because he thinks it sounds studly. He really, really plays the rock musician...down to the purple hair, pink eye shadow and studded leather chaps. We're on the same musical wavelength and my mom thinks he's "bad company."

Anyway, after seeing Plunger I realized there are no aunts, no uncles, and no neighbor kids from down the block. Just the people my mom found in my address book. Kinda cool. At least for awhile.

The next guest to arrive blew me away. Tracey Winthrop. I had just met her the week before at the Bel Air Country club with my dad. She and her mom teed off just before us. The look she gave me as she started down the fairway was... Incredible? Hot? Vulnerable? Sensual? All that and more. She was wearing this slinky thing like no other golf clothes I ever saw. Tracey Winthrop turned around six times on her way down the fairway. I counted. Does that seem conceited? Probably. But she did, damn it, and I loved it. I experienced... (I stop here looking for words an English teacher would like, like "a stirring in the loins.") Bottom line, she turned me on big-time.

Anyway, raging hormones didn't come close to what I was feeling, though. For the next 18 holes she kept playing in my head. I'd drift off in my mind and imagine these super conversations where we both said the most perfect things to each other—dancing with our words— like a scene in this ballet my mom took me to, where the prince kisses the sleeping princess, she wakes up, and they do this really sensuous dance that was a turn-on.

I'd imagine Tracey and me touching each other so our whole bodies vibrated and the air ran like a shiver between our teeth. We'd completely know what the other was feeling and we'd love being able to make each other feel that way. Is that what it means when they say "carnal knowledge"? That's what I think it means anyway.

I have to say something else about myself before I go on. Since I was about 15 years old I have had some kind of power over girls—even girls older than myself. I know that probably sounds awful and conceited, but it's true. I think that power is more than if you're good-looking or not. I think it has something to do with knowing this thing about carnal knowledge. If you can imagine it in your mind, and imagine them feeling it too, I think you somehow groove together on that vibe—like getting lost in a good beat. That's the kind of power I mean. I know firsthand that it's real.

Tracey and I had that moment on the fairway. So when she hung around on the terrace with her iced tea after her mother left, it was clear we'd spend the rest of the day together. It felt so natural. I just walked over to her table, sat down and said, "I'm glad you waited for me."

"There was no other choice was there?" she said.

"Not really," I said.

"Let me drive you out to Malibu for lunch," she said matter-of-factly. Her eyes grabbed mine in a hammerlock. (Is that a great line for a song or what?!!) She said, "I know a quiet, romantic little place you'll absolutely adore."

She was so completely direct—so mesmerizing. I said, "Are you always so..."

"Forward?" she asked. And without waiting for a reply she said, "No. But I don't fall in love every day either."

With that little bombshell she gave me a heart-melting smile, picked up her keys and headed for the door with supreme confidence that I was right behind her.

I was.

Personally I don't like it when other guys brag about how far they got (usually not very) so I won't go into too much detail here. Who knows who might read this someday? Let's just say that, short of getting the whole way there, Tracey and I shared some radically honest moments. We danced like the prince and princess!

Anyway, back to the party. Here she was, silhouetted in our doorway with the breeze blowing her silk party dress. I was so glad my mother had found Tracey's number.

Well, I was glad for a little while at least. But, you see, what I described about those first electrifying moments with Tracey is exactly the same thing I felt the week before for Melissa and the week before that with Adrienne and the week before that with Suzanne and the week before... you get the picture. How the hell do you feel you're in love every day of your life but with different people?

I thought it was just great, but guess what? I must, somehow, give the impression to the girl I'm with that she's the only one.

So, the next person on my mother's guest list to arrive was Melissa. Damn! Then Adrienne, then Suzanne. Double damn!

There's more to tell, but it's late. More later...

Claudia was shocked by the explicit candor. But it was a pleasant shock, she noticed, because she found herself smiling. The oven timer went off. Claudia ignored it and read the pages over three more times, each time savoring the images created and the obvious ease with words. The writing was directed at an audience. Most of Lance's classmates had done the, 'After I got home from school I talked to Bev on the phone for half an hour and then had a sandwich' kind of stuff. Written for themselves. Lance's style was somewhat novelesque, using dialogue and with a certain provocative edge. *He's writing for a reader outside himself,* she thought. *Me!*

On the one hand, this is why she chose to teach English. This elegant young man from a distinguished family was talented and deserved encouragement. On the other hand, his subject matter could be thorny. What the hell, she thought as she scrambled to find a pen and paper. She would be his mentor. Her heart was pounding and her Observer was noticing that the excitement of discovering a talented student mixed with the apprehension about his subject matter was exhilarating. She wrote:

> *To: Lance Van Arden*
> *From: Miss de la Rosa*
> *I must say that I was very surprised and pleased by your first journal entry. Your striking description of ballet-like conversations is quite good.*
>
> *"Her eyes grabbed mine in a hammerlock," is a vivid line. But I also liked the image you created with, "We danced like the prince and princess." Good poetry and good lyrics possess striking images. In reading your first installment, I was curious how being smitten weekly and having four girls (or more?) thinking you were their one-and-only made you feel. Maybe you could explore that a little.*
>
> *Regarding your question about how far you can go in your language and descriptions, I think that, since you have stated your objective as wanting to write*

better song lyrics about love and personal feelings, the boundaries must be set to allow you to explore those feelings. I'm a little torn by this because I can't put myself in a position in which anyone could ever say I encouraged prurient language or explicit sexual allusions for their own sake. I've already made the point in this assignment that what you write is totally confidential. I must ask that my responses to you must also be totally confidential if we are to continue in this vein. I am, in fact, only a few years older than you, so you have to understand how small some minds can be and realize that our discourse could be totally misinterpreted. I have to trust that you will protect me in this as I will protect you.

If that's understood let's proceed.

Claudia de la Rosa

She read her note several times, each time trimming a little here, picking a different word there until she felt that the fine line she was treading was safely drawn. Feeling somehow spent, she breezed through the other students' pages making short notes: "Good start." "Excellent work." "Interesting."

The casserole had burned and was now cold, but her hunger had diminished as her excitement and anticipation of a new day at school grew. A couple of Mallomars and a glass of milk took the edge off and she tucked herself in and reached for her diary. With pen and book in hand she began to think about the fading week, closed her eyes to remember the adventure of it all, wrote a little, then drifted off.

Claudia did not remember her dreams often, but when she did they usually had something to say that she figured she should pay attention to whether she understood them or not.

*

Claudia looked so peaceful lying there, Claudia thought, as she sat on top of the armoire looking down at herself in the bed. Did she always sleep like that, she wondered, her arm tucked under the pillow just so with one leg out over the covers? The window was open and the sheers fluttered lightly in a warm breeze scented with jasmine and wood smoke. She spread her arms and pushed off against the armoire knowing that flying would be effortless. Claudia in the bed will be all right thought Claudia in the air as she circled the ceiling once before floating out the window, accelerating upward over the house. Her vertical momentum shook thin leaves from the willow tree into the pond. A meadow stretched out before her with thatched roof cottages dotting emerald hills. Higher, she thought, and was instantly lifted on a current of fragrant air to what would be a dizzying height to a mere mortal. She looked out at the vast horizon, the red haze of dawn illuminating white smoke rising from the chimneys of the cottages. A cottage on the edge of a cliff drew her. She settled to the ground at its door. She'd felt blissful while several thousand feet in the air, but standing at the door of this cottage she felt uneasy and wondered if she should be back with her other self in her bed.

The door was ajar and she peered into the quaint darkness that was broken with an oil lamp on the table. Claudia saw herself sitting at a table with books spread out before her. Odd, Claudia thought, she'd just left her other self in bed in her apartment. What was she doing here? Did she fly too? Claudia looked up from her book and smiled at Claudia. There were no words spoken as Claudia One pushed off gently from the floor and circled the table as Claudia Two watched her. Claudia Two shut the book as Claudia One took her hand. The two Claudias floated out the door and soared into the morning sky.

When Claudia had first approached the cottage she had not noticed there was a vast city that lay beyond the cliff with its lights of night still ablaze in the approaching dawn. The two of them felt a rush as they reached the edge of the cliff and soared toward the city. They stopped moving and floated motionless over mansions with palm trees and swimming pools.

Suddenly like a movie cutting from one scene to the next, Claudia found herself standing in the middle of Rodeo Drive. Cars were whizzing by blowing their horns at her. Now there was only one of her. People on the sidewalks were yelling and waving their arms at her. She tried to move and couldn't. No voice, no legs. Suddenly there was a horrible screeching of tires behind her and she knew she would die. Then all became quiet. As she turned around, a beautiful young man jumped out of a Ferrari and ran to her. He picked her up, leaped in the air and suddenly they were sitting on the armoire looking down at the sleeping Claudia whose eyes shot open. She looked up at the armoire. Seeing no one there, she took a deep breath, closed her eyes and said, "Lance."

Get a grip! she thought. *What the hell did that mean?* Her Observer went into analysis mode: She flew out her bedroom window, found herself in a cottage lost in books, took herself to an exciting and spectacular city, got lost and scared, and a handsome knight in a Ferrari rescued her and took her back to her room.

She laughed. "I dreamed a sexist fairy tale." But she couldn't deny that the dream belonged to her, and its symbols seemed clear. In the last week she'd left the voyeuristic life of books, tasted an exhilarating evening with a rich and famous family in a spectacular city, experienced a lovely silence with Lance on the bench in the garden with Beverly Hills at her feet. Her senses were opened to a new world and, to be honest with herself, new feelings. She thought, *that must have been the flying over the city part.*

After reading the most revealing, intimate musings of a horny teenager she'd gotten scared. *That was the standing in the middle of Rodeo Drive unable to move part.*

Who was rescuing whom, though? She'd decided to be his mentor. Wasn't she rescuing him? 'Not really,' her little Observer answered. Lance was leading her into an intoxicating and unsettling adventure. In a strange way, he'd rescued her from being trapped in the pages of other people's far more distant dramas and dragged her unnervingly from the pages of his diary into the reality of his world.

She loved it.

Chapter 8

The next day Claudia handed the manila envelope, re-sealed, to Lance.

"You did a great job," she said.

Lance's smile spoke of relief. "You really think so?"

"I really think so."

"Everything's…ok? The language and stuff…?"

"Read my note." She pointed to the envelope.

The Van Arden mansion contained two master suites, each with a fireplace, marble bathroom, sitting room, and a walk-in closet the size of Rhode Island. Edward and Roberta had the largest suite and Lance the other. He'd turned half of his walk-in closet into a mini-recording studio and the sitting room into a study. He had read Claudia's note at school, but couldn't wait to read it again. He stretched out on the chaise in the study and perused it carefully.

She's so cool, he thought as he grabbed a pad and wrote:

To: Miss de la Rosa

From: Lance Van Arden

OK, it's our secret. Thanks. I like this.

There was an Edward Hopper painting secretly hinged to the wall over his desk. He swung it open, punched in the code to open the wall safe, put the note inside, took out his classified memory stick, popped it into his laptop, pulled up his diary and began to write:

Day 2: How does falling in love on a weekly basis feel? I like knowing I have this kind of effect on girls. I know I'm supposed to feel guilty about it but I don't. Is it so bad to romance a girl and make her feel how much you desire her? Why does it have to be one at a time? If I make her feel special—and she is!—why does she have to latch on to a guy like a possession? I know there's a time to settle down, get married and raise a family, but I'm 18 years old. Isn't this playtime?

Anyway, more about the birthday party. After Tracey came in we went down to the pool-house to change. I've been wearing Speedos since I was about 12. Most of the other guys wear these boxer things which I could never understand. Why are they so self-conscious? My mother, of course, hates Speedos because they show too much. I tell her, "If you got it, flaunt it."

Tracey wore this red, string bikini. She's got it. She flaunts it too. Very elegantly. We walked down to the deck below the pool where you can see all the way from Beverly Hills to Catalina Island. I stood behind her as she took in the view, wrapped my arms around her and kissed her neck. She turned to me and said, "With that bathing suit on, you're going to be very embarrassed if we start making out here."

I said, "It can't be a gun in my pocket because I don't have a pocket."

She guided me toward a chaise, pushed me down, leaned over and kissed me on the forehead. Then she sat down on the lounge chair next to me and stared out at the view."Do you think we're moving kind of fast?" she asked.

"Do you?" I replied

"A little, maybe. I've known you a week and I'm a little scared."

That old confidence of knowing I'd be right behind her when she left the club last weekend seemed to be wavering.

"Of what?" I asked

"Of feeling like I've known you forever."

As she said it, she hammerlocked me with her eyes again with that, "tell me you'd walk to the ends of the earth for me" look. Seemed like she was looking for the reason to take the next step.

At that moment I wanted her more than I can say. She was so beautiful and so vulnerable and so...

"Hi, Lance..." came this sexy voice from behind us.

I turned and there in a yellow bikini was Melissa!

When Claudia got home, she fished this latest installment out of the stack she'd dumped on the cozy table in her breakfast nook. She read it through without stopping and found herself smiling at the end. She cocked her head for a moment, puzzled by her sudden aversion to these pages. She turned them over, pushed them away, turned off the light and sat in the dark for a long time thinking about what she'd just read and what she felt about it. *What the hell is happening here?* she thought. *I absolutely cannot condone him writing this stuff. Can I?*

She turned it over, read it again and found herself undressing Lance down to his Speedo and imagined the bulge beginning to take shape as he stood behind Tracey and wrapped his arms around her. She noticed that she was glad when Tracey stopped him. And was there an instant of relief that tinged her amusement when Melissa arrived? It certainly must have undone both of those brief romances, she thought, and she was pleased about that. *Claudia de la Rosa!!* she lectured herself. *You absolutely cannot be jealous of an 18-year-old student!*

Her mind drifted back to the boy at the Holiday Inn pool in Flagstaff on her long drive from Michigan to L.A. He was lean and tanned as she imagined Lance was at his birthday party. Every time she glanced up he was looking in her direction with what could only be described as a horny grin plastered on his face. Once she had the nerve to smile at him, whereupon he got up from his lounger, tossed his sun glasses on it and made a spectacular dive into the pool. She knew it was just for her. When he came up for air, he let out a joyful cry, looked her direction and yelled, "Come on in. It's great."

Her heart had skipped a beat and a voice behind her replied. "Ok, I'm coming."

She turned to see a lithe and very young blond in a red bikini swish past her and fly into the pool.

Claudia snapped back to the present with Lance's diary spread before her and thought, *So much for lean, tanned boys. I'm a 26-year-old school teacher, for God's sake. There's no going back, dummy! Get over it, dammit!*

Claudia de la Rosa could, therefore, not deny to herself that she found Lance Van Arden attractive. *But, who doesn't?* she thought. *Most of the girls at school are dying to get in his pants and I'm sure a lot of them probably have. After all, he's already said he falls in love with a different girl every week.* She berated herself with a *Grow up!* and vowed that she could and, more importantly, would separate misplaced attraction from mature and responsible mentoring. She'd be very careful to indulge Lance Van Arden's talent and let him be the horny teenager he needed to be on paper and that's all. She was ready to respond accordingly:

> *To: Lance Van Arden*
> *From: Claudia de la Rosa*
> *Lance, I seem to be on the edge of my seat waiting for your new journal chapters. I can't say that about any of the other students' work. I've had to explore for myself why that is and I have a couple of thoughts that I'll share with you.*

First, you do not write like an 18-year-old. It's so great that I sit here wondering if someone is helping you with it. How much editing do you do? Do you spend a lot of time thinking about what you're going to write?

Second, I find myself captivated because your world is very different from mine. I grew up in a small Mid-western town and was, unfortunately, what you might call a "wall-flower." I was the girl who went to the prom with her cousin's best friend who was coerced into a "mercy date."

So, I suppose I'm a bit of a voyeur when it comes to youthful experiences that differ so vastly from my own.

As a writer you are drawing me into your world and that's good.

As your teacher—someone who is supposed to be guiding you—I am a bit confused about my role in nurturing what is turning out to be an exploration of your "coming of age." If you weren't so talented I'd tell you to stop.

Chapter 9

With Claudia's patient urging, the rest of her students continued to modestly improve their observational skills. Dutch even managed to craft a few crudely eloquent phrases about his mother whose health had recently been on the decline. Claudia's tender notes to him left him doe-eyed with respect and he'd become a model student.

Claudia collected the day's assignments and stopped at Starbucks on the way home from school to satisfy an overwhelming craving for a Venti Mocha Frappuccino. At least that's what she told herself as she wheeled into the parking lot and grabbed Lance's manila envelope from the stack in the trunk. More likely she wanted to rip open his latest installment and sip a blissfully sweet comfort drink while savoring some delicious new paragraphs. As she stirred the whipped cream into the heart of the drink she noticed that a man standing behind her table waiting for his Tall Chai Latte was trying to see what she was so eagerly reading. She shifted her position so the precious pages were out of his line of sight and read:

DIARY OF A TEENAGER WITH RAGING HORMONES
By Lance Van Arden
Chapter 3
It's great that you think I'm a good writer. To tell you the truth, I'm really getting off on this project. And no, no one is helping me. And I don't edit much

except I read over what I've read and if it's not clear to me I fix it.

I can't believe you were ever a wall-flower like you said. I don't know what you looked like when you were in high school, but you're a stunner now. I hope you don't mind me saying that. Besides being beautiful, you've got a really cute, deer-caught-in-the-headlights kind of look about you when someone surprises you with a smart remark or brings up something you never thought of. I mean that nicely. Some of the others in the class like to tease you to see that look. Some of them are maybe a little mean about it, but most of us really like you a lot and we find it cute. That's not a very good word, cute. Maybe charming or endearing is more to the point. Anyway, I hope you got over your wall-flowerness by now. You must be making some guy very happy. P.S. What I wrote before about Tracey? Forget it. She dumped me after the birthday party. Another one, I guess, who thought she had a lock on me. Oh, well.

She read it once and found herself smiling when she finished. *So much for Tracey*, she thought. She read it again and her brow furrowed a bit. A third read and her heart started to race. *He thinks I'm a stunner?! Beautiful?! Is he flirting with me in writing? What am I doing letting him talk to me like this? I have to tell him to stop!*

She read it a fourth time and thought, *He did say he wasn't coming on to me and the tone was gentle and sweet. Really kind of innocent. Don't over-react.* So she wrote:

> *To: Lance Van Arden*
> *From: Claudia de la Rosa*
> *I'm a little thrown by the personal reference to me in your last diary chapter. You start by answering my questions and then tell me I'm beautiful. That's probably enough to get me fired if I let you keep it up!! But you're so charming about it all that I can't get too*

angry. After all I did start it by telling you the wall-flower story. But, perhaps from now on you might want to avoid addressing me directly in the diary pages. If you want to communicate personally, please do so in our separate notes as before. If you become a successful writer, I'm not too keen on showing up in your published diaries with you describing your English teacher as a stunner!!

Tell more stories. From your life experiences. You have the heart of a writer. Observe and write. Who are your most interesting friends or relatives? What are their unique qualities?

There, she thought, *That ought to send him in a different direction.* Even though he's titled himself as a teenager with raging hormones, it would be best if he took his mind off his crotch for awhile. *Odd to think that way,* she thought. *He bares his soul about falling in love with a different girl weekly and makes it sound so right and so adorable and I characterize him as a crotch.* She declined to look at why.

Claudia handed back the diary assignments at the end of the next class. Most of the students stuffed them into their backpacks and vanished quickly. Lance pulled Claudia's note out of the envelope and read it eagerly as he zipped his bag and started for the door. Claudia watched as his face fell. Her heart sank the moment she saw the pain on his face. He looked up, shrugged and mouthed "I'm sorry."

She didn't mean to make him feel badly and wanted to stop him to say she didn't mean it—that he could write any damn thing he wanted. Her eyes must have said something like that because he strode to her desk and said, "I'm so sorry I made you uncomfortable. Sometimes it feels so natural to say things to you I can't say to anyone else that I forget."

"I know." After an awkward moment she blurted out, "I feel the same way. Maybe we're some kind of soul mates or something." As soon as she saw his puzzled expression she tried to back track. "I'm sorry. That was a goofy thing to say. I mean sometimes people communicate in ways they don't understand…and make up silly reasons why—like maybe we're soul mates."

"Actually, it's not so silly," he replied. "There's this really weird guy that I tutor who goes on and on about soul mates and spirit guides and channeling entities—stuff like that—and he actually makes sense when you sit and listen to him. His name's Marco. I told him about how you really get my writing and he said, 'maybe you're soul mates'."

Now it was her turn to look puzzled.

With a smile he said, "Don't worry I haven't told him anything *incriminating*. He's really cool. I was actually thinking about writing about him in my diary. Interesting family. I think his dad's in the 'trucking' business, if you know what I mean."

"Mafia?!"

"Shhh," he teased. "I don't want a horse's head in my bed. Seriously, no matter what his family does, he's kind of awesome for a sophomore."

"Then you should write about him. Give yourself a break from your libido. Me too."

"I don't know about that," he grinned. "Marco is as gay as you can get and started our first conversation with an assessment of my abs. Then he went on to blow my mind with a piece of information he couldn't possibly know without *extraterrestrial* help. It sure seems like there's some kind of awesome psychic ability there. I don't know whether to take him seriously or not."

"Sounds like a good story in there somewhere."

Chapter 10

Lance sat up far into the night thinking about Marco and writing:

> Lance Van Arden – Chapter 4
> Marco Cerasuolo has a tongue coated in honey and dipped in vinegar. From the moment I walked into his house he had me smiling and completely wrapped around his little finger.

Lance sat for a long time thinking about how to describe Marco. How do you adequately depict someone who cuts through to the core of your very being at the moment he meets you, whittles you down to size and makes you feel good about it?

He had arrived for the first tutoring session at the Cerasuolo home on Roxbury Drive one Saturday morning at ten sharp. It took at least five minutes for someone to answer the door, and when it happened he was greeted by what seemed to be a wizened widow from the vineyards of Taormina. The bronzed and withered woman in black peeked at him through a crack in the door. She croaked at him in caustic Sicilian, rattling on and on with appropriately accompanying gestures as if he'd come to assassinate the household. He deduced that if he kept saying "Marco" over and over she'd come to her senses and let him in. Fortunately Marco took her by the arm, spoke softly and propelled her toward the kitchen.

"Sorry about Nonna," he said brightly. "Sometimes she can't tell the difference between real people and dead people. Sometimes I can't either, but you are one hell of a real one, sweetheart. Cheekbones to die for and a six-pack like a rock.

"Excuse me?!" was all that a usually cool Lance could muster.

"Excuse you, what? You're gorgeous. Come on in. Don't be afraid. I'm sure your father's more my type anyway."

Marco led Lance through the living room filled with high-end rent-a-couches and lithographs of old masters printed on brush textured canvas. *Clearly temporary quarters. Best not to ask why.*

Marco's impeccably spiked hair had an overtly blonde and low-lighted aspect that screamed 'look at me.' Lance couldn't help staring at him as they walked toward the dining room. His hips swayed like a girl's but his tank-topped torso was muscular and masculine. His aura of self-assurance was impressive. Lance liked him. Marco pointed him toward the dining table. "You can dump your bag over there." Lance started to unpack the books he intended to use and Marco plunked down two bottles of beer and a deck of Tarot cards.

"Nobody's home but Nonna and she's on another planet," said Marco. "If we hear a car in the driveway we can ditch the bottles and pop an Altoid."

"I don't think we should..." said Lance nodding at the bottles. "If your parents found out I'd lose my tutoring job."

"Oh, for God's sake, lighten up. You don't need the job and I don't need the tutoring. Here. Drink up."

With that Marco pushed the books aside and shoved the Tarot deck toward Lance. "Cut the cards," he said.

"We're playing cards?"

"Not *playing* cards. *Reading* cards."

At that point, Lance gave himself over to the beer and the card reading. Marco didn't seem to offer any choices and Lance figured it might be fun to see where all of this went. This was definitely not your average high school sophomore.

"Anything in particular you want to know about?" Marco asked.

"I'm not sure I really believe in this."

Marco smiled, took a deep breath and closed his eyes. He knew his spirit guides would come through and give him a piece of information that would blow Lance's mind. It always happened that way. If you were going to help someone they couldn't be doubters. His eyes popped open.

"You had a girlfriend named Carla," he said.

"I think everyone at school knows that," said Lance with a tinge of triumph. So much for that mumbo-jumbo, he thought.

"But not everyone at school knows she had an abortion in August."

Lance caught his breath and blushed.

"How the hell do you know that?" he demanded.

"I didn't until they gave it to me."

"They? Who are they?"

"Daniel and The Bear," Marco said. "Daniel whispers in my left ear and The Bear whispers in my right. And they say not to worry."

"Worry?"

"It wasn't yours."

Lance's mind was appropriately blown. He was ready to pack up his book bag and flee, but Marco spoke softly and gently touched his arm. "Don't be afraid. They only make me do that when someone needs help and needs to believe." Marco's wry sarcasm had evaporated and he was speaking with a sense of clarity that no 16-year-old could have or should have.

"Maybe reading the cards is not a good idea right now," said a fearful Lance.

"I don't need the cards. They're just a crutch to get things started. I'm already tuned in and they're asking me to tell you something. But you have to ask me if you want to hear it."

Lance looked into the dark, bottomless eyes of this strange young man as tears suddenly welled up in his own. His body felt like he was leaping off a cliff and able to fly. "Yes," he said. "Tell me."

"Sometimes they talk in riddles. This is one. You are embarking upon an adventure. Be careful. You can learn much and you can teach much. Do not lead someone up a mountain unless you are willing to risk everything if they fall."

"What does that mean?" asked Lance.

"Whatever it means." said Marco. "To you."

"It doesn't mean anything to me. Aren't you supposed to tell me what it's about?"

"Not unless they tell me I can."

Lance chose not to write about the abortion in his diary. Instead he wrote about the questions he asked Marco about his powers, how it worked and how he got them.

He's been this way since he can remember and it wasn't until about four years ago that he put all the pieces together to realize he wasn't crazy. He calls it a gift.

His grandmother—Nonna he calls her—had the gift too. She taught him how to cast and break spells. He says he mostly doesn't cast spells because it's interfering with the natural order of things. But when people come to him to break spells others have put on them, what she taught him comes in handy.

Do I believe any of this? Before I met Marco I'd have said it's all bullshit. Now...??? He's VERY self-confident about it all and it's hard to poke holes in what he says. And, he gave me some information that absolutely no one on this earth knows but me. I'd say the jury is still out for me.

Meanwhile, he passed on a message from his *guides*. Something like I'm not supposed to go mountain climbing with someone who might fall off the mountain. And if I do, it's risky for me. Whatever the hell that means. He said he couldn't tell me what it means until "they" tell him he can. What good is that?! They, by the way, are Daniel and The Bear. He said The Bear is not really a bear, but someone who in his life on earth was big and burly, drank a lot of whiskey and smoked Cuban cigars. Am I nuts for listening to this stuff or what???

Lance pondered what he'd written. As odd as it sounded when he wrote it, he really thought there was something to it all and that Marco really was put in his path for a reason. He just couldn't figure out yet what that reason was. *All in good time*, he thought.

Chapter 11

Claudia realized that she'd created a new habit of making the Venti Mocha Frappuccino stop on the way home from school in order to pop open the manila envelope to sample Lance's latest. *Excellent*, she thought as she breezed through it. *I've re-directed him away from his libido.* She loved the way he populated his life with rich characters and found enjoyment in writing about them. She resolved to encourage him to dig a little deeper into Marco, perhaps because her own grandmother fancied herself a bit of a *bruja*, rattling bones, throwing them on the floor, and pouring elixirs of honey and herbs over photos brought to her by needy neighbors. Most of her aunts and cousins were embarrassed by *abuela's* antics, but when they had some problem with their husbands straying or their bosses harassing them, who did they run to for extraterrestrial help?

And then there was *Viejo Paulo* who inhabited a cave in the nearby mountains. No one ever saw him in the village. It was rumored that he never ate anything and drank his own urine. Claudia had heard the story about the parish priests who preached against the evil of witchcraft, but when the mayor's daughter turned into a real-life monster, like the little girl in The *Exorcist*, and bit off the little finger of Fr. Francisco when he ineptly waved his cross at her, they summoned Viejo Paulo to deal with it. And deal with it he did.

Claudia was, therefore, inordinately interested in finding out more about Marco the sophomore brujo.

As she sat savoring Lance's latest she became aware that the bookish-looking man at the next table kept glancing up from his laptop to stare at her. He reminded her of what she thought her ill-fated paramour, William Potter, III, must look like a dozen years later. Not what you'd call handsome exactly, but clean-cut, intelligent and driven behind those wire rimmed glasses. As she cocked her head slightly to assess the similarities, he smiled at her, took off the glasses, closed the lid on his laptop and slid into the empty chair at her table.

"I can't imagine what you're reading, but the look on your face is absolutely transfixing," he said. "Mind if I join you?"

"You already have," she mused.

"Want to share it?" he asked.

His directness and the simplicity of his smile appealed to her. It had been a long time since a man had showered such attention on her and she thought she'd see where it went.

"Just an essay by one of my students," she said.

"Must be good. What's it about?"

"Sexy young men and magic. But I'm sworn to secrecy," she said with a conspiratorial gleam in her eye. *You want to flirt,* she thought, *I'll flirt right back at you.*

"You're gonna tease me and leave it right there?"

"Actually, he's a very talented writer with some remarkable friends and I really enjoy reading his work."

"And the secret part?" His question invited confessions.

She pantomimed zipping her lip. "It's actually a deal I made with the whole class. They're keeping diaries and I'm the only one who can read them. It helps them open themselves up to more candid self-expression."

"I can respect that."

"Good. I'm Claudia de la Rosa."

"Clay Brooks. I'm a talent manager." Clay was no William Potter, III. He definitely knew how to take matters into his own hands. Over another Venti Mocha Frappuccino he regaled her with stories from his days at The William Morris Agency—the big deals with big names and bigger price tags. He forgot to mention, however, that his paycheck was actually four credits earned as part of a DeWitt College internship. Over dinner at

Dan Tana's he told her how it always takes a little time for big things to gel in Hollywood. He assured her he was a man on the move.

Clay had a good heart, but had never succeeded at much. School had never been his thing. He'd tried acting school and had made a valiant effort to learn to play the guitar, but hadn't quite found his niche. His one gift was an ability to recognize talent and schmooze convincingly. Three of his acting school friends had no clue about the mechanics of finding work as an actor so Clay took them under his wing and *signed* them. Josh Van Alden was one. Josh was riotously funny with a mobile, Jim Carrey face. He was also a pathological liar and had convinced everyone that he was related to the Van Arden fashion dynasty even though his name was spelled Van Alden. Clay had gotten him a couple of under-five-line roles in primetime. Another of his clients got a beefy role as a short order cook in a Garry Marshall film (that ended up on the cutting room floor), and another got a recurring role on *The Bold and the Beautiful.* Not enough commissions to quit his day job yet, but he was sure he'd be a major player within a year. Some really hot deals in the works now, he told her.

"With whom?" Claudia asked.

With an impish smile he replied, "Now that's my secret!"

He insisted that she come back to his apartment to view his collection of menus. Yes, menus. He had one from every restaurant that had ever opened its doors in Hollywood. He'd even been written up in Variety. "And over my sofa, I've got the menu from Sardi's final day framed in Plexiglas."

"Really?"

"Isn't that the coolest thing?"

Claudia was speechless. She felt like rolling her eyes, but just smiled sweetly, cocked her head a little and said, "Wow."

This is sounding more and more like William Potter, III, said the little Observer on her shoulder. A bit weird, in a charming sort of way. She would put the visit to his apartment off until another day.

He insisted that she was the most special woman he'd met since he got to Los Angeles and made her promise they'd get together again.

He's a bit odd, she thought, but she loved the attention and he was, after all, a Hollywood 'player'. Worth at least another dinner. Or, hmmm…she'd been invited to a benefit at the Van Arden mansion this Saturday night. Why not show up on the arm of a Hollywood manager?

Chapter 12

That evening Claudia breezed through her usual, cursory comments on the class diary homework, saving her comments on Lance's until last.

> To: Lance Van Arden
> From: Claudia de la Rosa
> I thoroughly enjoyed your chapter about Marco. You asked yourself if you're nuts for believing any of it. Doubt and questioning are very healthy. Rest assured that there have been many brilliant writers before you who have asked the same questions. Carlos Castaneda comes to mind. He wrote a fascinating series of novels about a shaman named Don Juan. Very controversial at the time. They were presumably drawn from his own personal experiences.
> For my own part, I believe! Personal experiences with my own grandmother made it very real for me. When my parents brought her from Mexico to Michigan she hated it at first because she didn't know where to go to find her "tools"—things like powdered sulphur to do 'spell breakings,' herbs like ajenjo and star anise. There is no such thing as a botanica in

Harbor Point, Michigan. We finally found a mail order one. I can't imagine what the postal inspectors must have thought. I'd love to read more about Marco. From your description I think I've seen him in the halls.

By the way, your mother sent me an invitation to the benefit at your house on Saturday night. I've actually met someone and I'll bring him along. He's a talent manager.

Claudia stuffed the marked papers in the plastic supermarket bag she'd been using as a carry-all since school had started. She kept reminding herself that she had to buy something Beverly Hillsish that was large enough to carry the mounds of homework she accumulated every day. Her budget wouldn't quite manage Louis Vuitton or Gucci at the moment. She'd have to make do with something inexpensive but cool.

At the very moment she was pondering this dilemma the doorbell rang. It was her next door neighbor Monica who proudly proffered a navy blue canvas tote with red piping and red and gold lettering that said 'La Biennale di Venezia—1970.' "Sweetheart," she said, "I just could not abide seeing you dragging that ragged Vons bag to school every day. Here. I'm a pack rat. Had this stuffed in the back of my closet. I actually sang at the Biennale in 1970, would you believe. One of my good years. I was a bit of a star then, you know. It'll be very chic on your arm, dear."

Monica and Claudia shared a narrow balcony in one of those aging, beige apartment complexes with cookie cutter boxes of studios and one bedrooms that mostly housed attractive, young transplants from Ohio and Kansas newly arrived to find fame and fortune, and old people whose moment of fame had never happened or had come and gone. Monica fell into the latter category. She was a sweet soul whose heart had led her astray more than once and whose career as a singer had catapulted her briefly to a top ten spot in the '50s. Monica had her social security now and free rent as manager of this creaking haven for those whose hopes had not yet been dashed. She was young-at-heart enough to enjoy the bright-eyed enthusiasm of the young hopefuls and wise enough to be able to console them in their disappointments.

"Monica, how lovely. I was just thinking about having to buy something chic and trendy and, I swear, you rang as it was going through my mind. Thank you so much. It's perfect."

"Yes it is, isn't it," Monica replied wistfully, clearly parting with an object of some sentimental significance.

"I'll just borrow it," Claudia said, picking up on Monica's moment of almost regret. "Until I buy something else. I know it must bring back wonderful memories to you. It's so sweet of you to loan it to me."

Monica paused ever so briefly to consider this and said, "No, dear. It's yours. I'm goin' on 80 years old and I don't want to die with a closet full of things that…" Tears welled up in her eyes as she paused to collect herself. "…things that the people who'd paw over them at the Salvation Army when I'm gone wouldn't know were important. This was important—to me. I carried home a carnival mask in it from Venice once. Maybe, for some reason, it will be important to you too."

Now they were both teary-eyed. "Oh, Monica," said Claudia. "It's important to me because of what it means to you and because you chose to give it to me. It's beautiful. And so are you." Claudia drew Monica into her arms to say "thank you" in the most profound way she could think to do so. Claudia felt this frail lady's loneliness that, somehow, mirrored her own and she was overwhelmed.

Claudia's Observer noted that, once again, life presented her with the right thing at the right time. She missed her family. She was alone in a place foreign to her experience. And here was a kind, motherly soul who gave her a piece of herself. She heard the Observer tell her to remember this—a moment in time when strangers meet to form a bond of trust and love. She knew that one day she would write about it.

Claudia made mint tea and they sat at her kitchen table for hours talking about their lives and loves, bad times and good times. Monica rattled off the names of friends from the '40s and '50s many of whom were *names* in their day. Some of them had sent her checks when they knew she'd fallen on hard times. Most of them were now dead.

Claudia told her about growing up in Harbor Point.

"Why did you move to California?" asked Monica.

"I figured if I'm going to be a writer, I need to experience life in a more enlightened environment."

Monica laughed. "I think you might get some argument about Beverly Hills as an enlightened environment."

"Well, fast-paced and exciting then. With interesting people doing interesting things."

"Such as?"

"Well, this boy in my class for instance. He's a wonderful writer for an 18-year-old, and he's living a fabulous life I could only dream about. His family has this mansion up in the hills overlooking the world. They're rich and famous fashion designers and they know everybody! They invited me to dinner right after I started teaching Lance and it was fabulous. Monica, you wouldn't believe their house. Well, I suppose *you* would. When he walked me to the car after dinner the entire city of Los Angeles was like a carpet of light. We sat down on a bench and it just overwhelmed me. That's why I came to California. I couldn't find that in Harbor Point, Michigan."

"And this Lance? What's he like?"

"Fascinating. He writes the most intriguing diary."

"You're reading his diary?"

"It's an assignment. The class is keeping a diary and I read them all."

"That must be enlightening. I don't think I'd have the nerve to read the diaries of teenagers in this day and age."

"Mostly they write about what they had for breakfast or the fight they had with their mother. Lance is different. It just reads well. Like a writer. I've sort of become his mentor. I find I just can't wait to rip open the envelope to read the next installment. He's that good."

"Does he have a crush on you?"

"What?!!" No! Why do you ask me that?"

Monica smiled. "Sounds like the English teacher has a crush on the 'intriguing' Lance."

Claudia blushed. "Oh, please! How could you even suggest that? He's only 18."

Monica raised her eyebrow with a knowing smile and reached for the Vons bag. "When did that ever matter? Which one is his?"

Claudia panicked. "No. Monica, I can't. I made an agreement with the class. No one ever sees them but me."

"Why?"

"It protects their creative freedom if they don't have to share what they write with the class."

"Sounds like a recipe for disaster to me, dear. But, who am I to judge? Just be careful. This town does strange things to those of us who arrive with stars in our eyes and loneliness in our hearts." Monica paused thoughtfully. "I've never even told my own daughter this…" Monica said looking into Claudia's eyes for a reason to continue.

Claudia felt such a strong note of sadness in Monica that she cocked her head slightly signaling her to go on.

Monica took a deep breath. "When I was 26 I had an absolutely torrid affair with my agent's 17-year-old son."

For some reason that she didn't quite understand, Claudia flushed. "What happened?"

"Cost me the best agent in town and, if I let myself be completely honest about it, probably ruined my career. Things were never the same after that."

"How did it start?"

"I've asked myself that a thousand times. I don't know. Really, I don't. I didn't mean it to. He was very attractive. Tall, dark and handsome as they say. Charming. I was his friend. We were pals. I even baby-sat him when he was younger, for God's sake!

I'd been through seven 'relationships' with the most despicable men. They breed in this town like flies. You've seen the type. Or you will. Power brokers. The world is their oyster and I was delicious in those days. Tell you anything to get in your pants and suddenly you're old hat and they're on to the next challenge. I was easy pickin's. Low self-esteem my therapist called it.

I'd just been dumped by number seven and, David was his name, David was consoling me. Claudia, I was so destroyed. I thought it must be my fault. I was not good enough for these 'important' men. I felt ugly. Worthless. I'm not exaggerating

53

when I tell you I wanted to die that night. David drove me home. He was my friend. I could tell him anything—and I did. I told him everything. He told me I was wrong to blame myself. It wasn't my fault. I was beautiful and kind and loving and he couldn't stand to see me like this."

Monica took a long moment, reflecting deep within herself, then turned and looked into Claudia's eyes with the most profound pain Claudia had ever seen.

"Then he took my face in his hands and kissed me. Not hard or brutal like the others. Just kissed me. He said… he said, 'I love you.' And I believed him because he did. It was beautiful, Claudia. From that moment on for two months it was just beautiful." Monica's face glowed as she recreated those moments in her mind. Then her face clouded and her body slumped. "And he was 17; his father found out and I was finished."

Claudia found herself breathless. "But, didn't he defend you?"

"Defend me?" asked Monica. "His father was the most powerful agent in Hollywood, his mother sat on charity boards that controlled millions of dollars. They had a 'reputation' to uphold. He was 17. They told him that if he ever saw me or spoke to me again they'd have me arrested. They sent him to school in Switzerland. What could he do?"

Claudia thought to herself that he could have done something. She didn't know what, but something.

When Claudia returned to her apartment, she sank into the big leather reading chair and picked up a *New Yorker* to try to unwind from Monica's unsettling tale. After spending 10 minutes on one paragraph and still not remembering what she'd read, she decided it was time to call Sally.

Sally Stewart was her best friend in college and after they got past the then-uncomfortable fact that Sally was a lesbian with an undeniable crush on Claudia and Claudia had a thing for men, they found they could talk about anything—and did. If things had been different, they'd have made a good couple. They shared their dreams and broken hearts and vowed they'd always be there for each other when the chips were down. Claudia had gotten an MFA in English and a job in Beverly Hills and Sally had become a big deal veterinarian specializing in wildlife who darted between Europe's major zoos to solve large problems with large animals.

Claudia calculated the time difference and dialed Sally's cell.

"Stewart," she answered.

"Hi, Sal. Did I wake you?"

"No, doll. Got a hippo emergency. Can I call you back?"

"I guess." Claudia's tone said *help*.

"All right," Sally said, picking up on the plea. "Give me a second." Claudia heard several minutes of muffled shouting and swearing before Sally came back on the line with a "Holy shit!! And I mean that quite literally, doll. Vet school never adequately explained what it's like to give an enema to a hippo!" With that she let out a victorious hoot and screamed, "Mission accomplished!"

Sally found a quiet spot away from the cacophony of animals agitated by their hippo friend's predicament. Claudia launched into her just-finished conversation with Monica.

"So," asked Sally with her usual bluntness, "you're thinking of doing it with this kid?"

Claudia laughed. "No," she said with certainty. "I just needed to hear you ask that question in the way you just asked it to make it absolutely clear to me that I could not possibly be that stupid."

Weight lifted. Dilemma dismissed. They chatted about lions and tigers and hippos, lunch at the Four Seasons and a benefit at the Van Arden estate to which Claudia, quite happily, announced she would be taking a date. Sally agreed that it was a wise move to send that kind of message to the young heartthrob just in case he had any sort of crush on the teacher.

On the next day after school, Lance sat in the school parking lot and eagerly opened Claudia's note to see how she'd reacted to his latest installment. She met someone? He didn't quite know why he didn't like the idea. It would be interesting to meet him. She'd probably be entertained if he wrote a diary chapter with his thoughts about the guy. Maybe not. She'd asked him not to get personal.

Chapter 13

On Saturday night, Clay was 45 minutes late. Claudia fumed impatiently by the window in the Carolina Herrera cocktail dress she'd picked up at a studio re-sale shop and the new shoes that had cost a month of lunches. He finally screeched to the curb in a hot, red Lamborghini.

"Wow. This is amazing" she exclaimed, letting the car dazzle her into forgetting how annoyed she was by his tardiness. "I was just about ready to go by myself."

"Sorry," he purred. "Had to take a meeting and it took longer than it was supposed to."

She poured herself into the seat and with an unnecessary squeal of tires they were off. She said, "Straight up Doheny and make a left…"

"Uh, uh, uh, uh," he interrupted while pushing a button on the dash.

"Your route is being calculated."

"I already programmed their address. Don't you just love it?"

"When did you get this?" she asked.

"Just picked it up today."

"You just bought it?"

"Let's say it's one of the perks of my job."

There was something in the way he said it that seemed mysterious and a little naughty. Right now, it only mattered that he was a successful Hollywood insider who seemed to fit right into her sudden immersion into the high life. "I could get used to this."

As they arrived at the Van Arden valet station, they had to wait behind two Bentleys, a Jaguar, a BMW and two Mercedes before a handsome young man took the car.

"They're all actors," said Clay.

"Who?"

"The valet parkers. Actors wait tables or park cars. Goes with the territory."

Claudia remembered that when she'd come to dinner with the Van Ardens the motor court was ringed by a lovely selection of tropical palms and tree ferns. That tropical motif was now richly amplified with a vast amount of lush vegetation and special-effects rain in selected areas (certainly not on the arriving guests). There were parrots and monkeys in the trees (unobtrusively tethered mind you) chattering loudly enough to visually and aurally announce to the arriving visitors that this very evening they'd have the opportunity to *Save the Rain Forests.*

The Van Ardens had polished the charity event to its most lustrous. Inviting a cross section of the rich and famous to see and be seen with one another, with an equal portion of those aspiring to be rich and famous along for the star gazing and the photo ops, brought tens of thousands of dollars into the coffers of worthy causes. Clay Brooks had lucked out to find a pretty girl in a coffee shop who just happened to be coming to one of the season's hottest tickets. He showed up in style and was intent on working the room.

Roberta and Edward were ensconced at the door to greet their guests with 10 charming seconds of small talk and kisses on the cheek as if they were the best of friends. Their social secretary who had memorized the photos, names and a personal nugget or two on each individual stood discreetly by to prompt them as needed. But Roberta and Edward seemed to know everyone and the human prompter was rarely called upon.

Lance had just finished piling a plate high at the buffet table when he saw Claudia and Clay waiting their turn at the door. He surprised himself with a visceral reaction to her date. First impressions are always right, he'd heard. Who's the nerd? How could she be with someone like that? He put hunger aside, stowed his plate and headed across the room as Roberta greeted them.

"Claudia! We're so glad you could make it."

Edward said, "You were such a charming dinner guest we knew you would thoroughly enjoy our little soiree."

"Thank you for inviting me. I'd like you to meet my new friend, Clay Brooks."

Edward's line: "So nice to meet you, Clay. Glad you could come."

Roberta's line: "Welcome to our home. Please come in and enjoy yourself."

That little script usually ushered the guests on into the house so the line of guests waiting at the door could continue to move. But Clay didn't quite pick up on that. He continued the conversation with, "I was so pleased when Claudia invited me to be her guest. I believe we have something in common. Your nephew."

The dramatic pause invited some kind of response—albeit a puzzled one from Roberta. "Our nephew...?"

"I manage actors and just signed one of your nephews—Josh."

"Josh..." The formerly charming smiles on Edward and Roberta now became masks. The mouths were still smiling but the eyes were saying, 'Who the hell are we talking about?'

Clay was quick enough to pick up on the fact that they hadn't the foggiest notion who Josh was. "Well, he said he was your nephew."

"Last time we looked," Roberta replied, "we had three nephews between us and none of them are named Josh."

Clay said, "Cousin, maybe?"

Edward laughed. "A long lost one maybe."

At that moment, Lance breezed into the picture. "Miss de la Rosa!"

His smile was a lifesaver for Claudia. Clay's strange start to the evening became a small bump and the path forward seemed smooth to her now that Lance had arrived.

"Lance," said Edward, "do we have a relative named Josh? An actor? Meet Claudia's friend, Mr. Brooks. He's a manager who represents someone claiming to be related to us."

Lance extended his hand. "He must be lying. Your client I mean, not you of course," Lance said, making eye contact with Clay that could be read to mean 'Yes, I mean you.'

Trying for a recovery, Clay smiled broadly and said, "You're Lance, Claudia's student, right? You're not the one writing about 'sexy young men and magic' are you?"

Claudia turned crimson and said, "What?!"

Roberta's antenna went up with the sexy young men and magic remark and she took charge with a sharp look to Claudia and an intense look to her son. "Lance, why don't you show our guests to the bar. We're holding up the line... Evelyn, so delighted to see you, darling. Thank you for coming. How's Carl?" The door ritual had begun again.

Lance took Claudia by the arm and led her into the atrium. Clay tagged along behind them. Claudia leaned into Lance and said, "I'm so sorry. It's not like it seems."

Lance squeezed her arm comfortingly as Clay struggled to keep up with them. It was a reassuring touch and Claudia was emboldened by it. As Clay grabbed her arm she stopped, turned on him with fire in her eyes, led him to a vacant chair, and said, "Sit down and shut up! You have said entirely enough to last you the whole evening. If you move a muscle from this chair ..."

Lance finished her sentence, "...she'll ask the sexy young man who writes about magic to escort you bodily to your car."

With that, Lance and Claudia walked arm in arm across the atrium to the bar.

Clay, feeling thoroughly humiliated, couldn't imagine it getting any worse. But there was a rustle of activity at the door. Edward and Roberta were intently discussing something of import with four uniformed police officers and one of the valet parkers. They had all turned scouring the room with their eyes. The valet parker leaned over to speak to one of the officers, pointing at Clay. The officers, hands poised on their holsters, crossed the room.

The commotion had caught the attention of Claudia and Lance who witnessed the officers approach Clay and ask, "Sir, did you arrive in the red Lamborghini, license number 5KLI64X4?"

"What if I did?" said Clay.

"Sir, did you arrive in it?"

"Uh, I'm not sure that's my license number."

"Did you arrive in a red Lamborghini?"

"Uh, yes."

The officer turned to the valet parker, "Any other red Lamborghinis here tonight?"

The valet parker nodded 'no.'

With that they whipped him around, patted him down, cuffed him, told him he was under arrest for grand theft auto, read him his rights and marched him out the door.

Clay was not really a car thief in the gang-banger sense. He had wanted to make a big splash with Claudia and the Van Ardens. What seemed like a harmless opportunity had presented itself and in a moment of temptation, he couldn't resist. "I can clear this up. The owner gave me the keys."

The lieutenant said, "Tell it to the judge."

"Really, this is all a mistake. I know the owner. I'm supposed to have it detailed."

Claudia was mortified. She looked at Edward and Roberta and they were clearly distressed. There was a palpable sense of anxiety among the guests piled up at the door. The Van Ardens pulled themselves together, put on the hosting charm and ushered them all in at once without individual greetings. The guests who had seen Claudia arrive with Clay were nodding toward her. She could only imagine what they were saying. Roberta and Edward were approaching with a police officer. They were clearly trying to defuse his interest in interrogating Claudia who had, of course, arrived with the thief. Once more she was feeling like 'Señorita Stupid.' Roberta managed to convince him that Claudia was an innocent bystander and assured him that she'd make sure Claudia came down to the police station during the week to give a statement. When Edward and Roberta took the officer's arm and escorted him, somewhat unwillingly, to the door, Claudia lost it. Lance tried to calm her as she wept about how sorry she was and how she needed to get out of there, begging him to call her a cab.

Edward and Roberta reappeared after managing the officer. Claudia sobbed, "I am so, so sorry."

Roberta demanded, "Who was that?"

"I don't know him, really. I met him day before yesterday in Starbucks. He said he was a talent manager. I'm such a fool."

"Perhaps a little foolish," Edward said kindly. "But not a fool." You just learned a very big lesson about being careful who and what you believe in this town."

"He was so convincing! I've created such a mess." Tears welled up in her eyes once more and she said, "Please, could you call me a taxi."

"You're certainly welcome to stay if you'd like, but I know you've been through the wringer," said Edward.

"I would like to go home if you don't mind."

"You'll come visit us again when it's a bit less stressful."

Lance smiled wryly and said, "Next time we'll send a car for you."

They all laughed and Claudia had to smile a little too. Just like Lance to lighten the mood and make her feel better.

"Lance, why don't you take Claudia on home."

"Cool," Lance said.

The Van Ardens' eight car garage sat just off the main motor court. To Claudia, walking there took an eternity—past arriving guests buzzing about the yellow police tape surrounding the red Lamborghini, past whispering valet parkers, past the incredible view of twinkling lights that on her last visit had dazzled her as she sat on a bench with the warmth of Lance's jacket soothing her. Now she couldn't wait to dive into the passenger seat of Lance's Prius and escape the nightmare this evening had become.

Lance sped quickly past the prying eyes and noticed that Claudia heaved a great sigh as they left the Van Arden gate and rolled down the hill toward the ordinary life she thought she was escaping. Her head was turned toward her side window so Lance would not see her tears. She didn't know what to say to him. She'd said "I'm sorry" so many times that evening and it never seemed enough. What more could be said?

Lance had experienced tearful exchanges with various girlfriends when they'd accused him of doing something stupid or insensitive. Those tears had baffled him and left him annoyed. Claudia's tears, which he couldn't see but knew were there, were different. Her pain wounded him.

He kept trying to find something to say to her but nothing sounded right. 'It'll be ok,' didn't work because she'd never forget this night and it would never be ok. 'Don't worry about it,' wouldn't work because she will worry about it. She'll worry that she humiliated herself in front of him, that he would tell someone and everyone at school would find out about it and laugh at her.

61

He knew they would, and he knew he would never tell. He struggled to find something that would comfort her. Nothing came and there was a cloud of dark silence for awhile until, for the umpteenth time Claudia said, "Lance, I'm really so sorry about this."

"No. Don't say that! You didn't do anything wrong. The guy was an asshole. You're really one of the kindest people I know and it kills me to see what he did to you. Please," he pleaded, "don't be sorry."

She turned and looked at his face. The oncoming headlights made his eyes shine with the almost-tears lingering there. "Thanks," she said so simply that he knew how much she meant it. He thought, *how perfect was that?*

They both simultaneously heaved a relieved sigh and then laughed that they had done so.

The tension broken, Lance said, "You want to stop for a burger or something?"

"God, yes!" she said. "I'm starved and here I'm keeping you from the feast you're missing at your house so it's my treat."

"Deal," he said.

They settled into a booth at Johnny Rockets and dug into burgers, fries and chocolate malteds.

"Nothing like comfort food to soothe the injured spirit," Claudia said. "We had a place like this in my hometown and every time high school ganged up on me I'd take a novel, grab a stool at the counter, order this, and forget about the world."

"Where is your hometown?"

"Harbor Point, Michigan."

"How did a hot tamale like you end up in Michigan?" Lance asked.

"My God! What did you just call me?"

His face darkened. "I'm sorry…"

"No," she said. "I'm not offended. Just amazed. Some of the guys in high school used to call me that behind my back. And I could never figure out why."

"Why not? You are."

"Strange how we never see ourselves the way other people see us," she said.

"How do you think people see you?"

She thought for a long moment. "The geeky girl with her nose buried in a book who tries too hard at everything she does and makes a fool of herself at every turn."

"No!"

"Really. Haven't you noticed? Look at me tonight. I thought I was being so cool to invite a 'Hollywood manager' to your parents' party, arriving in a Lamborghini, for God's sake, and whamo, right between the eyes!"

"Stop me if this is too personal, but I hated him the moment I saw him. I wondered why you were attracted to him. You could do a lot better, you know."

Claudia looked at his earnest face and did understand. "Thanks," she said with such grateful simplicity that he replied, "You did it again."

"What?"

"The way you said 'thanks,' it was just so… I don't know, so honest. Like when you said it in the car."

It was a moment of nakedness between them that somehow, for all its sincerity and goodness, seemed forbidden.

The burgers and fries had been consumed, the seconds of chocolate malteds had been drunk. "Time you should get me home and get back to your party," she said.

"If we have to," he said. "I'm really having a better time here."

"Yeah, sure."

"Really. You don't know what these Beverly Hills parties are like. A lot of 'grownups' pretending to like each other because they're meeting 'important' people.

They continued to enjoy their oddly begun evening all the way to Claudia's apartment building. They parked out front and talked for another hour about vastly different childhoods, great disappointments, great hurdles and great joys. Lance played some of the songs he and the band had recorded in his mini-studio. Claudia found the bittersweet one that spoke of Majorcan mists and tender goodbyes particularly compelling.

"How on earth does an 18-year-old come up with lyrics like that?"

He grinned. "Actually, I was 17, well almost 17, and she was 26 or 27 I think. About your age." She ignored his sly wink. "My parents took us to Europe for a month and she was our tour guide in Majorca. Maria was her name. It was only four days and I think I got about four years experience out of it if you know what I mean."

Claudia was certain she knew what he meant. For an instant she thought, *Would that I could have been in Maria's shoes*, but she quickly pulled herself together. *Not going there*, she said to herself. *I'm the responsible adult here.* So she ignored his wink and said, "You certainly got a good song out of it. Where else did you go in Europe?"

He told her about falling into an Amsterdam canal, climbing the Eiffel Tower, and water-skiing in Italy. She told him about art-overload in Florence, imagining Shakespeare walking the streets of Stratford-on-Avon, and falling in love with love upon seeing a wedding party emerge from St. Mark's Basilica in Venice.

Strange, thought Claudia, how what had started out as the most horrible night in her life had turned into what, in other circumstances, would be considered a great first date. Oh, well.

Like the gentleman she knew him to be, Lance walked her to her door. She thanked him for salvaging the evening and he told her he had a really great time. She extended her hand. It was an awkward moment until he finally said, "Oh, what the hell. I think you need a hug after what you went through tonight." He drew her into his arms and gave her a hefty squeeze that lingered a moment. They separated briefly, both smiling shyly. Propriety was regained in a moment as he turned and strode toward his car feeling somehow taller. She found herself smiling and shaking her head in disbelief as she softly closed the door behind him.

She kicked off the new shoes and dropped the Herrera dress in a heap. So much for dressing up in case she needed to pretend to like someone 'important' as Lance had so bluntly described the game being played. She really did hope it was a lesson learned. After putting a kettle on to boil, she showered with the rose bath gel carried home from the five star hotel she'd splurged on in St. Thomas last year. Anything to wash away the lingering smell of Clay's cheap cologne and leave only the freshness of Lance's presence.

Now for a cup of chamomile tea and the last three Mallomars she'd been saving for a moment of indulgence. She turned on the ugly monstrosity that passed for a lamp in her furnished-as-is living room and decided it was too much hideousness to deal with after such a lovely evening, so she snapped it off. Lovely evening? She laughed at herself. Be honest, the little Observer on the shoulder said, you do have a bit of a crush on the kid don't you? Maybe, she thought. But so what? And why is that? She lit the dozen candles she'd carefully arranged for some as-yet-unrealized romantic evening, and slipped into the Chinese silk robe she'd bought on a whim. After pouring the tea, she sat back in the worn leather reading chair pondering the question she had asked herself: What exactly is this crush all about and why does Lance Van Arden's presence in her life seem so important?

For some reason, she thought about the bag boy, whose name she never knew, at the supermarket in Ann Arbor, remembering his ripped abs through the damp tee shirt on those 95 degree afternoons as he gathered up the carts in the parking lot. The way he smiled at her made her wet. To this very day, it was the image of him that she re-wound and played over and over whenever she couldn't stand it anymore, found her vibrator, smiled back at him in her mind's eye and let him follow her home. Him or Derek Malone—the one who stood her up in high school and didn't even remember he'd asked her out. If Derek was the evening's choice she'd take him into her bed, forgive him and make love to him like he'd never had it before and never would again. He was hers and when she was done with him he would be out of her thoughts until time to forgive him again.

She was sipping her tea, munching on the last Mallomar, smelling the sandalwood that had permeated the air, watching the flickering shadows of the candles on the ceiling, when the doorbell rang. *Monica*, she thought, *wondering about the big Van Arden evening?*

She opened the door eager to share the disaster and the wonderfulness of the evening with Monica—and there was Lance.

"Hi," he said awkwardly. "I've been sitting outside in the car thinking about everything and... Would it be ok if I came in?"

Claudia stepped back in awe. Lance walked in and rattled on, "You've read a lot of stuff I wrote about girls and falling in love every week and a lot of other bullshit and I'm sitting out in my car thinking about it realizing I don't know Jack shit about anything." He brushed back a strand of hair that had fallen over Claudia's face and said, "All I know is you make me feel something I've never ever felt before. And I don't want to let it go. I just need to ask you one thing—am I crazy here or do you feel the same thing? I'm really sorry if I'm making a fool of myself, but part of me knows you feel something. I just don't know if it's what I think it is. If it's not, I'm really stupid so if it isn't... Oh, God! I'm sorry. This is really dumb. It isn't is it?..."

Claudia reached up and put her fingers on his lips. "It is, Lance."

He pressed her fingers to his lips in a gentle kiss, then brushed his lips against hers and the air shivered between them.

All doubt vanished and both of them knew where they were going. Their first embrace was a tableau of exquisite proportions, his left hand firmly spread across the small of her back, his right hand behind her head just so. Her hands softly stroked his face as their bodies began an exploration that revealed how very much they wanted to know each other. They broke from a long kiss and both exploded simultaneously with a joyous laugh. Claudia was remembering Lance's diary observations about carnal knowledge. Mind reader that Lance had become, he said, "carnal knowledge?" They laughed again and she pushed him playfully down into the leather chair. In the last few moments their hands had explored the contours of each other's bodies. Pieces of clothing had miraculously been dispensed with. Claudia thought she had successfully imagined what Erica Jong wrote about in *Fear of Flying* when she described the 'zipless fuck.' The pas de deux she was dancing with Lance proved her prior imagination about that concept to be woefully inadequate.

Lance settled into the leather chair knowing where Claudia wanted to go. He arched his back and lifted his hips offering her the firm youth he knew with certainty she wanted more than anything she had ever wanted. Her eyes grabbed his in a hammerlock and she watched him watching her slowly descend upon him. His adoration of her was immense as her thumb and forefinger held him firmly while her lips and tongue learned more about him than anyone ever had. The softness of her fingers as they explored the firmness of his hips and buttocks and stroked the hair on his abdomen and below made him lift himself even higher to give her the tautness he knew she wanted. Claudia was amazed by the gift they were giving to each other. She had never willingly done this for any man or boy. Well, not any real boy. Derek and the bag boy had been given this pleasure in her mind's eye, but the intense contentment of acknowledging Lance's gift with her own was pure, blissful ecstasy.

As one they broke from the peak of this tableau. Lance leaned forward, took Claudia in his arms and lifted her to her feet. They stood with their bodies immersed in each other; an enormous desire building in Claudia for Lance to be inside her in a way she knew would lock them into a destiny fraught with passionate danger. Caution had been thrown to the wind the moment Lance had walked across the threshold.

He swept her into his arms and carried her into the bedroom. The intensity of their love-making did not surprise either of them. When their lips touched there was a velvet softness that made them smile as one. As each sensation peaked, they moved from one exquisite position to another, each responding to the other's needs as if a choreographer had planned the phrases of their movements as an enchanting ballet. When they reached that place where final communion would begin, he hesitated and she knew his thought. "It's all right," she said with a wry smile. "I've been on the pill for months. Just in case." He smiled and when he finally placed himself inside her the wonderment on both their faces was a joy for each to behold.

Lance was 'everyman' to her that night. All fantasies more than fulfilled.

Lance had done what many handsome, teenage boys have done since time began. He'd learned to enjoy conquest and took pride in adding notches to his belt. He'd found girls who easily responded to his charming advances. Adrienne loved nipple play. Susan had a mouth made of silk and knew what to do with it. Juliette loved a tongue in her navel. Each had a favorite place to go to find extreme sensations. But, they were only sensations. They found pleasure in giving each other the sensations; then ardor faded and conquest was savored.

With Claudia, Lance found passionate sensations wrapped in a timeless cocoon of something he'd never experienced. He'd read about "oneness." His mind understood it, but he never really knew what it meant. Now he knew. There were no separate and unique erogenous zones to find and focus upon. Both of their minds, bodies and spirits were one gigantic erogenous zone. A finger tracing the spine, a cheek brushing a shoulder, a sigh whispered in an ear, witnessing a blissful smile; all became one seamless whole.

After the intense rush to completion, they lay silently in each other's arms without doubt or guilt, knowing that what they had done was perfect. The world and what it would think was nowhere in sight.

Then Lance's cell phone bleated "The Saints Go Marching In" and the world came rushing back like a tidal wave.

"Oh, shit," Lance said, looking at the caller ID. "My mom. Oh, fuck, it's 2:30. Mom, hi," he said too brightly. "No...I'm ok....Five hours?! I just lost track of the time. Miss de la Rosa was super upset so we stopped to get something to eat. She was so buzzed about what happened that we just, you know, I just thought I'd hang out with her until she was feeling better..."

His bumbling panic struck Claudia as funny and she buried her face in a pillow to keep from laughing aloud. But her laughter now infected Lance as he tried to wave her into silence before his dutifully serious masquerade cracked. He managed to say, "I'll drop her off and come on home," before snapping the phone shut. "Must have hit a dead spot."

They collapsed into laughter made ripe with the implications of what they had done and what they would do.

Chapter 14

Lance turned off his headlights as he opened the gate and shot up the driveway into the garage. Thank God the lights were off on the main floor and in his parents' bedroom. As he crept through the kitchen he noticed the light under the door of Maria's bedroom. The door opened a crack and Maria peered into the kitchen darkness.

"Mr. Lance?" she whispered.

"Yes, Nana. It's me."

"Is everything all right?" Her tone implied that it wasn't.

"Everything's cool, Nana."

"Your mama, she is *furioso*. I never see her so."

Lance thought the spontaneous excuse he'd laid on his mother had passed muster. "What did she say?"

"She thinks you and the *maestra* are...up to something."

"Up to something?"

"You know. Something." Maria's knowing look spoke more than her words. "Mr. Lance, I know you since eight years old and I know when you have crush on girlfriends. I know that look. You be careful, *mijo*."

Oh, shit, thought Lance. *Gotta defuse this one.* "Thank you, Nana. But everything is really ok. I promise."

He'd never been able to successfully lie to Maria who continued sternly, "She is very nice lady but she is your teacher!"

"Yes, ma'am. I know."

There was a long moment between them during which Maria's eyes seared him with a truly loving admonition. She had a son Lance's age whom she'd chosen to leave with her parents in

Guatemala 10 years ago. The Van Ardens provided her with a place to live, three meals a day and a decent salary, three quarters of which she always sent to her family who lived in the poorest district of Guatemala City. It was a modest sum, but it allowed her son, her aging parents, her sister and three nieces to survive. There was much love pent up in Maria that she couldn't give to her own son and Lance had become the lucky recipient.

"Thanks, Nana." His grateful look told her that he understood her concern.

Lance slipped past his parents' room, quietly closed his door, stripped down to his briefs and crawled under his satin sheets. His body still tingled from the intensity of the night. The smell of Claudia clung to his body. He smiled at the thought that he didn't want to shower for a week to hold on to her. Maria's words echoed through his consciousness, troubling his mind and furrowing his brow.

Tonight had presented him with an undeniable quandary. If Maria knew, then his mother would figure it out soon. Roberta had always been one step behind Maria in her understanding of her son. Maria had known that 12-year-old Lance was smoking a week before Roberta began to suspect. Roberta raged and threatened. Maria listened to Lance, and then made him understand why he should stop. Maria discovered that Lance was cutting his violin lessons before the teacher called Roberta to report his truancy. Roberta grounded him for two weeks. Maria listened to why he couldn't bear to hear himself screech and bought him his first guitar for his 13th birthday.

As he drifted off, the sensations and emotions of the night flooded Lance's being and he found himself smiling at his monstrous erection. He chose not to touch it. Somehow it wasn't about relieving the itch but about reliving each of tonight's tableaus in his mind. He'd fucked girls and thought he'd figured out what carnal knowledge meant, but until tonight he had no idea you could know someone so totally. He heard what Maria was trying to tell him, but how could something that the world would judge as wrong be so right? He'd never felt so relaxed, so at home in his body, so happy. There was a strange buzz in his forehead and he felt like he was leaving his body. He remembered Marco telling him about out-of-body experiences and wondered if he might be having one.

The buzzy spot felt like it was trying to leave from the top of his head so he pulled it back. It kept wanting to creep there again and he thought, Oh, what the hell, let it go. So, he watched it this time going up and up. Not feeling like he was flying, more like it was flying. Then he stopped focusing his attention on the buzzy spot and started to look around at where the buzzy spot had arrived. He saw that he was the buzzy spot when he felt himself sitting at an enormous table in the center of a gothically grand room. The cases of ancient books that framed the room looked to be miles high. As he reached forward to dip a quill pen in an ancient inkwell made of stone, a deep, echoey voice whispered, "The stone is lapis lazuli." Lance smiled at the thought that this might be a movie on the SyFy Channel and James Earl Jones was playing the voice of God. He thought, "What is lapis lazuli?" and instantly the voice answered, "The stone of truth and harmony." Lance somehow understood that the ink held the essence of the stone and that it was necessary to sign the scroll. As he dipped the quill in the ink and directed the pen across the scroll, he noticed that his sleeve was part of a flowing, white robe that was cinched at his waist with a red sash. Hesitating, he looked up, noticing for the first time that there was a row of straight-backed wooden benches across from him—like the choir stalls at St. Patrick's, he thought. They were full of people all dressed in white robes. People? He was certain he had seen them all somewhere before and wondered if they were dead people. He realized they weren't all dead people when he saw Marco who smiled at him. Although Marco's lips didn't move, Lance was certain he said, "Welcome to *my* world."

He was surprised to see Claudia sitting in the front row, also dressed in white. Then, like an instant fast forward, she was kneeling with him at a triangular table, each facing one of the three sides. On the third side sat a luminous being whose robe glistened like diamonds and whose face was so bright that Lance could not see the features. With the scroll now before them on this table, Lance handed Claudia the quill and, without hesitation, she signed it.

Music that sounded like a million-voice choir swelled to an awesome crescendo as the luminous being took a knife-sharp stone and made a small cut in Lance's wrist, then in Claudia's. Taking their two hands in his, he entwined their fingers and pressed their wrists together in a bond of blood.

Suddenly, shafts of an intense light burst through the windows high above and the roof opened to the sky. A limitless expanse of light lay beyond. Lance and Claudia ascended into it and the rapture of the moment brought tears to the eyes of both.

It seemed to Lance that they had become one with the light. He felt the buzz in his head again as he and Claudia began to descend in a grand spiral, their hands clasped together until they reached a cloudy membrane through which they dropped together, then separately as they let go of each other.

The heavenly choir still echoed in his ears as his body stirred in his bed and he awoke, finding tears on his face. The clarity with which he remembered everything surprised him.

He bolted from his bed, grabbed his laptop, wrote it all down and, changing the names to retain his and Claudia's anonymity, posted it on his blog. That'll give them something new to chew on, he thought.

Chapter 15

Claudia had stood on her balcony watching Lance disappear around the corner below and was suddenly struck with a profound sadness. She wanted to call him back but it seemed too late. Too late for what, she wasn't quite sure. She listened for the little Observer on her shoulder to comment one way or another about the momentous thing she'd just done. But there was no voice that came. No witty thought. No wry commentary. She knew, of course, that the little Observer whose company she sought was just a compartment in her own mind that allowed her to be detached enough from herself to look at a moment in time from a little outside herself. The Observer would, undoubtedly, say *What in God's name were you thinking?!* Answering that question right now was not something she wanted to do. Savoring the contentment that pervaded her every cell was a better choice. Having never experienced such erotic fulfillment, she didn't want to look at the possibility that it could never happen again.

Claudia sighed deeply, turned to go back inside and heard Monica's voice through the oleanders that separated their terraces: "Sweetie, I think you'll probably sleep very well tonight."

"Monica. You're awake."

Monica's head popped up over the bush. Her cat-that-just-ate-the-canary grin said it all. "Of course I'm awake. The walls are very thin."

"My God. I'm so sorry. I didn't know we were that noisy."

"Honey, don't worry about it. At my age some of the best moments in life are lived vicariously. You've kept me up half the night, now you have to tell me everything."

Claudia wasn't sure she wanted to tell Monica anything. It became clear to her in a flash that from now on she had a secret that must be guarded very carefully. Monica picked up a bottle of brandy and two glasses, walked around the oleander to Claudia's side and said, "I saw that car he picked you up in. Wow! Who the hell is he and where did you find him?!"

"Just a talent manager."

"A manager! My God. Well then, take this for what it's worth—be careful. Use him for the best sex you ever had and don't be surprised when he doesn't turn out to be who you thought he was." Monica noticed Claudia's dazed and anguished look and thought she'd been insensitive. "I'm so sorry, dear. I'm a crusty old fool who's had one too many heartbreaks and one too many brandies and I'm rattling on-and-on just ruining your beautiful evening with your new gentleman caller. I'm sorry."

"It's not that," said Claudia, not wanting to elaborate on what 'that' really was, but her eyes told Monica that there was much more to tell and that the pain of telling it was almost too much to bear.

"What happened? Did it end badly?"

"No. It ended beautifully. It was the most beautiful thing that ever happened to me. It was magnificent. I'm so happy and miserable at the same time."

"Why?"

"It wasn't the manager I was with tonight. Turned out he wasn't a manager after all. He was a valet parker pretending to be a manager to get me to take him to the party. He stole the damn car and got arrested right there at the Van Arden estate. It was horrible, Monica. I was so humiliated."

"So, someone else brought you home and you drowned your sorrows in wild sex. No big deal, honey. I'd say you deserved to find some happiness at the end of that kind of evening."

"No, it wasn't like that. It was more. Better." Claudia paused. If anyone could understand, Monica could. "I've fallen in love, Monica. And it's impossible."

"He's married?"

"Worse."

74

Monica threw up her hands. "What could be worse?"

Claudia needed to tell someone and life had presented Monica. "My situation is as impossible as yours was. He's my David."

Monica sank back in her chair. "Oh, my God. Lance Van Arden."

Claudia and Monica talked until the brandy bottle was empty. Monica understood the depth of Claudia's feelings for Lance but also understood the pain of secrecy and the wrath of those who could not possibly understand. By the second drink Claudia knew that she had to end the richest love she had ever experienced before it was too late. Monica finally said goodnight, hugged her and reassured her that it was the right choice.

Claudia was exhausted. The smell of Lance's body was still richly trapped in the folds of her bedding As she drifted off to sleep she kept trying to formulate the words that she'd say to him to let him know that she loved him and that they could not see each other like this ever again. She had to be the adult. She was more experienced with life, more mature, was his teacher and… Oh, hell, she thought, it sounded like the up-tight speech of someone firing someone. She knew it would be terrible and that it was something she must do.

Sleeping fitfully until noon, having stirred often with a vague awareness of dreams, she awoke somehow feeling rested and centered. She knew she must call Lance, see him this afternoon and find a way to make him understand.

She wouldn't say it should never have happened. That would demean what they had done. It was beautiful and she'd want to make sure to tell him that. But, they had to live in the real world and in the real world a teacher couldn't sleep with her 18-year-old student no matter what they felt about each other. Plain and simple.

Reluctantly, she took a hot shower trying to wash away the smell of him. Holding on to that smell would only bring back the images of the night and that would make it much harder to do what she had to do.

As she mentally prepared herself to make the call, she realized that she didn't have his cell phone number. Calling the house would definitely not be a good idea. It would be agony to put this off until she saw him on Monday.

Chapter 16

Lance had popped his X-rated USB drive into his laptop and written feverishly since he awoke. In his most troublesome moments he always found that asking questions and writing what came to him sometimes gave him the answers he was desperate to find. At the very least, his meandering words sometimes pointed him in the direction he needed to go. As the dream images drifted back into his consciousness he began to question what they meant. It somehow felt like he'd been there before and that he was a part of a class. It made no sense. And what was it he signed? It seemed like something serious, a contract of some sort. Claudia signed it too. And the blood ritual. The faceless guy who took some kind of sharp stone and cut his and Claudia's wrists. What was that about? Thinking about it made him look down and turn his arm over. My God! There was a cut there. Impossible! He must have hit that sharp edge on the headboard again. Just a coincidence. Or was it? It seemed like a marriage. If he was to think about the kind of woman he would want to marry, the feelings they shared last night would certainly go a long way toward fitting the picture. It was all very confusing.

He wrote:

> I'm only 18. It can't be about marriage. And we can't date. Mom already suspects something. Nana is right. This is <u>impossible</u>! I can honestly say I'm in love, but is this one for real? How am I supposed to know??? This

is whack! Last night I called her Claudia while we made love and this morning I'm writing about her and I'm thinking Miss de la Rosa. That's mega-trippin'. I don't even know what to call her! This is all my fault. I'm the one who went back up to her place. I knew she wanted it and so did I, but I'm the one who started it. Dammit, I love her. I know it's real.

He pondered his dilemma and knew he was on dangerous ground. He closed his eyes and silently asked, as he'd done in such moments before, for his hands to be guided to the answers he needed. "Did I make a horrible mistake? What should I do?" he asked as his fingers started to move over the keyboard.

A mistake? What's a mistake? Something bad. This was definitely not something bad. Nothing that good could be bad. Yeah, not bad for *me*. But for Claudia? I got her into something that we can never tell anybody about. And if anyone ever found out, she'd be in trouble. People go to jail for having sex with students, don't they? This is bad for her. No way around it. What should I do?

His fingers stopped. Nothing else came. Maria knocked on his door and came in with breakfast and, it would seem, to help him find his answer. He closed the lid of his laptop sheepishly. She noticed and gave him her 'I know you're up to something' look.

"Morning, Nana," he said. "Got inspired and had to get up and write it down."

"Inspired," she repeated with a knowing glance. "Why you hide it? *Cuidado, mijo.* Be very careful."

"OK," he replied. "*Sí.* I will." And he meant it. When she put his bagel and orange juice next to him he took her hand, kissed it and said, "Nana, *gracias!*"

"It's only a bagel, *mijo!*"

"It's not about the bagel. *Gracias!*"

When she left, he opened the laptop lid and was very clear about what he had to do.

I got her into this and it's my responsibility to get her out of it. She could lose her job or worse. I have to make her understand I think she's majorly hot and I love her, but we can't do this anymore. I don't want her to think it wasn't the best. It was.

He picked up his cell phone and realized he didn't have her number. Just as well since Roberta barged into his room after a perfunctory knock on the door.

"Well, young man!" An off-putting opening gambit if ever there was one. "I hope you have a very good explanation for last night's shenanigans."

"Shenanigans. Mom, this is the 21st century. Shenanigans went out with bell bottoms."

"Don't you dare change the subject. You spent over five hours with that woman and I want to know why."

"Why? What the hell do you mean why? She was really zoned out over what happened. She needed somebody to talk to."

"For five hours? And don't you use profanity and that tone of voice with me. I'm going to be very direct about this. Did she try to seduce you?"

"For God's sake, Mom, she's my teacher."

"Exactly!"

"Mom! How could you even think that?"

"Did you try to seduce her?"

"Mom!"

"I know you. You're young, rich and handsome and every young woman you take a fancy to falls all over you and you fall right back. I'm putting two and two together."

"Well, it equals five this time. That's really lame. We just lost track of the time. That's it."

"That better be it. If your Miss de la Rosa tries to be anything other than your English teacher she'll have me to answer to. Do you understand?"

"You are way off, Mom."

"Do you understand!?"

Lance thought that this would get worse if he argued it any more. So he just said, "Yes, ma'am. Of course I understand." Which only heightened Roberta's suspicions.

Lance showered away the night's bliss along with his mother's venom. He'd decided to drive over to Claudia's apartment and do the proper thing. Not the right thing, he thought, but the proper thing. At this moment Claudia appeared to be the best thing that had ever happened to him and he had to end it—for her sake.

As he dressed, his iPod shuffled to Andrea Bocclli and Celine Dion—"The Prayer." He was irritated that he hadn't remembered to take the time to transfer his mom's albums to her own iTunes library. But before he could pull up one of his own playlists he was surprised to find himself clobbered by the words he was hearing about finding another soul to love.

He so desperately wanted to do the right thing and at the same time wanted to have another soul to love and to feel as happy, always, as he'd felt last night with Claudia.

It was a muggy and oppressive Indian Summer afternoon as Lance slowly drove the route. He parked a block away, not really knowing why.

As he turned into the walkway that led to her building, the crimson roses lining the path sent an intense fragrance into the dense, humid air that overpowered him with a sense of regret. He looked up and stopped when he saw her standing on the terrace looking off in the other direction. She was wearing a diaphanous white skirt that blew softly around her legs in the breeze. So beautiful, he thought, remembering the whiteness of her flowing robe in his dream. Mesmerizing. He realized he could not stay there looking at her or he would never be able to do what he knew he had to do.

"Good morning," he said.

She looked down at him and a brightness crossed her face. "Hi."

"Can I come up?" he asked tentatively.

For a moment she looked uncertain. She knew she could never again let it happen. "Sure," she finally said waving him in.

Lance noticed the hesitation and wondered if she regretted what they had done. As he climbed the stairs he found himself hoping she'd be as heartbroken as he was when he explained to her that it had to end.

She opened the door and let him pass her threshold one more time. She'd hoped they could have this conversation in a coffee shop or on a walk in the park. But here he was in the place where they had experienced something profound. Every word she would speak to try to break it off would be haunted by last night's images and feelings that would make a mockery of everything she knew she had to tell him. How could she begin?

Lance had not anticipated what this first moment would be like. It was clear that neither of them was rushing into the other's arms. It was also clear that they both wanted to. He had a sudden realization and smiled.

"We're both in the same place," he said.

"What do you mean?"

"We both know that last night was super-awesome and we also both know it can't happen anymore."

"Oh, God," she said. "I've been thinking for hours how I'm going to explain that to you and you just took care of it in one sentence."

"I didn't know how I was going to say it either. It just came to me when I saw that look on your face."

"What look?"

"The look that said 'I love you' and also said 'but this is impossible.'"

"Yes. That's exactly it. God, I'm feeling like Mrs. Robinson."

"Who's Mrs. Robinson?"

Claudia smiled, motioned Lance toward a chair in the kitchen and poured two cups of coffee. "Anne Bancroft? Dustin Hoffman? *The Graduate?* Oh, never mind. Generation gap alert. That's one of the reasons this could never last. I can be your friend. I can be your mentor. But nothing more."

"I know. But how do we do that? Every time I see you in class I'm gonna think about last night."

"And so will I, but we have to be very careful to let those feelings remain a part of the past. If we're overly familiar, people will notice."

80

"Some people already have. My mother asked me this morning if you tried to seduce me."

Claudia blanched visibly. "Oh, my God!"

"Don't worry. I told her you were so upset I just stayed and talked to you and lost track of the time."

"Did she believe you?"

"More or less."

"More or less?"

"Yeah, she has no reason not to believe me. I'll never tell her or anyone else. I promise. But, she's like Sherlock Holmes sometimes. If she invites you to the house again, we can't ever let her see us being too friendly. She already put two and two together, she said, and I told her it equals five. She backed off."

"Lance, I'm so sorry."

"For what?"

"For putting you in this position."

"What position?"

"Of lying to your parents."

"You didn't. I'm the one who came back up here last night. I could have left it alone."

"I'm glad you didn't."

Lance thought for a moment, wanting to choose his words carefully. "I thought I knew a lot about 'making love.' Truth is, I don't think I ever actually 'made love' until last night."

Tears sprang to Claudia's eyes. "Me too," she said. "I don't want to make this any harder than it already is, but I really do want you to know how extraordinary it was." She paused, knowing she was treading on a risky path. She smiled shyly. "I never before in my life had 13 orgasms in a row."

"You counted?"

She laughed. "I sort of knew when we got to number four that it was going to go on forever and somehow I wanted to know how many more there would be so... Yes, I counted."

"That's great," he said, beaming with a pleasure that felt right but seemed wrong.

"And on every one my eyes rolled back in my head and I heard singing."

"Singing?"

"Like a choir almost. It was pure ecstasy. I've never had that feeling—ever!"

Lance remembered the awesome choir he'd heard in his dream. For a moment he was tempted to tell her, but thought better of it. No sense confusing the issue. He'd come to end it and they'd both come to the same conclusion. Best leave it alone.

Claudia lost herself for a moment as she remembered the ethereal music. It had been wonderful, but there was something vaguely troubling about it too. She couldn't remember quite why.

Suddenly they felt awkward again. The easy rapport they had developed last night could no longer be. No more affectionate kidding around, no more gentle kisses. Hanging out here any longer just wasn't an option and they both knew it.

"This is really hard," she said. "You should probably go."

"Yeah, I guess," he said unconvincingly. *Should I kiss her goodbye?* he thought.

Claudia was thinking the same thing. *No,* she thought, *that would be dangerous.*

Trying to lighten the moment, Lance extended his hand, made a courtly bow, and said, "Very nice to *know* you, Miss de la Rosa."

Claudia laughed, took his hand and said, "The feeling is entirely mutual, Mr. Van Arden."

Lance pulled her into an easy embrace and said, "I'm sorry, but I do have to give you a hug."

They held each other tightly for a moment, then looked into each other's eyes with an exquisite longing.

Claudia said simply, "I know that from now on we'll never be able to relate to each other like this, but I'll never forget."

"Neither will I," he said.

"Bye," she said simply.

"Bye," he replied with a sad smile.

As Lance walked across Claudia's threshold for the last time, she watched him descend the stairs. As he reached the landing he knew he couldn't look back. She knew that he wouldn't look back and thought, that's the way it has to be. As he descended out of sight, her face flushed, her heart felt like it would explode, her breath came in short gasps and she clasped her hand to her mouth to muffle the sob that emerged from the very depth of her being.

She closed the door quickly lest he should hear and return to comfort her. She'd never had a panic attack before but was sure she was having one now. Her sense of loss was overpowering. Never again to have the intense feelings of the last 24 hours seemed like a life sentence. *Maybe if I meditate,* she thought, *this will go away.*

Throwing a pillow on the floor, she assumed the lotus position, closed her eyes, took three deep breaths and tried to relax. As much as she tried to focus on her breathing, her mind's eye kept seeing Lance's face. She could no longer hold back the dreadful sounds that erupted from a place of sorrow never before experienced.

At first her unyielding sobs masked the quiet knocks on her door. As the knocking became louder and more insistent, Claudia finally became aware and for a brief moment she was hopeful that Lance had returned. Then she realized she mustn't hope that and knew she could not let him in. She wiped the tears from her face and pulled herself together. "It's OK. Really. I'm all right," she said through the closed door.

"You sure as heck don't sound all right. Open the cotton-pickin' door." It was Monica.

Claudia opened the door and Monica swept her into a motherly hug. "You did it, didn't you?"

"I did it."

"Good! I was afraid you wouldn't. You did it. It's over and now you have to put your life back together."

Monica poured a brandy for them both and Claudia poured out her heart. "I was agonizing over how to tell him and it turned out he was agonizing how to tell me the same thing. In the end he said he knew we were both in the same predicament, that we both knew what we did was awesome but we couldn't do it any more. It was really quite beautiful."

"Beautiful, indeed, but a sad story at the same time."

"Some story. No happy ending. Girl meets boy, girl loses boy. Period. End of story." Claudia waved it all away with a sweep of her arm.

"What did you do to your wrist?" Monica asked.

"What?"

"You're bleeding a little."

Claudia looked down. "Oh. I don't know. I woke up with it. Must have scraped myself somehow during the night." As she dabbed at it with a tissue, she stared at it for a moment and said, "Wait. I think I did it in a dream."

"You cut yourself in a dream?"

Claudia thought for a long moment and said, "I don't think I cut myself. Somebody else cut me."

"Who?"

"I'm not sure." Claudia cocked her head and furrowed her brow. "It seems like there was some kind of ceremony. I was kneeling down next to a table. It had three sides. There was a kind of transparent man on one side of the table and me on one side and... Oh, my God!"

"What?!"

"It was Lance."

"Lance cut you?"

"No. Lance was on the third side of the table."

"I don't get it."

"Let me think." Claudia closed her eyes to focus on the dream images floating through her memory. "Holy shit!" she finally said.

"Tell me."

"The transparent guy had a sharp stone in his hand and he cut my wrist and Lance's wrist and put our hands together so our wrists were touching."

Monica got goose bumps. "A blood covenant."

Claudia had goose bumps too. "This is spooky, isn't it?"

Monica felt the need to steer Claudia away from making too much of this. "Honey, remember it was just a dream. Most likely wishful thinking. Especially after the night you'd just had."

Claudia thought that seemed like a logical explanation. And it felt much safer to leave it at that. The alternative seemed to have no harmless promise in it.

Chapter 17

Lance drove home, pulled into his space in the garage next to his dad's vintage Pierce-Arrow and walked toward the front door. Not wanting to go in and face the possibility that his mother might be waiting to ambush him while he was in such a black mood, he strode to the bench he'd shared on that lovely evening when Claudia made him appreciate the beauty that surrounded him on this hilltop. As he thought back to the feelings of that magical night, he realized he'd fallen in love with her right here on this bench when she sighed as he wrapped his leather jacket around her shoulders to protect her from the autumn chill. He remembered how vibrant and alive she had been at dinner. She had charmed his parents that night and she'd enchanted him. Although she was smart, well read and a take-charge teacher, she also revealed a delicate vulnerability that he found endearing. He remembered thinking how he wanted to put his arm around her on this bench to show his gratitude because she was valuing him like no one had ever valued him. He'd offered his jacket instead and knew she was feeling the warmth of his body. She was his teacher and he'd reprimanded himself for even daring to think about her in that way. *What is it that made me fall in love with her?* He knew when he asked himself that question that he really was in love with her. Not some high school romance. Not some new conquest. Not another notch on the bedpost.

When Lance was troubled he found it comforting to log onto his blog to play with his fans. Right now he needed to connect to someone who wasn't Claudia. So he went to his room, logged on and read the responses to this morning's entry. It didn't actually help him stop thinking about Claudia because the story he had posted that morning was about the dreamed marriage. As he read the responses he was glad that it was an anonymous page and that he hadn't revealed names or places. He would be very careful to never put Claudia in jeopardy.

Some of the regulars had very definite interpretations. Toe-tagger was a mortuary employee whose dreams always seemed to be communications with someone he'd embalmed that day. His observations were always tinged with death and destruction. Lance never answered him directly but others did which kept him coming back. He thought SuperDreamer's marriage dream was about a mutual suicide pact. Lance knew that some of the other dark-sider fans would elaborate on that and he found it amusing.

Candlepower was a 43-year-old actress who lived in North Hollywood. She had never acted 'professionally' she admitted. Her day job, as she called it, was in phone sales. She pitched generic printer ink cartridges to unsuspecting clients dialed at random from a computer library of yellow pages covering every city, town and village in the U.S. The best customers were church secretaries. They were usually volunteers who served for a couple of months before being replaced by another volunteer. After a little fishing expedition, Candlepower would "confirm" the make of printer used and rattle off a convincing pitch that implied she was calling about their HP or Canon account with a reminder that prices were going up and it was time to reorder. One secretary checked the supply room and couldn't understand why there were 36 dozen printer cartridges there. Candlepower, of course, knew exactly why. Lance liked Candlepower. She may be a cartridge hustler, but she was sweet, supportive and usually right-on with her dream interpretations. She had a special, intuitive talent for it. She asked if SuperDreamer thought it might be a shared dream. "Have you asked," she wrote, "if the lady had the same dream?"

Given Candlepower's customary accuracy, Lance briefly pondered Claudia's mention of hearing a heavenly choir, but recalled that it happened while they were making love, not in a dream, and dismissed the possibility of a shared dream as preposterous.

It's so odd, Lance thought, that, filled with the whirlwind of the last couple of days, it was now Sunday evening and he was faced with writing a diary chapter to hand in tomorrow. The diary would now be a whole different experience. Regardless of the subject matter, every word would now be tinged with this awesome thing they had done together. He couldn't think of a thing to write about and stared at the blank screen for a long time before deciding to put his hands on the keyboard and just type whatever came into his mind. What came was about falling in love with someone he could never have—someone with whom he'd been bound together in a powerful dream. Wishful thinking.

He read it over and thought it was sufficiently vague to cause no trouble. But he wanted to send a final message to Claudia before he went on to more mundane subjects in his future entries. He printed it, put it in his bag and got ready for bed. Although he hoped he would dream about Claudia one more time, if he did he wasn't sure he could take the disappointment of waking up.

Chapter 18

Claudia arrived in class very early the next morning feeling somehow that she needed to organize her desk. She made neat piles of the assignment sheets and graded homework, cleaned the chalk board twice and rehearsed how she'd react with ordinary disinterest when Lance walked in.

He arrived with the three prettiest classmates in tow. Lucy, the blondest of the blondes had draped her arm possessively over Lance's. They were laughing about something and Claudia was instantly jealous. Lance knew that Lucy's arm lock on him would upset Claudia and he was hoping she wasn't looking. She was. Their eyes met and there was no way she could hide her distress. He dropped a book on the floor. She knew he'd done it purposely so he could disengage from Lucy to pick it up and to distract everyone from Claudia's obvious agony. This was going to be a lot harder than either of them had thought.

Claudia struggled through the hour. She tried to focus on the subject matter and fought to keep her eyes off of Lance. Why in heaven's name hadn't she remembered that today's topic would definitely not work? UNREQUITED LOVE! Her list of quotes from the great writers ran from Abraham Cowley who wrote "A mighty pain to love it is, and 'tis a pain that pain to miss; but of all pains, the greatest pain it is to love, but love in vain" to James Blunt singing about seeing his ex with another guy.

She muddled through the hour as best she could, hurriedly handed out some assignment sheets, collected the diary entries and dismissed the class 10 minutes early. The students were puzzled. As they filed out they whispered about Claudia's odd mood and wondered what was wrong. In the short time she had been their teacher most of them had somehow bonded with her and it was distressing to see her so undone.

Lance didn't look up at Claudia, but she knew he was taking his own sweet time packing up his things in order to be the last one out. Lucy wasn't having any of it, however. She called brightly to him, "Lance, we've got an extra 10. Let's go grab a latte."

Claudia turned her back to wipe the board and hide her anxiety. Lance poked around in his bag and responded, "Thanks, Lucy, but I think I left my history homework at home. I better bounce and get it. Mr. Bell marks you down for excuses. See you later."

Lucy gave him a disappointed pout and said, "Ok. See you at lunch?"

"Uhh…" Lance hesitated, "Can't today."

Lucy seemed to get the message that she was being brushed off. Lance had sniffed around her like a buck in heat at the student government meeting last week. What the hell was going on with him? With a disdainful shrug she said, "Your loss," swung her bag over her shoulder and strode out the door. Whether she saw David Shaw in the hall Lance couldn't tell, but she shrieked as she turned out of sight, "David. Love your hair. Wait up."

Claudia turned, Lance grinned and they both laughed aloud.

"My God, this is hard," Lance said.

"What turning down girls?"

"Pretending to be something we're not. Unrequited love?!"

"I didn't remember what I planned for today until I opened my bag. I was a mess, wasn't I?"

"Yes."

"Do you think the others noticed?"

"Noticed? Deer-caught-in-the-headlights times 10."

"I don't know how I'm going to get through this. And when I saw you coming in with Lucy on your arm…"

"I saw."

"That's why you pretended to drop your books."

He smiled and shrugged.

"Thank you," she said. "Well, I did get through it."

"With 10 minutes to spare."

"I'll get better at it."

They'd moved close enough to touch each other, but didn't.

Principal Adashek gave a passing glance through the window of the closed classroom door as he hurried toward his office. Something made him stop, step back and study what seemed to be an intimate moment. There was an odd ease between Miss de la Rosa and her star student—she had raved to him last week about what a talented writer Lance was becoming.

Claudia spotted Mr. Adashek over Lance's shoulder and quickly turned to take another wipe at the chalk board.

"Mr. Adashek is at the door," she whispered as she turned.

Lance didn't turn to look. He gathered up his books and quietly said, "I only wrote a couple of diary paragraphs, but I think you'll like them," turned and left waving cheerfully to the principal who was still standing at the door. "Hi, Mr. Adashek. Have a nice day."

Claudia's little Observer warned heads up as Adashek strode into the classroom. "That boy has a bad case of testosterone overload, I think. Don't let him beguile you with the Van Arden charisma, Claudia. He's been known to charm better grades than he deserves out of members of our staff. Quite a reputation with the girls, you know."

"No kidding," was all Claudia could muster.

Principal Adashek was considered an odd bird. Officious and well-meaning, he was the sort of person who stood a couple of inches closer to people than the usual limits of personal space invasion would allow. Roberta had once speculated that it was his subconscious way of getting close to people because warmth was not a natural state of his being.

He was not evangelistic in a church-going way, but had a puritanical streak that no one could quite understand. Everyone accepted his quirky behavior as just a part of the Principal Adashek myth. He'd been haranguing the board-of-directors for years to require school uniforms and was, once again, trying to gain support of the teaching staff for the idea. Since Claudia was new, he figured she'd go along easily and help him start a peer pressure bandwagon rolling.

"I'd like to enlist your support in a cause dear to my heart, Claudia. May I take a few moments of your time?"

"Of course."

"I just don't understand parents who let their girls come to school with these low cut jeans, rings in their navels and God knows what else. It's just too tempting for the boys, don't you think?"

Adashek promptly whipped a clipboard from under his arm and presented a petition to a bewildered Claudia. "Direct to the point. I'm asking our staff to support me in this. We desperately need school uniforms. I hope you agree."

"Well… I don't know. Are the other staff members behind it?"

"I've just started collecting signatures, but I assure you, they will be."

Claudia tried to stall. "What kind of uniforms do you mean?"

Adashek was prepared. "This," he said, thrusting a dog-eared catalog page at her with photos of girls in calf-length plaid skirts.

Claudia had her own thoughts about the culture of consumerism, celebrity obsession and sexual liberation, but her principal's tactics seemed strangely repressive and he, obviously, didn't see oddness in believing that wrapping Scotch plaid around girls would make them chaste. She thought maybe she could lighten him up a bit. She grinned and said, "I'm sorry, Mr. Adashek but doesn't this seem a little Talibanish?"

No lightening up happened. "Miss de la Rosa, I expect our teachers to hold themselves as morally correct and to discourage the licentiousness we see around us every day. I hope you will keep that in mind in your work and," he paused meaningfully, "in your personal interactions with your students." With that he spun on his heel and exited like a vanquished general intent on regrouping.

Chapter 19

Claudia pondered skipping the Starbucks stop today. After the strange confrontation with Principal Adashek she somehow didn't feel like reading Lance's diary in public. But, the traffic was stop-and-go and it would be another 20 minutes before she got home. She couldn't wait. She picked up her Mocha Frappuccino, settled into the easy chair in the dark, back corner and ripped open the envelope.

This was the most awesome weekend of my life. I can honestly say that I fell in love. I can't reveal her name and we've decided never to see each other in the same way again. She's 26 and I am 18. There's nothing wrong with that, but for reasons I can't go into, there is no future for us.

Ever since I was a little boy I've had extremely vivid dreams when something huge is going on in my life. After the most incredible night of making love I had one of those dreams about her. It was awesome. We were all dressed in white and we were in this ceremony where we were bound together in this sort of mystical place. Undoubtedly wishful thinking. I just want her to know that even though we've ended it, I'll never forget her and I hope I can at least dream about her when I miss her.

Claudia was stunned. She read it over and over to make sure it said what she thought it said. She had dreamed about him too. They were both dressed in white. It couldn't possibly be the same dream! Could it? Lance had told her he had a blog where he posted some of his dream stories. She grabbed the laptop from her bag, booted it up, connected to Starbucks' wi-fi and, cursing at the slowness of the process. She'd been wracking her brain to remember Lance's URL. She knew he'd told her. It had something to do with dreaming. *Dream Maker? Dream Weaver? Dreamer? Something Dreamer.* "Yes!" she said aloud, typing in *TheSuperDreamer.com.* Enter! And there he was.

Greetings from the land of the subconscious. I just had such an awesome dream I jumped out of bed to get it to you before I forget. It was a flying dream, like an out-of-body thing.

I ended up in this huge room, sort of a library but also like a church or cathedral. There was an audience there and I recognized some of the people. Not dead people. I don't see dead people!! I have a friend who does, but that's another story. He was actually there in the dream, this friend who sees dead people, and he said "Welcome to my world." So I guess there must have also been some dead people there. Who knows? I'm getting off the dream.

Claudia instantly saw the grand room.

Anyway, I'm sitting at this table and there's some kind of scroll in front of me. I don't know what it said, but it seemed very solemn what I was doing. I picked up a quill pen—you know one of those old-fashioned feather things where you dip it in ink. I sign it. Oh, also there's this choir singing and it's fully awesome! Back up a minute. When I was signing the scroll, I looked up and saw this girl—woman that I just met and am really in love with. Nothing can happen between us, but that's another story.

She's at the table, I hand her the pen and she signs the scroll.

Claudia quickly closed the screen of her laptop. She'd learned to recognize the signs of an anxiety attack and she was having one. *This can't be*, she thought. She was gasping for breath. *Breathe slowly,* she thought. *Relax your body. Pull yourself together.*

Two women at the next table with sleeping toddlers in strollers had noticed and one said, "You ok?"

Claudia had gotten it under control and nodded yes with a reassuring wave of her hand. She couldn't bear to not read the rest so she opened the screen again.

> **Next thing I know, we're kneeling down at a little triangle table, maybe two feet on each side. There's me and her and a... I just paused to think how to describe him *or it*. A very tall man in a white robe that glowed and a face that was so bright you couldn't even see it.**
>
> **Anyway at the triangular table, I'm kneeling down and the guy with no face is kneeling down and this beautiful girl kneels down also and the faceless guy takes a white stone, sort of like an arrowhead that's been filed down to make a sharp edge, and he cuts my wrist and her wrist and holds our hands and arms together like a blood brother sort of thing. I know I'm rambling, but I have to get this out before I forget it.**

Claudia was reading with both hands over her mouth and nose to keep from hyperventilating. The toddler women eyed her edgily as they sipped their drinks. Claudia continued.

> **When the guy puts our arms together and mixes our blood, the whole roof opens up and the two of us just float up into the light. We were holding hands. I don't have words to explain how that felt and I certainly don't know what it means except I'm sure it's some kind of wishful thinking after the weekend I just spent**

94

with her. It is definitely a dream I'd like to have again. And again and again!!!!
Curious what you guys think. ?????
SuperDreamer

Claudia was on her feet. She left the Frappuccino undrunk, grabbed her bag and laptop and fled. The toddler women raised their eyebrows. "What was that about?" said one. The other shrugged. "Gotta be about a man don'cha think?"

Claudia waited until she got in her car to let it out. She was shaking. "No, no, no, no, no. This is impossible." She grabbed the Lays bag on the passenger seat, dumped out the chips and held it over her mouth and nose. Calm down, she thought. Breathe slowly. She closed her eyes, leaned back against the headrest and wailed. "Why? Why? Why is this happening to me? This is wrong! This just cannot be happening." She reached for her cell phone and dialed Lance.

He'd gone straight home from school and was playing a vicious game of tennis with his dad and he was winning. He didn't want to stop the momentum of the game, but was feeling something urgent about the way the phone was ringing and said, "Ok, old man. Rest. I'm still gonna whip your butt." Edward smiled, grabbed a towel and felt a swelling pride about how well he had taught his eldest son to play tennis.

"Yo," said Lance.

"It's Claudia. I need to see you."

"What?!" he responded hearing the urgency in her voice.

"Right now!"

"What's wrong?"

"Maybe nothing, maybe everything."

"Where are you?"

"In the Starbucks parking lot. The one on Beverly Drive."

"I'll be right there."

"Wait." She'd resolved that he would never again come to her apartment, but was falling apart over a potentially life-changing dream and knew there was no way she could handle this in a coffee shop or its parking lot. "You'd better come to my apartment."

"Are you sure?"

"I'm sure."

"Tell me what it is," he said, not wanting the suspense hanging over him on the drive over there.

"Not on the phone. Please, Lance. Come now!"

"Ok. I'm on my way."

He flipped the phone shut, paused a moment to process what he'd just heard and said to his father, "Dad, I gotta go. Friend of mine is in a jam and I've gotta pick him up. I'll fill you in later."

"Sure."

He grabbed his keys, sprinted to his car and sped down the driveway leaving Edward to wonder if there would be a phone call later that had to do with booze or drugs or sexual improprieties. He was fairly certain that Lance was not in trouble, but Lance had a habit of taking odd-balls and losers under his wing. Sometimes the consequences bubbled over into straightening out problems that really should have been someone else's parent's job. Ah, well, he should be grateful that Lance had such a good heart.

Lance worried over every possible disaster scenario that popped into his mind. Principal Adashek had confronted her. His mom had called her. Someone had seen his diary and her notes to him and figured it out. Someone had videotaped them making love through her open window. She was being blackmailed. And on and on. He kept checking his rear view mirror to make sure there was no cop behind him on his 60–mile-an-hour ride down Sunset Boulevard.

The only place he could see to park in a hurry was a spot near the hydrant on the corner. He didn't care. Let them give him a ticket. Screeching to a halt, he jumped out, took the stairs three at a time and arrived at her open door. Sitting with her laptop in the breakfast nook, she looked up and beckoned him in. He could see she'd been crying.

"What's wrong?"

She turned the computer around so he could see the screen and saw his blog with the story of his dream.

"My God," he said. "I'm so sorry. I didn't use our names."

"That's not what I'm upset about," she said.

"What?"

She paged down. "I also read what Candlepower had to say about it."

He couldn't remember exactly what that was.

"Read," she said.

As he read it he realized Claudia was really asking him the question. *Have you asked if the lady had the same dream?*

There was a calmness in Claudia's eyes. She'd given over to the idea and Lance instantly knew it was a shared dream.

"Did you?" he asked—just to make sure he wasn't mis-reading her look.

"I told you I heard the music," she said.

"I remember you said that but it was while we were making love, not in a dream."

"In the dream too," she said.

"Was it all echoey-like?"

"Yes."

"And you remember signing the paper?" he asked. She nodded. "And the triangular table?" She nodded again. "And the guy with no face with a sharp stone?"

She took his right hand, turned it over, looked at the cut on his wrist, then turned her arm over to show him the cut on hers.

Panic in his eyes, he said, "Holy shit! This is weird."

Claudia was calm. She'd had a little time to process all this.

"We had the same dream!" he said. "What have we done? This is bad. This is really bad."

Claudia hadn't expected that.

"Maybe not," she said. "Remember how it ended? We floated up into the light hand in hand. It was quite beautiful."

"Look," he said. "I've got goose bumps. Honestly, I'm blown away by this. And scared."

"I've got goose bumps too. But I'm not scared. What can this mean?"

"Show me your arm again," Lance said.

He entwined his fingers with hers as in the dream and pressed their arms together. The position of the cuts matched perfectly.

"I know what it means," he said solemnly.

Claudia searched his eyes and felt that she also knew.

"We really are soul mates," he said.

The wind had changed. The air had become dry and fresh and the white sheers that flanked the French doors billowed around Lance and Claudia as they stood for a very long time in each other's arms. Lance stroked her hair and kissed it gently. Claudia's head rested on his chest and she could feel the beating of his heart. *If only it could always be like this,* she thought, knowing that it could not.

Lance was certain that no other 18-year-old boy in the history of the world had ever received the gift of such profound love. He'd never had such feelings for any other person. He loved his parents, he loved Nana, he loved falling in love every week with a different girl, but he'd never felt the absolute bliss he felt at this very moment with a woman he was satisfied to just be holding. With this kind of proximity he would normally have an erection by now. He didn't and he didn't care. This was better. He found he was smiling. He looked down at Claudia and saw that she was smiling too.

The world disappeared for them that afternoon. All that existed in this moment of divine certainty was love—heaven-sent and blessed. It didn't matter that they could never be seen together in public. It didn't matter that they'd have to act like an ordinary student and teacher in school. It didn't matter that their entire relationship would have to be a lie to everyone except themselves. All that mattered right now was the exquisite tenderness that made their minds, bodies and spirits as one.

Both lost in thought, they nestled together on the couch. Claudia was the first to speak. "Are we sure that's it? That we're soul mates?"

"What else could it be?"

"Don't you have doubts?" she asked.

"Do you?"

"I don't want to," she said, "I just want it to be like it is right now, always." She smiled a bit sadly. "But I think we both know life doesn't quite work that way."

The real world had begun to make its presence known again. But Claudia settled back against Lance and said, "I have no idea what any of this means. We meant to break it off until the dream showed us something we can't ignore. I can't imagine being anywhere but here with you holding me. I feel at one with you."

Lance too felt a oneness at the way their bodies fit together as she leaned against him. Her bare arms felt magical to his touch, her bronzed skin melting from the heat in his hands. When his lips touched her neck she smiled. And when his fingers brushed her nipples they hardened instantly sending a wave of intense pleasure through her body. No one and nothing had ever made her feel this way.

The experience had become so trance-like for both of them that he found himself not remembering how he could possibly have gotten his clothes off while backed into a corner of the couch. Claudia had simply dispensed with her diaphanous white dress in one simple motion.

Still sitting with Lance behind her, Claudia felt the hard strength of him pressing against her. She lifted herself and settled on him. The feeling of being inside her was so intense that Lance had no need to thrust. They found their lovemaking to be different than before; slower and more deliberate. He had a far greater awareness of the exact curvature of her breasts and how the nipples throbbed if his touch was soft enough. For her part she realized she'd stopped breathing. It was somehow a way to stop all movement and feeling in her body except for that single spot where she felt the power of his life force merely by his presence in her.

She threw her head back to rest on his shoulder, her neck stretched and exposed, inviting whatever he chose to do with it. As she surrendered completely, he slid his left hand across her abdomen and brushed his fingers lightly through the hair below. She spasmed and let out a cry as his finger found that heavenly spot. They spent what seemed to be an eternity sending alternating messages of concentrated pleasure—all in a state of near-suspended animation. They both knew that a thrust—that fucking—would destroy the moment. Everything was focused on their nearly immobile joining. Her spasms would cause him to throb intensely which would cause more spasms in an endless rhythm.

They would reach plateaus of such great passion that it would cause them to simultaneously bubble up with joyful laughter. She'd turn her head so her lips could find his and their kisses and laughter would give them a few moments to express their shared surprise before losing themselves in each other once more.

During one such recess Claudia said, "This is awesome!"

Lance laughed and said, "It would be more awesome if I didn't have a cramp in my groin."

"Oh, Lance, I'm so sorry. Stand up and it'll go away. What happened?"

He looked at the clock. "We've only been in this position for 20 minutes!"

She grinned. "I didn't hear you complaining."

"I could've had a heart attack and I wouldn't have stopped."

"Me too. I've never felt anything like that." She led him limping into the bedroom and said, "Here, lie down and I'll massage it."

"You've been doing that for 20 minutes."

"I don't mean *that*."

He responded playfully. "I know what you don't mean."

"Ok, where does it hurt?" He pointed to the spot and she leaned in, kissed him on the thigh and dug her thumbs into his groin. The pain was intense, but just when Lance thought he was going to scream, she backed off then dug in again, increasing the pressure each time to the point just this side of torture.

"You're very good at this," he said.

"I went to massage school for awhile. Wasn't really my thing."

"I would seriously disagree with that."

"You ever massage a three hundred fifty pound guy?"

He grinned. "I see."

"I do know how to batter a hard muscle into submission." With a seductive grin she whispered, "Don't I?" She had to move only slightly to the left to kiss the still-strong other muscle and tease it with her tongue. That started another round.

After a break for banana splits and another break for peanut butter and jelly sandwiches and another break for strawberry cheesecake, they lay hand in hand and exhausted on Claudia's rumpled satin sheets with blissful smiles.

Lance finally spoke. "Now tell me we're not soul mates."

Claudia replied, "I can't tell you that. I can only tell you I've never been more in love." She thought about what she'd just said and continued. "Actually those words don't do justice to what

I'm feeling now." She paused, cocked her head in that way that meant she was searching her interior literary encyclopedia. "You ever hear of János Arany?"

"No."

"Hungarian poet." She shook her head in wonder. "Tell me this line doesn't say it all: 'In dreams and in love there are no impossibilities.'"

Lance smiled. "That's tight."

"Tight?"

"You know. Sweet. Sick. Tight. Excellent."

"My God, how is this ever going to work? We even speak different languages."

Lance leaned over and kissed her on the forehead. "It works."

"Yes, it does."

As they settled into feathery kisses once again, Lance's cell phone rang.

"Please, God, not my mother." He looked at the caller ID. "Damn. I totally spaced. I had a tutoring appointment with Marco a half hour ago." He flipped it open. "Marco. Sorry, dude. I got involved in something and spaced."

Marco replied, "Get your exhausted butt dressed and get over here. We need to talk."

Chapter 20

Lance sprinted up the driveway to the Cerasuolo house. He was desperate to find out how Marco knew he was undressed and exhausted. He could hear Marco's mother, father, grandmother and sister screaming at each other through the open front door.

Lupo, the father, was a bear of a man; the kind you wouldn't want to start an argument with in a bar. You could imagine his wife, Angelina, flattening him with a cast iron skillet if properly pissed. Lupo had undoubtedly had that experience so his at-home bark was far worse than his bite. Nana was even more agitated than when Lance encountered her on his first visit. Lance could see her standing on a chair waving a cross at everyone in the room. He assumed she must be begging God to exorcise demons from these lunatics.

The object of Lupo's ire was Marco's 13-year-old sister, Capricia. Much of the shouting was in Italian. In the tutoring sessions, Marco had taught Lance more Italian than Lance had taught Marco English. Most of it the bad words—enough for Lance to pick out some doozies from Lupo's rant. *Donnaccia, prostituta* and *baldracca* popped out at him mostly because of Lupo's vehement emphasis of them. When Lupo repeated the tirade in English, Lance confirmed that Lupo was calling Capricia a slut and two kinds of whore. He was demanding that she not leave the house wearing a next-to-nothing outfit of studded leather shorts and halter top.

Capricia screamed back at him, "I'm wearing what I damn well want to wear!"

Angelina chimed in, "Capricia, listen to your father."

"It's not fair! Look at Marco. You let Marco wear shorts up to his balls and get away with it."

Lupo replied, "He's three years older than you. He's in high school and he's… he's…" Lupo was reaching for something he couldn't or wouldn't say.

Marco had been sitting in a corner with his feet propped on a table, his head pivoting back and forth between the combatants like watching a tennis match. "Papa is trying to tell you that I can wear shorts up to my balls because I'm gay and it's expected."

"*Sí*," said Lupo, "*Omosessuale. Finocchio.*"

Nana shrieked and made the sign of the cross.

Lance decided it was now or never and pressed the doorbell. All heads turned toward the door. After a moment of readjusting attitudes, they all rushed to admit Lance with warm smiles and gracious offers to share the feast they had been eating before the altercation that now seemed never to have happened. Being a Van Arden, Lance had learned, often prompted that kind of over-lavish indulgence.

Angelina took Capricia by the hand and led her to meet Lance. "Capricia," she cooed, "this is Marco's friend, Mr. Lance Van Arden. Mr. Lance, this is my beautiful daughter, Capricia."

She's actually twirling the girl around so I can get a good look at the goods, thought Lance. *One minute they're calling her a whore-in-training and the next minute they're actually pimping her.* "Nice to meet you," said Lance as he looked over at Marco who rolled his eyes and grinned. He whipped his feet off the table, gave Lance a push toward the garden door and said, "We have to talk."

As Marco led him toward some supermarket lounge chairs by the pool, Lance said, "Dude, your family is a trip."

Marco answered wryly, "I'm a lost cause, so Capricia is their only chance now, although respectability may not be her thing either. You may have noticed. Mama thinks you're a good *compagno*. A good match."

"For Capricia?!"

"You're respectable."

"How old is she?"

"Thirteen."

Lance laughed. "They're trying to set me up with her at 13?"

"Too much age difference?" With a knowing look that stopped Lance in his tracks, Marco said, "You're screwing the English teacher all night and all day and my sister is not good enough for you because she's 13?"

Lance's face froze. Marco laughed. "Relax, I am...*irritante*. Teasing you." Marco's demeanor changed to all-business. "Sit! What do you want to know?"

Lance didn't ask how Marco knew what he knew. He had already learned that Daniel and The Bear told Marco things that would blow people's minds if proof was needed. Lance didn't need proof anymore. He said, "Is she my soul mate?"

"Yes. But maybe not in the way you imagine."

"Meaning?"

"Meaning, it's not all going to be like the last 24 hours. I'm supposed to tell you that you are bound together for a purpose." He reached for Lance's wrist and turned it over. He looked Lance in the eye and said, "You made a pact and you should keep your end of it."

"You were there weren't you? In the dream."

"I was a witness."

"What do I do now?" Lance begged.

"I have no idea. Whatever the purpose is, it was your choice...and hers. You have to figure it out." Marco paused, cocked his head as if listening, and said, "I'm supposed to tell you that if it's a bumpy ride, just remember one thing: *Uomo d'onore*. Be a man of honor."

Lance was awed and humbled, his 18-year-old bravado a bit shaken.

Marco continued. "And don't worry about me. If I said one word to anyone about you, they," he said pointing up, "would have my head. One more thing."

Lance said, "I'm not sure I can handle one more thing."

"This one you can. You don't need to come for tutoring lessons anymore. We both know I didn't need them. You were here for you."

Lance looked stricken. Cut loose in a leaky boat without an oar.

Marco saw the look and said, "You can always just come as a friend. To talk, play chess, whatever. You're not alone. I can't tell you anything unless I'm allowed to. You'll be alright—if you believe you'll be alright. I believe it."

Lance wanted to hug him.

Marco said, "I know you want to hug me, but don't. Mama would kill me for stealing you away from Capricia." He tilted his head toward the house. Lance followed his cue and saw Angelina and Capricia peeking through a crack between the slightly parted curtains. Lance and Marco turned their heads away from the house to mask their stifled laughter.

Chapter 21

Lance invented elaborate excuses to cover his frequent absences from the family dinner table and from the customary weekend tennis matches he would most likely have won.

His stolen moments with Claudia were always fresh and different. Each time they made love it was virginal, as if they'd never done it before. He loved to bear witness to those moments of pure ecstasy when she'd close her eyes and her face would glow with a transcendent beauty. At other moments, he would throw his head back and she would explore every chiseled inch of him with her hands and her eyes. The world completely disappeared around them at these times and would come crashing back in class. They had learned how to play-act the teacher-student thing. Now and then he would tease her with a flirtatious look that would leave her wondering if their cover was blown. They'd laugh about it later when he'd give her that same flirtatious look and they'd fall deep into the bottomless well of each other all over again.

Lance had fallen into the habit of staying behind for a brief conversation with Claudia after class. To all appearances these seemed to be tutorial moments but they noticed that Mr. Adashek strolled by quite often, always taking a curious look inside the classroom. They tried not to get paranoid about it, but twice when they'd left the classroom together they discovered him lurking in a shadowy corner. From the way he too-casually looked away when they noticed him, they were clear that his curiosity was not a good thing. After that they were careful to have no more after-class encounters.

Once they both slipped into a dark place of doubt. Sunday afternoon they had gone to a secluded spot on a Point Dume bluff overlooking the ocean. As the waves crashed on the rocks below, Claudia burst into tears and asked, "Do you think this has to end badly?"

"What?"

"Us."

Lance sighed deeply and replied reluctantly. "I sometimes wonder the same thing."

"What we're doing is definitely not politically correct."

"You being my teacher and all."

"We've convinced ourselves we're soul mates and that we have a purpose. Is that delusional? Societies make rules for a reason and we've broken one of the biggest. Can that be a right thing to do?" Both of them had wrestled with that question.

Lance said, "What if we were both 17 and we felt about each other as we do now. We just know we're soul mates and we make love and know it's right. Most people would think that's ok, right? And it's legal. But if I turned 18 before you did they could send me to jail for statutory rape. How does that make any sense? And who makes up the rules anyway? For sure not somebody who's ever had a transparent dude do this to them." He entwined his fingers in hers and pressed their wrists together.

Claudia smiled and said, "If only we can just be us and stop buying into what others would think is something bad, we'll be all right. We *are* all right!" They were back on track and again it seemed that nothing could intrude in their private heaven.

Thanksgiving would be coming in another week and they knew they'd not be able to share it even though the thing they were both most thankful for was each other. Claudia's parents would be arriving from Michigan on Tuesday for their first visit to Los Angeles in twenty years.

Once, after they had exhausted each other and lay quietly together, Claudia asked, "Do you ever wonder where we go from here?"

"I try not to," said Lance. "But yes, I do."

"What we do in this room is wonderful," she said. But it's impossible to have a life beyond this, isn't it?"

"Now, yes."

"You've applied to all the best Ivy League schools. I'm in a very different place. You'll be leaving and I'll be here. I don't want it to end."

"I don't either. I've also applied to UCLA and USC you know."

"Yes, but if you got accepted to Harvard you would be a fool not to go."

"Maybe you could come with me."

She gave him an are-you-kidding look. "Who's gonna tell your mom?"

That silenced him. At last he said, "We haven't found our purpose yet."

"What do you mean?"

"Marco told me not to expect it to always be like it is now. That we had to find out what our purpose together is."

She snuggled against his chest and said, "Meantime, I'm not complaining."

Chapter 22

Lance got home that Sunday evening around 10 o'clock, exhausted and with a blissful smile on his face. Roberta had been noticing the extended absences and the missed tennis matches. She was in the kitchen when he went in to get a bedtime snack and thought he was high.

"Well!" she said. It was the well from hell. The one that said *I'm going to get to the bottom of this.*

"What?" he said jostled from his contented space.

"Have you been drinking?"

"Mom!! No!"

"Drugs?"

"Why do you ask that, do I look high?!"

"High. On some other planet. In love. Something! You're never around anymore. What did you do today?"

Lance had mentally prepared a whole litany of believable excuses in case he needed them for just this kind of moment. "Drove out to Malibu with some friends," he said with what he hoped was an air of finality.

"Which friends?"

"Couple of guys from the band and we met a couple of girls at Moonshadows."

"The couple of guys don't have names?"

"Of course. Jason and Plunger."

"All right. Sorry. I didn't mean to pry. It used to be nice spending Sunday afternoons at home. Playing tennis. Having your friends over here."

"Things change, Mom," he said. *Haven't they ever,* he thought.

Lance knew his mother well enough to know that she would somehow investigate if he was, indeed, with Jason and Plunger in Malibu today. He'd already warned them to cover for him if anyone asked. He'd told them he was spending time with this chick from San Diego and he didn't want to have to answer any parental questions. They wondered why and he told them that she was an older woman. They were lecherously intrigued, assured him their lips were sealed and begged him for details.

Lance thought it best to re-direct Roberta. "Who's coming for Thanksgiving this year?"

Roberta knew this was a diversion, but played along. "Just us, Uncle Hans, Aunt Elsa and Biddy."

Hans and Elsa had emigrated from Holland when Biddy was four. In kindergarten, Biddy was an easier name for schoolmates to remember than Betje. Biddy stuck.

"Not Biddy's fiancé?" said Lance with a smile. Biddy was his aunt and uncle's slutty daughter who was always engaged and never married. The parade of fiancés fueled an endless soap opera that embarrassed Hans and Elsa and amused everyone else.

"Now, now," Roberta scolded.

Roberta finished dunking her tea bag, meticulously squeezed the water out of it and, with what could be read as a mischievous look that she was careful Lance didn't see, said, "We still have room at the table. Your English teacher is new in town and I'll bet she doesn't have somewhere to go. We had such a lovely time at dinner with her at the start of the semester, it would be fun to have her here. Maybe it'll keep Uncle Hans from discussing his hemorrhoids and ulcers ad nauseum."

"She can't come," he said too quickly.

Roberta raised her eyebrows.

"Her parents are coming for Thanksgiving." That sounds like she told me, he thought. "She told the class last week that her parents are coming from Michigan to L.A. for the first time in twenty years."

"Wonderful," Roberta bubbled. "What better way to celebrate Thanksgiving than having dinner here. It would be such a treat for them, don't you think? It'll be good for us too. We live in such a rarefied atmosphere it'll be good to have an honest conversation with real people for a change. Remind us of our Midwestern roots." She grabbed her Blackberry from the counter and said, "I think I put her number in my address book. De la Rosa."

Lance's panic was bubbling to the surface. "Mom, I don't think that's such a good idea."

Roberta looked him directly in the eye and said, "Why not, dear?"

"It's such short notice," was the only thing he could come up with.

"Nonsense," she said as she dialed. "It won't hurt to ask."

The ringing phone broke Claudia's reverie. She was still savoring the warmth from Lance's side of the bed and was completely unprepared. The caller ID said Van Arden but it wasn't Lance's cell number. Why was he calling her from home? That was dangerous.

"Hi," she said.

"Claudia, this is Roberta Van Arden."

"Oh! Hello. I thought it was my mom calling me back."

"Lance told me that your parents are coming to L.A. next week?"

"He did!?" Something felt very wrong here. Why was he talking to his mother about her?

"Yes. Said it was their first visit in 20 years. I insisted that we should invite you and them to our house for Thanksgiving. I do hope you can make it. I'm sure they'd enjoy it."

"Well…" Claudia fumbled. "I don't know."

"Do you have other plans?"

"Yes. I made reservations."

"Where?"

"The Four Seasons." It was the first place that popped into her mind.

"Well, call and cancel, my dear. I won't take no for an answer."

Claudia could think of nothing that would sidetrack the potential disaster of having Thanksgiving dinner at the Van Arden table. She would be spending the first major family holiday with her soul mate and his family and there was no way they could be who they knew they were.

She couldn't believe she would ever be invited back to the Van Arden estate after the disastrous rain forest party she'd nearly ruined. Since then she hadn't seen or talked to Roberta, and Lance was living in fear that his mother suspected something. *Is this a setup? Why else would she invite me to spend Thanksgiving with them? She thinks she can trip us up. And with Mom and Dad there. My God! This woman has balls.* Claudia was feeling something very like a thrill in the challenge. She would not let Roberta Van Arden win this round. *Wait,* she thought. *I'm being paranoid. We did have an absolutely wonderful dinner in September. And Edward was very sweet and forgiving after the party. Maybe they like my company.*

She cocked her head listening for guidance from the little Observer voice which said, *You'll have friends and enemies there. Charm them. Go for it.* She knew the role she had to play and she knew she could give an award-winning performance. Whatever Roberta's motives, Claudia's Latina feistiness had bubbled to the surface and she found herself relishing the test.

Claudia called her mother and father to get them excited about having Thanksgiving dinner in a Beverly Hills Mansion with people they didn't know. She'd gushed to them about the wonderful Van Arden dinner in September so it ought to be a little easier to convince them that they'd have a good time.

When her mother picked up she said, "Hi, Mama."

"*Mija*, hold on. I'm on the cordless and the big suitcase is stuck halfway off the shelf."

"Mama, you're four foot eight. Let papa get it down."

"I don't want him to push himself."

"Why?"

"He isn't feeling good."

"What's wrong?"

"He worries too much. About business. Since the mill closed, nobody in town has money to eat out anymore. Now they're talking about closing the auto parts plant too."

"It's that bad?"

"It is. But I'm not going to let it spoil Thanksgiving. We haven't taken a real vacation in I don't know how long. Years. And we miss you. We are coming!"

"Mama, that's why I'm calling. We have an invitation to Thanksgiving dinner at one of my student's houses—with his family. Do you remember I told you about going to dinner with the Van Ardens?"

"The dressmaker?"

"Yes, the ones with the fashion house."

"Your papa won't like that."

"Why?"

"You know he's not too happy with the clothing business. The mill fired twelve hundred people and all that work went to China. No, Claudia. You cancel Thanksgiving dinner with those people."

"Mama, *they* didn't fire the people." Claudia was tempted to give in but her combative nature kicked in and took over. "I can't cancel it. They would be insulted."

"Your papa's grabbing for the phone. Ask him. He'll tell you."

Esmeralda handed off the phone to Leonardo and Claudia told him about the Van Arden invitation.

"I know who they are," he said. "Tom told me they were one of their last good customers before they had to close the mill."

"Mama was worried you wouldn't want to go."

"Your mama worries too much about me worrying too much. Life is too short. What kind of people are they?"

"They're rich and famous, but they're just like you and mama. They started with nothing, worked their butts off, got lucky and got successful. Just like you and mama. They lived in a little apartment over a bar and used to change Lance's diapers by the light of a neon sign outside their apartment window. They're just people."

"Who's Lance?

"The student in my class. The one I told you about who's a good writer. I'm kind of his mentor."

Leonardo seemed won over to the idea, and Claudia suddenly wondered how on earth she could be selling something to her mom and dad that could turn sour. But, when she got into this *I can conquer the world* mood she usually won the war through sheer determination. In this way she was very much like her father. His buoyancy about trying new things had infected her at a very young age and made her follow her own dream. Besides, she loved Lance and refused to be ashamed of their unlikely soul mate status. They'd never find their purpose by hiding in the bushes.

Chapter 23

Edward Van Arden liked his sauna and ice cold shower before bed. It was a comfort that took the place of the sensual adventures he and Roberta had shared in the early years. He was slipping into his silk pajamas and smoking jacket (even though he didn't smoke), when Roberta charged in as if she'd just trounced someone on the tennis court.

"You'll never guess who I just invited to Thanksgiving dinner," she said.

"If I'll never guess, just tell me."

"Claudia de la Rosa."

"She's not bringing a guest, is she?" he teased.

"She's bringing her mother and father who are flying in from Michigan for the holiday."

"That's a lovely thought, Robbie." Noticing Roberta's cat-that-ate-the canary contentment he continued. "Or is it? What are you up to?"

Roberta smiled. "You know me so well."

"Fess up," he said.

"I just want to see her and Lance together."

"Not that again. Roberta, give it up. She's a charming young woman and Lance enjoys the attention she's lavishing on his literary talent. Don't make more of it than there is."

"Where is he going all the time? He's never home. He moons around like a lovesick adolescent and never brings girls to the house anymore. Honestly, Edward. What's he hiding? Open your eyes."

"So you're going to invite her to our Thanksgiving table to expose them? With her parents there, no less. What, in God's name, are you thinking?"

"You think there's something going on there, too."

Edward rolled his eyes and threw up his hands. "So what if he has a crush on her. Just leave him alone. You've complained since he was 14 that he runs around with too many girls, goes to too many parties, hangs out with the wrong friends and writes lyrics that are not for polite company. And on top of that, you ransack his drawers looking for condoms and drugs."

"I take my responsibility as a parent very seriously," she huffed.

"So do I and I appreciate how he's mellowed out in the last couple of months. We don't have to know who he sees or where he goes all the time. So what if he's spending time with his English teacher if that's what it is. It does seem to be good for him."

"You can't be serious. She's his teacher! People are thrown in jail for molesting their students. I'm appalled that you don't think there's anything wrong with it."

"I don't know what it is. He's not a minor anymore. And frankly it's none of my business. Or yours."

Roberta was now in attack mode. "Laying his teacher is not your business?! That's macho bullshit." She turned and stalked out of the dressing room with the last word. "If you won't do anything about it, I damn well will."

Edward knew that there was no reasoning with her when she reached volcanic mode. He sighed, ran a comb through his damp hair, poured a glass of brandy and sat down to brood about the potential for warfare on the Thanksgiving horizon.

Chapter 24

After Lance witnessed his mother's overly gracious invitation to Claudia, he was certain something was amiss. He'd seen Mom on a quest and this seemed to be just that. He called Claudia in a panic and kept getting a busy signal while she was wooing her parents on the idea of a Van Arden/de la Rosa Thanksgiving. When he finally reached her he was surprised at her calm self-confidence as she reassured him that there was nothing she would like to do more than bring her parents for Thanksgiving dinner. He'd never seen her quite like this. Almost obsessive, he thought.

"I'm sure Mom's up to something," he said. "You have to call her with an excuse."

"Don't worry about it. It will be fine."

"You're sure about this?" he asked.

"Listen to me. Calling with some lame excuse would really make her suspicious wouldn't it?"

He had to admit that was probably true.

"I'll gush about your talent and you'll be embarrassed and shy. They'll burst at the seams with pride. Our parents will charm each other, we'll be enjoying our first Thanksgiving dinner together with our families, and only we will know the truth.

"It's dangerous!" he said.

"Yeah!" she replied with mischief in her voice.

"You're a lunatic. This could be a total disaster."

"Or another step forward."

School was closed all of Thanksgiving week. On Monday, Claudia spent the afternoon shopping for the perfect gift to give her Thanksgiving dinner host and hostess. She looked in the wine and spirits shop on the corner. A fine champagne, perhaps? A lovely wine? Nothing seemed right. The Van Ardens' wine cellar had been featured in Gourmet. How could she top that? Certainly the hundred dollar cheese/caviar/fancy cracker basket wouldn't do the trick either. *Something personal*, she thought. *Something money can't buy.*

She stopped at Cost Plus in The Grove to pick up some candles since she and Lance seemed to use them up by the gross. A lacquered wooden box with a gold Buddha on the lid caught her eye. It had been carefully distressed to look as if someone had lovingly rescued and treasured it for centuries. *The Van Ardens probably have the authentic antique box this one was copied from,* she thought. She almost passed it by but the size of it inspired a brilliant thought. The box would just be the wrapping for something special and she knew what that something special was going to be.

Chapter 25

When Claudia called Hertz to reserve something larger than her Miata to accommodate her parents' visit, she'd already considered what would look good when they arrived on Thursday in the Van Arden motor court.

It was only a three day rental so she splurged on a BMW 740il and arrived at the airport an hour before the flight was to arrive. She didn't want to risk a traffic jam on the way because she knew her mother would be a nervous wreck if she wasn't waiting at the foot of the escalator.

As she spotted them wrestling with their carry-ons, her heart skipped a beat as she saw how fragile her father looked. In the three months that had passed since she'd last been home, Leonardo seemed to have aged three years. He was pale and sweating profusely. He brightened when he saw Claudia and for a moment the shock of his appearance passed as he became the beaming papa she missed terribly. She hugged them both and rushed to take his duffel bag.

"*Mija*," he crowed. "*Muy bonita.*"

Claudia suddenly teared up and the hugs seemed never ending.

Leonardo pulled out a handkerchief, wiped his brow and said, "It's so hot here! And the plane too."

Claudia smiled. Of course, she thought. Maybe her father's damp and pallid appearance was just a result of being overheated. After all, they just left a 20 degree cold snap in Michigan and arrived to a Los Angeles heat wave.

"Leo," Esmeralda said, pointing him toward a bench. "Sit down a minute. Rest."

That admonishment from her mother quickly erased Claudia's short-lived relief. "Papa, are you ok?"

"I'm fine," he said brushing Esmeralda's concern off with a wave.

"He's not fine," Esmeralda said. "He's tired all the time and worries all the time and I can't get him to go see Dr. Butcher."

Leonardo pushed the concern aside with a laugh, "Who wants to see a doctor named Butcher?"

"Oh, stop!" Esmeralda said.

"Papa, you've used that excuse every time you didn't want to go see Dr. Butcher. You don't look like you've been taking care of yourself."

"I'm fine. Let's go. I'm on vacation from work, from snow and from everything wrong with Harbor Point, Michigan. We've got five days in the sun and I'm going to make the most of it."

Claudia had to admit that her father did have a point. Clearly he was overworked and needed a rest. For a moment she had second thoughts about submitting him to the possibility of a stressful Thanksgiving with the Van Ardens.

"And," he said emphatically, "I'm really looking forward to a fancy dinner with the rich and famous. Look," he said, proudly pulling from his bag a Tupperware bowl wrapped in a towel filled with dry ice. "I even brought something for dessert that all the money in Hollywood can't buy. A tub of my famous arroz con leche."

His delicious self-confidence infected both Claudia and Esmeralda.

"He's going to improve the gringos' Thanksgiving," Esmeralda said with a reluctant grin.

"Hollywood, here we come," Leonardo said as they picked up their bags and headed out of the terminal. Esmeralda had to have the last word: "Fine. But next Monday we go see Dr. Butcher."

Leonardo turned to Claudia. "I don't have a choice do I?"

Claudia draped a conspiratorial arm over her mother's shoulder and said, "No choice. None."

Claudia had splurged on a room for her parents at the Hotel Mondrian. On Wednesday morning, feeling properly pampered, Leonardo had regained his color and was looking forward to a guided tour. Claudia picked them up at the hotel and drove them to Beverly Hills.

They parked the car underground and took an elevator up to the little fake street called Two Rodeo that resembled a European village in a Vegas kind of way. The uniformed guard at the elevator was always amused by the Midwestern tourists who browsed at Tiffany and Versace and, after observing an overwhelming glut of ostentation, rushed out the doors marveling about forty five thousand dollar watches and seven hundred dollar scarves. The experience caused Esmeralda to fret that she had absolutely nothing to wear to a Beverly Hills Thanksgiving dinner.

Claudia took her down the block to Neiman Marcus and bought her a divine little eight hundred dollar black dress. It fit perfectly and Claudia knew she could return it with impunity next week.

Before Claudia had even thought about rolling out of bed to go fetch her parents at the airport, Lance had been wide awake at five worrying about Thanksgiving. Deciding to keep himself busy to keep his mind in a more positive space, he picked up three friends with wet suits and boards at 6:30 a.m. to take advantage of the high winter storm waves rolling in at Malibu Cove.

Jason had brought along his guitar to play the new song he was working on for their band. After finishing the last verse and polishing off the chorus, the guys were appropriately appreciative in a laid back, cooler-than-thou sort of way. *Sweet, dude. Tight, man.* That sort of thing. Lance had his eyes fixed on the road ahead and was in another world. He managed to grunt, "Excellent."

Lance's approval of lyrics was always paramount to Jason and he couldn't believe the trance his lifeless buddy seemed to be in. "Dude, what the fuck are you on? We haven't seen you in two weeks. You're not you, man. You high? This mystery bitch in San Diego got you by the nuts? What?"

If you only knew, thought Lance.

"He's in love," volunteered Plunger. "Didn't you read his SuperDreamer blog? You gotta drag yourself loose from this one, dude. She's ruining our lives."

Jason said, "You're the chick magnet, man. You don't hang out with us anymore and we never get laid. And on top of that, we gotta cover for you if your mom calls."

That jarred Lance loose from his reverie. He wished he hadn't given them his otherwise anonymous URL. It had gotten a whole lot more complicated since he'd posted that dream. He couldn't risk posting more clues.

"Ok," he said. "After we hit the waves, lunch at Moonshadows is on me. I'll see what I can do to pimp you out one more time, then you guys gotta learn to fly on your own."

Chapter 26

Roberta rarely cooked. She was used to having Maria or one of the others on their household staff prepare the meals, but she always got up early on Thanksgiving morning to make the oyster dressing, stuff the bird and get it into the oven. Next she would open the big cans of yams, mash them up leaving them a bit lumpy, copiously lace the dish with rum, brown sugar and a dash of nutmeg, then set the bag of marshmallows out for spreading on top for the last 10 minutes of baking. Maria did the shopping, of course, and had learned by now that the string bean casserole must be made with canned beans. The frozen French cut ones always tasted better, but Roberta's mother, and grandmother before her, had always done Thanksgiving with canned beans, canned yams, oyster dressing, mashed potatoes, gravy from scratch with the turkey drippings and jellied cranberry sauce. The memories of those holiday dinners always promised a time that was simpler, when the warmth of the kitchen's anticipated gifts and the expectant relatives arriving to the smell of the traditional gustatory treats joined her sometimes peevish family in a few hours of relatively loving togetherness.

Roberta had always reached for that feeling on the holidays and as she started the morning ritual this year she realized that she was on the brink of spoiling it with a devious little scheme she'd concocted in an impulsive moment of suspicion. Why was she so intent on seeing what kind of attention her eldest son lavished upon his English teacher? Why did it upset her so much? No matter, she thought. This was Thanksgiving and she would not let her vigilance stop the warm and inviting holiday wonderland that had become a Roberta Van Arden hallmark. She resolved that Claudia and her parents would never forget this Thanksgiving dinner.

Claudia had called Roberta to ask if it would be all right for them to bring dessert. She explained that her father always made this wonderful rice pudding that had become a holiday specialty at Cocina de la Rosa. She described how he'd lugged it all the way from Michigan in his carry-on bag past suspicious airport security agents and through a plane change in Chicago. Roberta's first reaction was to panic at the thought of no pumpkin pie with made-from-scratch whipped cream. But Claudia was genuinely protective of her father in a way that surprisingly melted Roberta's heart and she was powerless to do anything but graciously accept the offer of Leonardo's thoughtful gift.

Chapter 27

As Claudia pulled the BMW up to the call box at the massive Van Arden gate, Esmeralda was very glad she was wearing an $800 dress. She and Leonardo had only seen such extraordinary wealth in the movies. They were feeling a bit intimidated when Leonardo, Roberta and Lance opened the front door and met them with warm smiles.

Much like a bride and groom remember very little of their wedding in the rush of the happening of it, Leonardo and Esmeralda floated through the welcoming pleasantries overwhelmed by the sheer grandeur that surrounded them. As Roberta and Edward led them through the living museum that was their home, they pointed out where, in their travels, each of the fine paintings, remarkable sculptures and exquisite rugs had been found. It was clear that their pride of ownership was much more than just ownership. Each of these objects was a part of the fabric of a creative life force that fueled the remarkable success of these two extraordinary people.

Lance and Claudia followed a short distance behind, chatting amiably and a bit formally about how good it was to see each other again without being in a classroom setting.

Leonardo did a double take as he glanced down a hallway that led toward the kitchen. As if drawn by a magnet he strode down the hall past a long row of vibrant paintings and sketches, stopping before a serigraph that dominated the wall. He was awed by what he was seeing.

The others had no choice but to follow Leonardo's detour. Claudia hadn't remembered noticing the painting when she visited in September. She would have been as stunned then as she was now to see something that hung both on a wall of the Van

Arden mansion and in her parents' living room. "Bordando," she said.

"*Sí,*" Leonardo said. "Rodolfo Morales."

Edward, Roberta and Esmeralda gathered around Leonardo. Esmeralda exclaimed, "Our painting."

Leonardo laughed, leaning in to look at the signature block. "You have number 6 of 10," he said. "We have number 7 in our living room." He looked up at the recessed halogen light focused precisely on the painting and turned again to look at it. "In our house it's beautiful too, but with this light it's *alive*." Leonardo was so lost in the painting that tears came to his eyes. Roberta had always loved this painting and as she looked from Leonardo's moist eyes back toward it, she suddenly saw it in a new way.

Lance and Claudia stood a little away from the small cluster of parents that had crowded around the colorful image of a dark-skinned woman with bright eyes doing needlepoint in a yellow dress with puppies at her feet. "Small world," said Edward. "We picked this up in a gallery in San Miguel de Allende maybe six or seven years ago. Is Morales well known?"

"You are kidding," Leonardo replied.

"I don't really know," Edward said. "We saw it in the window and bought it because we fell in love with it. And because she's doing needlepoint. Seemed appropriate given the business we're in. I don't even know what Bordando means."

Leonardo grinned. "Needlepoint."

They all laughed.

"Where did you get yours?" asked Roberta.

"Morales was my cousin's father-in-law's nephew," Leonardo said. "We saw it on the floor behind a door at my cousin's house and Esmeralda begged him for it."

"I asked him for it. He wasn't using it."

"He wasn't loving it," said Leonardo. "We love it." Again he looked up and pointed at the halogen light. "But, we sure as hell are going to get one of those."

As they continued on their house tour, Roberta led the way, arm in arm with Leonardo. Edward and Esmeralda followed behind, Edward touching her gently on the arm or shoulder now and then as he pointed out a particularly beautiful jade carving or another striking painting.

Lance and Claudia followed in awe. Claudia was pleased that, so far, her confidence about the likely success of this day hadn't been misplaced.

They joined Uncle Hans, Aunt Elsa, Biddy and Biddy's new fiancé, Liu Minjie, a 27-year-old vice president of one of China's largest garment manufacturers.

Lance didn't understand why, but Biddy had always confided her innermost secrets to him. She pulled him aside to say she'd met Liu three weeks ago at her girlfriend Frederika's weekly *pool party*. Lance had been amused the first time she'd told him about the select group of invitation-only gentleman callers Freddie gathered every Sunday afternoon. When Biddy had told him that Freddie always gave her five hundred dollars for cab fare, he surmised that the fine gentlemen were accustomed to helping out with the rent and other expenses.

Lance couldn't tell if Biddy was boasting or if she was just an innocent airhead when she'd said, "I don't know why she thinks a cab costs five hundred dollars."

She was sure, she told Lance this Thanksgiving afternoon, that Liu was finally the one. Lance had his doubts, however, because he'd seen that these wedding-bound liaisons never seemed to pan out. It was pretty clear to Lance that when Liu found out her last name was Van Arden it made business sense to hang on to her. Manufacturing for their mass market division would be a coup.

Sure enough, two weeks later she called Lance with a sad story. Liu's wife and son had arrived to set up housekeeping in the Bel Air mansion his company had bought. He wanted to set her up in an apartment, but she refused. "Mr. Right still has to be out there somewhere," she'd said.

Two uniformed servers offered trays of a fine 1996 Dom Perignon and tables were loaded with warm brie, stuffed mushrooms and luscious fruits. Uncle Hans and Leonardo bonded fairly quickly by comparing their respective bouts with ulcers and gout. Aunt Elsa and Esmeralda were comparing schoolgirl stories of horrors at the hands of militant nuns.

Claudia had never met Lance's brother and sister. Michael at fourteen was consumed by video games. Roberta dragged him away from his Xbox to join the family gathering but it was clear his brain was still on another planet fighting aliens. Jennifer at 10 found her time consumed by American Girl dolls, American Girl Theatre productions, American Girl birthday parties (with a special Treat Seat for your doll) at the American Girl Café in The Grove. Three American Girl dolls would attend this Thanksgiving dinner with the family; Felicity and Elizabeth, colonial young ladies from 1774, along with Kaya the Nez Perce girl who wants to be a bold warrior woman like Swan Circling. Not quite pilgrims, but as close as Jennifer could get.

Claudia tried to relate to Jennifer. "I had a Barbie collection when I was your age."

"Oh, Barbies," Jennifer said but with a disdainful undercurrent that indicated that Barbies were not cool.

Biddy and Liu had backed Edward into a corner so Liu could extol the virtues of his factories in Guangzhou. Edward had felt duty-bound to have his garments American made and had been holding out as long as he could afford to do so. But the big discounters kept demanding lower and lower prices on the mass market goods. The design firms that wanted to stay in business had to farm the work out where labor costs were next to nothing.

"I still have about 60 percent of my stock made in the U.S.A.", he said proudly. "I'm sure the quality of your work is excellent, Liu, but the U.S. is becoming a country with no middle class because we're outsourcing everything to you guys. I think we're giving away the store. I for one am doing my small part by resisting as long as I can. No offense, but my dad did honest work all his life in a shoe factory. He was a craftsman, worked hard, supported a family, paid off our house, retired to Florida and died an honorable man. Not so easy to do that these days."

Leonardo had heard this last exchange and joined them. "Can I butt in?" he asked.

"Of course," Edward replied.

Liu had a plastered smile on his face, but his eyes were saying, *Oh, shit. This isn't going to be an easy sell.* "There is some truth in what you say, sir," he countered. "But the world is changing. We have no choice but to adapt or perish."

Leonardo's pulse had quickened. "Well, I'm perishing. I don't know what the hell to adapt to. I run a restaurant in a town where half the jobs have gone. I have half the business I used to have. I've laid off half my employees and my employees are a brother-in-law, two cousins, two nieces and a nephew. They've run up credit card bills, just to survive, that they'll never be able to pay off. They can't even declare bankruptcy anymore. Christmas is coming and I'll end up giving them all money I don't really have to buy gifts for their kids. What the hell do they adapt to?"

Liu was struggling. "Perhaps they could find out about re-training for something else?"

"Something what else?!" Leonardo said. "How to deep fry chicken tenders part time for minimum wage? How to point somebody to a shopping cart and say, 'Welcome to Wal-Mart'? I've worked my ass off for thirty years to get where I am and now it's going down the damn toilet. You ever hear of Michaelson/Donovan Fabrics?"

"No," Liu said cautiously.

"Nobody ever will anymore. Two guys in their 70's, been making high class fabric for 50 years. Gave it up. Couldn't compete anymore. Didn't have the damn will to fight it anymore. Fired twelve hundred people! You can't fry enough chicken tenders to employ twelve hundred people."

Edward rather enjoyed Leonardo's blunt tirade and was silently relishing Liu's discomfort. Not only did he and Leonardo share a painting, they had some similar thoughts about corporate greed, and were connected to two men who had played an important part in both their businesses. He smiled at Leonardo and said, "I know them—Tom Michaelson and Jack Donovan."

Leonardo winked and said, "I know you know them. You were their best customer."

"At the end I was their only customer. Made the best damn fabric in the world. And I was proud to pay a premium for it."

"You're a damn hero in my book," Leonardo said.

Edward shrugged self-consciously. "Well, thank you. Not that I accomplished that much."

Roberta had overheard most of this exchange and breezed in from the kitchen taking the tension temperature as she approached. She'd decided on the seating plan for the dinner table yesterday. But, managing a fashion house had taught her how to turn on a dime when necessary. Her brain instantly reshuffled the plan.

"Dinner is served," she announced, leading the guests into the dining room. She wished there was a children's table to accommodate Biddy and her friend. How dare they try to buttonhole Edward with a sales pitch before dinner?

"Leonardo, why don't you sit here next to Edward? Esmeralda right here next to me. Lance you there across from Claudia." That was actually part of the original plan. "Hans and Elsa down there. Michael and Jennifer next to them and Mr. Minjie and Biddy down at the end.

They all settled into their places and Maria entered with the bird, glistening and perfectly browned. The ooohs and aaahs over with, the turkey was placed next to Edward for the ritual slicing.

"Let's join hands and say a little prayer," he said. "Heavenly Father, this is a day to give thanks for everything we have and everything we are. We're thankful that we can spend this day with friends and family and we ask for your blessings on this feast as we say, thank you. Amen."

They took part in the traditional binge of too much of everything. Something brought them together in harmony that day, even the outcasts at the end of the table. Maybe it was the canned string bean casserole or the dousing of rum in the canned yams. Maybe it was that, in spite of their differences, they had come together for a purpose called giving thanks. There was laughter at the table. When Leonardo's *arroz con leche* was served along with the pumpkin pie, it perfectly symbolized the sweetness of the day.

Roberta noticed that Claudia and Lance had chimed in with quips and comments and teased each other with an intimate comfort. She was surprised that it didn't bother her as much as she thought it would.

Edward had noticed as well and kept his eye on Roberta to see if meltdown was imminent. He was amazed when Roberta turned to Claudia and said, "Claudia, I've never enjoyed Thanksgiving as much as I have today. I want to thank you and your amazing parents. Leonardo, if you'll give me the recipe for your *arroz con leche* it will be a part of every Thanksgiving dinner from now on to remind us of you and," she said looking directly at Claudia, "remind us how very fortunate we are to entrust our talented son's literary education to your charming daughter." That last remark was delivered with a sincerity that could be read as either a warning or a measure of acceptance. Even Roberta was not quite sure how she meant it.

Claudia seized the moment to take the box with the Buddha on it from the bag she'd stowed under her chair.

"I don't know what to say but thank you, Roberta. I brought a little something for you and Edward. She handed the box to Roberta who looked at it and said, "It's lovely. Thank you, Claudia." She passed it to Edward.

Claudia smiled, savoring her surprise. "The box is just the wrapping. Please open it."

Edward lifted the lid and found a dog-eared, hardbound copy of *The Artists Way*. "Oh, my dear," he said as he opened it to the flyleaf. "This is your autographed copy. The prized possession you told us about in September."

"You have been so kind," Claudia said, "that I wanted to give you something special."

"It doesn't get any more special than this," Roberta said. "Thank you, Claudia."

It had been a beautiful day. To complete it they adjourned to the south portico. From their lofty perch above Beverly Hills they could see all the way to the Pacific some 10 miles away. As the sun set they sat by the four-tiered Italianate fountain that had once graced a monastery garden in Bellagio. Maria brought coffee, chocolates and decanters of liqueurs. Leonardo, ebullient and charming during dinner, had become quiet. Esmeralda was engrossed in a conversation with Biddy and Liu.

Roberta noticed that Leonardo seemed a bit pale.

"Leonardo, are you ok?"

He brightened for a moment. "Yes, I'm fine. Just way too much to eat, I think."

Lance and Claudia had taken a little walk along the rose garden path, consciously staying within sight of everyone on the portico.

"Do you believe how this day went?" Lance asked.

"I hate to say I told you so," Claudia teased. Then she sobered a little. "What do you think your mom meant when she said my dad's *arroz con leche* would remind her how fortunate they are to entrust your talent to me? Was there just a little too much emphasis on talent?"

"Don't be paranoid," he said.

"The way she looked at me when she said it—I was confused. She looked like she was confused too. As if she really wanted to like me but couldn't quite get there."

"She likes you."

"How do you know?"

"Do you remember when Jennifer introduced you to Felicity, Elizabeth and Kaya?"

"Yes, she's really into those dolls, isn't she?"

"Yes, and so were you. Biddy was rolling her eyes and whispering something to her boyfriend. You and my sister were having an intense conversation with three dolls. And my mom was watching. I saw her face. Believe me, she likes you."

"I hope so."

They desperately wanted to touch each other. Even holding hands was impossible. "Later," said Claudia.

The air was sweet, the sun was setting over the Pacific, but the sound of the wind softly rustling in the trees was suddenly shattered by Esmeralda's scream.

Lance and Claudia turned to see her mother and Roberta on their knees and the others rushing to cluster around someone lying on the terrace floor. Claudia knew instantly who it was. "Papa!" She ran down the path toward the portico and, in spite of her heels, took the steps two at a time. Lance was right behind her.

Leonardo was clutching his chest, gasping for breath. Claudia met her paralyzed mother's eyes and saw terror in them. Lance turned to his father and said, "You have your cell phone?"

Edward was also paralyzed and Lance's question jolted him into reaching for it.

"Call 911," Lance said as he raced into the house nearly colliding with Maria who was on her way out to see what was happening. "Nana! Come with me." Maria looked confused. "Now, Nana! It's Mr. de la Rosa." She followed him into the kitchen. "Get me a bottle of water!" Lance pulled open the pill drawer and started pulling out bottles of vitamins, diet pills, and cold medicine, throwing the rejects on the counter. "Damn, where are they?" He found what he was looking for and shook the bottle. "Who the fuck put an empty bottle back in here!" He threw it angrily on the floor and kept looking. "Here," he said with relief. "Hurry, Nana. Give me the water." As he ran back outside he could hear a siren and figured it was maybe a minute or two away. He shouted over his shoulder, "Nana, open the gate and show the paramedics where to come. Run!"

Leonardo was conscious and still breathing very heavily when Lance returned. Claudia and Esmeralda were gently stroking him. "Hang on, Papa. Hear the siren? The paramedics will be here any minute. You're gonna be ok." She looked up at Lance not quite so sure that this was the case and silently imploring him to do something.

"Nana's opening the gate for the paramedics. Here. This is aspirin," he said handing two to Claudia as he opened the bottle of water. "If it's a heart attack they say taking two right away could help."

"Yes, he's right," Roberta said.

"Give 'em to me," Leonardo gasped.

"Chew them before you swallow, sir," Lance said. "They'll get digested quicker."

Biddy and Liu were watching from a distance and Biddy whispered to him, "Happy Thanksgiving." Liu looked at her a bit strangely. "Don't worry," she said. "I'll be damned if I'm going to let this spoil a perfectly good holiday."

Roberta overheard. The bitch! she thought, and had to restrain herself from bodily dragging her out by the hair and kicking her butt halfway to Tarzana. This was one that she would not let pass. She knelt down next to Leonardo, took his hand and Esmeralda's and said, "Leonardo, if this had to happen, I'm glad it happened here among friends on Thanksgiving where help is close at hand." Shooting a look at Biddy she continued, "That is truly something to be thankful for."

Lance had gone back to escort the paramedics. "It might be a heart attack," he said to the one with the clipboard. "He's breathing hard and holding his chest."

"What's his name?" asked the paramedic.

"Leonardo de la Rosa."

"Are you a relative?"

"Not yet," Lance said, wondering immediately why in God's name that had come out.

The family clustered around Leonardo parted as the paramedics breezed in and started the process; taking vital signs, asking questions that needed swift and accurate answers, setting up the EKG—the scary looking one with defibrillator paddles in their holsters ready to give a jolt if necessary. Their sense of urgency was palpable.

"Leonardo," said the paramedic, "are you allergic to any medications?"

"Nothing," Esmeralda replied. "Is it his heart?"

"We're not sure yet, ma'am." Another paramedic pulled out a packet with two pills in it. "Sir, I'm going to give you a couple of aspirin."

Lance said, "I did that already. Two of them."

"Three hundred twenty five milligrams or baby aspirin?"

"Three twenty fives," said Lance "I made sure. Two of them."

"Good thinking, kid."

Lance had taken charge, made the right choices, acted swiftly, maturely and confidently. *I'm not a goddam kid*, he thought.

He looked at Claudia. She saw the pain in his eyes and knew exactly what it was. "He's not a goddam kid!"

The paramedic was surprised at the vehemence of her response. "Sorry," he said. "Sir, you did exactly the right thing."

Roberta and Edward had also seen the pain flash across Lance's face and were also thinking, he's not a goddam kid when Claudia had the nerve to say it. Edward stage-whispered a *thank you* to Claudia. Lance's face softened and his look to Claudia was a silent expression of love. Anyone observing the two of them had to notice. Roberta did and tears sprang to her eyes for a moment. Then reason prevailed and a wave of confusion swept in. Wasn't this exactly something she had feared? She'd witnessed something beautiful yet wrong. She would process this later, she resolved. Now only one thing mattered—the life of a good man.

Edward helped Esmeralda to her feet as the paramedics got Leonardo on to the gurney. "I knew I should have made him see Dr. Butcher before we left," Esmeralda moaned.

"Don't blame yourself," Edward said. "He's going to be fine. I know the best cardiologist in Beverly Hills. I don't care if he hasn't finished his turkey yet, he owes me one. I'll make sure he handles Leonardo's case personally."

Roberta put her arm around Esmeralda as they followed the gurney to the ambulance. Esmeralda insisted on riding with Leonardo.

Claudia realized there wasn't room for her and said, "Papa, you're going to be ok. I'll meet you at the hospital."

As the paramedic closed the doors he said, "We're taking him to Cedars if you want to follow us." Claudia turned and looked past the BMW wondering in her confusion why she couldn't find her little red Miata. Lance was out of sight talking to the driver on the far side of the ambulance. Claudia felt overwhelmed and alone.

Roberta, noticing Claudia's disorientation said, "Claudia, you're too upset. Don't drive. Lance, you take her in the BMW. Your dad and I will say goodbye to Hans and Elsa and we'll come right down."

Lance tailed the ambulance closely. The urgency of the speed, the siren and the flashing lights fed Claudia's worst fears that her father was in deep trouble. *Don't die, don't die*, she kept thinking over and over as they drove in silence. Lance reached over and held her hand. There was nothing more he could do at the moment and it was enough. She started to cry softly and said, "I just had a thought that maybe you came into my life to save my dad's life. Do you suppose that's our purpose for being together?"

Lance thought for a moment. "I hope there's more than that."

"So do I," she said lifting his hand to her lips. "So do I."

Edward had rushed into the study to call Bernie, his cardiologist friend and tennis partner. Edward had dressed Bernie's daughter's entire wedding party two months ago for a song. "Bernie, sorry to bother you on Thanksgiving, but we just had a dinner guest collapse at our house and he's on the way to Cedars. Looks like a heart attack. Could you get on top of this one for me?"

"Sure thing. I'll put myself on call to come in as soon as the workups are done."

Not good enough for Edward. "Why don't you just meet us over there? Roberta and I are on the way now."

"Ah…well…" Bernie hesitated.

"Bernie, come on buddy I need you on this one. I know the E.R. staff is good and they have to run every test in the book and you could sit home and wait for them to call you with the results. But just come on over—as a friend."

"What the hell. Now that you put it that way. Meet you there."

Roberta was unusually silent on the ride to the hospital.

"What's on your mind?" Edward asked.

"This has been some day! I'm sure as hell confused."

"About what?"

I absolutely adore Leonardo and Esmeralda de la Rosa," she said with an almost annoyed certainty. "And I like Claudia."

"Well, good. So what's confusing?"

"It's clear as a bell that she and Lance are sleeping together and if they're not they soon will be. That's horrible. Isn't it?"

"Is it?" he asked.

"You don't think so?"

"Truth of the matter is, I don't really know. Look how they were today and how we got along with her folks like family. Lance probably saved her dad's life. If she wasn't his teacher and if there wasn't eight, nine years difference in their ages it would seem ok whatever's going on with them. Wouldn't it?"

"I think we need a little distance from this before we can figure it out," she said.

"Meanwhile," he replied, "Whatever we decide to do, I like them all a whole lot too and we've got to do what we can to get them through this crisis."

"Yes," she said simply, then stared out the window deep in thought as they approached the oasis of medical towers that promised both the hope of help and healing, and the fear of irreparable sickness and death. She felt not the least bit resentful that Thanksgiving had taken this turn.

She recognized a sense of inevitability about what had happened this afternoon that felt both strange and beautiful. In a few hours she'd grown to feel she had known Leonardo and Esmeralda for a long time; that they were somehow connected on some timeless path. Their parallel life struggles and successes were oddly similar despite the economic gap. Through the sheer force of will, hers and Edward's dream had paid off handsomely by the nature of the business they had chosen. Leonardo's and Esmeralda's dream had been realized on their terms and was close to failing through no fault of their own. Their paths had crossed on this day and there was a bizarre purposefulness in it that Roberta had sensed from the beginning.

She turned to Edward and said, "We're in this for the long haul aren't we?"

"What do you mean?"

"We've only known this family for a few hours and yet there's something binding us together. They somehow belong to us. That sounds crazy doesn't it?"

"No. It doesn't. I knew it from the moment Leonardo saw the painting that belongs to both of us."

Roberta smiled. "That's when I knew it too. You and I are some team aren't we?"

"You just figuring that out?"

In the E.R. Esmeralda sat next to Leonardo's gurney surrounded by instruments of survival attached to the walls. Nurses were attaching monitors and drawing blood. A technician wheeled in a portable X-ray machine and asked her to step outside. This mechanical need for even a few moments separation caused anxiety in them both. She kissed him and said, "I'm right outside."

He said, "I'm going to be ok."

Something in the way he said that made her know it was true. "I know," she said. "Next time I say see Dr. Butcher you see Dr. Butcher."

He smiled. "*Sí.*"

Lance sat on the arm of Claudia's chair in the E.R. waiting room. Both lost in thought, she rested her head against him as he stroked her hair.

Edward and Roberta rushed into the waiting room and stopped short as they witnessed this intimate moment. Lance and Claudia saw them simultaneously and pulled away from each other.

As much as a part of Roberta wanted to feel that the reality of a relationship between her 18-year-old firstborn and his 26-year-old teacher might somehow be acceptable, it made her uneasy to see them together like this. Something about the way Claudia's head rested against her son and the way that he was stroking her hair was both beautiful and horrifying. There was also something oddly familiar about it that she couldn't quite put her finger on.

Roberta was not used to a lack of clarity in her life. She usually knew exactly what she felt, what she knew and what actions she must take. In those rare moments when her certainty was shaky she'd learned that if she just took whatever the next step seemed to be, it was usually right. So, she sat down next to Lance and said quietly, "We're not sure what's going on between the two of you but it's clear that this is more than a teacher student relationship."

Lance and Claudia's faces froze. Edward put his hand firmly on Roberta's arm as if to pull her back from the brink but she continued. "Truthfully, I don't care at this moment what it is." She looked squarely at Lance and said, "The tenderness we just saw between the two of you was actually quite lovely, but…"

Edward interjected, "I think what your mother is trying to say is we are both a little conflicted about your *relationship* but we all have to focus on only one thing right now and that's your dad. Have they told you anything yet?"

"Nothing yet," said Lance.

"They'll only let one visitor back there at a time so my mom is there."

"My friend Bernie, the cardiologist, is on his way over."

"Thank you so much," Claudia said.

"Edward and I were talking on the way over and we know we're all in this together. We'll get your father through it."

Edward held Claudia's hand and comforted her with words of reassurance. Roberta sat next to Lance and took his hand. "I don't think," she said, "that I've ever been more proud of you than I am today. The way you took charge when the rest of us stood around like dazed chickens was wonderful."

Whether it was the intensity of the medical crisis at hand or whether it was the instant sense of kinship that she and Edward had felt with Leonardo and Esmeralda, Roberta was experiencing a revelation that was both freeing and disturbing: Her son was no longer the little boy whose life she felt compelled to guide (read control). Today she saw him as the man he'd become. Were these tears of joy or loss in her eyes? Perhaps both.

Bernie had come in the back way, wherever it is that doctors arrive avoiding the horde of desperate people waiting their turn. He'd briefly seen Leonardo, scanned the EKG and made sure the blood work would be moved to the top of the lab's priority list. He was genuinely pleased to be able to help his friends Edward and Roberta, but he hadn't had his pumpkin pie yet. He asked a nurse to go find his friends in the waiting room and bring them back to Leonardo's cubicle. After all, the best cardiologist in Beverly Hills is entitled to break the visitor rules once in a while.

Claudia came in first and was relieved to see that Leonardo's color had returned. "Papa, you look better."

"I feel better," he said.

Bernie said, "Your father is a lucky man. The EKG and the X-ray aren't too bad. Looks like you had a small heart attack but you got some aspirin in you right away which got the blood flowing a little better and you're stable. When we get the blood work back the heart enzyme tests will show us how much damage there is and we'll take it from there."

"We've got a flight back to Michigan on Sunday," Leonardo said. "I've got a restaurant to run next week."

"Well, sir," Bernie said, "we're going to admit you and I'm probably going to keep you here for a day or two until we get you properly medicated and stabilized."

"Then we'll fly home Monday. No later!"

Bernie turned to Esmeralda and smiled. "I hope you can tie him to a bed for a couple of weeks. I don't advise getting on an airplane right away."

Esmeralda gave Leonardo a 'you're-going-to-listen-to-me-this-time' look and reinforced it with, "You wouldn't listen to me about Dr. Butcher but you're going to listen to me this time. We're staying here! Jaime and Lourdes can keep the place going for a little while."

"He can't make a tortilla worth eating. We'll go bankrupt."

"Your mother can make the tortillas."

"She's weak and too old to work."

"If she's so weak, how did she chop through three inches of frozen dirt last week to dig up my spring bulbs so she could bury her baby food jars full of *bruja màgica*?"

Roberta and Edward were smiling at this exchange because it sounded a bit like them. Esmeralda could always get Leonardo to change course if she escalated a battle publicly. So could Roberta.

"I give up. You win." He turned to Claudia. "But we have to move out of that fancy hotel. I saw how much it costs on the back of the door."

"Papa, you and mama will use my bed and I'll sleep on the couch."

"I have a better idea," Edward said. "We have a guesthouse no one is using. You'll stay there."

"Oh, we couldn't do that," Esmeralda said. She'd always had this thing about not imposing on people.

"Of course you can," Edward said. "What? You can't stand the idea of your own little hacienda with a stone fireplace and a Sub-Zero refrigerator? Of course you're staying there. Leonardo didn't have a heart attack at our house for nothing, you know."

They all laughed.

Roberta said, "Edward's right. On the way over here we realized that we've only known you for a few hours, but you've become friends—maybe more." She didn't know quite why she said that, or if she did know she didn't want to go there. "And we said to each other, we're in this for the long haul, aren't we?"

"Maybe after a week or two we won't be able to stand each other," Edward said, "but right now fate has thrown us together and this is the right thing to do."

Bernie had watched this exchange in awe. "Wow. You guys are awesome. I'm glad you're my friends." He turned to Leonardo and Esmeralda. "If I were you, I'd say yes."

Leonardo was beaming. "Yes."

Leonardo was settled in a room on the cardiac floor. Edward and Roberta quietly asked Bernie to take a look at the financial situation and were relieved that Leonardo had a decent Blue Cross plan. They would have volunteered to pick up the tab if it had been necessary.

When they got home they were surprised at their eagerness to have Maria put the guest house in order, pick up some groceries and lay in some firewood. No matter how many rain forest benefits they hosted or how much money they gave to the

ACLU or Children's Hospital, helping new friends in need was tangible and fulfilling. The highbrow atmosphere in which they lived rarely offered such an opportunity.

When Lance walked Claudia to her apartment, they were both feeling a delicate uncertainty about whether they would or should make love. This was so unlike any other time they had closed this door behind them. He took her in his arms and she began to cry as the stress of the day's events finally overwhelmed her. It was one of those moments when words were unnecessary. Tenderness did not lead to passion because she was spent and he was content.

After she finally quieted he gave her a gentle push toward the bedroom. "You go get ready for bed. I'm going to make you some chamomile tea, tuck you in, and go home." And he did. That said more about their relationship than all of the passionate moments of the last couple of months rolled together. Neither spoke the word, but after he kissed her on the forehead and shut the door behind him, they both thought, *soul mates.*

Chapter 28

On Saturday afternoon Lance and Claudia picked up Leonardo and Esmeralda at the hospital and brought them to the guest house.

The Van Ardens had furnished it in the Southwest style—terracotta floors, rustic furniture, colorful paintings and sketches by Latin American artists, and a fine collection of Aztec and Mayan pottery spotlighted on custom shelving surrounding the stone fireplace. Pottery because Roberta had never cared much for the pre-Columbian attempts at the human form. She could never get the image out of her head that a pre-Columbian sculpture looked like an unsuccessful something that one of her children might have brought home from art class. But the 13th century bowls and jars were stunning examples of the period.

Edward, Roberta and Maria had spent the last half hour fussing with the welcoming decorations. Fresh flowers had been delivered an hour ago. Delicate bowls of Belgian chocolates and *dulce de leche* were set about. Mindful that Leonardo should probably not be eating cholesterol rich cheeses and meats, they had put out beautifully cut and arranged plates of fresh and dried fruits and there was a bottle of Martinelli's sparkling cider on ice. Since Lance had picked up their bags earlier, Maria had already unpacked them, done the laundry and set the two small framed photos she found in one suitcase on the mantle. One was a photo of Claudia in her U of M cap and gown. The other was a formal portrait of Esmeralda's mother and father whose memory was all she had left of them. When she was a child, they departed before dawn every morning to collect the catch from their lobster pots in the bay. One morning, when Esmeralda was 13, they never came home. Since that day, she carried them with her wherever she went.

Esmeralda was the first to walk across the threshold. She was moved by the warmth of the welcome and the elegance of their temporary home. Her eyes explored the beauty that had been created just for them. When she spotted her precious photographs on the mantle, tears welled up in her eyes. She repeated "*Dios Mio!*" several times. "*Gracias*, thank you!"

Esmeralda's reaction was Edward and Roberta's reward for the effort they had made. "It's our great pleasure," Edward said.

Claudia had tried to hold on to her father's arm to help him through the front door, but he pulled away to manage on his own. Leonardo had the constitution of a bull. You could count the number of days he'd ever been sick enough to *need* a hand on *one* hand. Lance read his body language and knew what he was feeling. Claudia was momentarily puzzled when Leonardo disengaged from her. When she saw Lance's knowing smile, she understood that it was a guy thing.

"I must admit," Roberta said, "that we've had a great deal of enjoyment the last couple of days getting this place ready for the two of you."

"It is so beautiful," Esmeralda said.

Leonardo too had seen Esmeralda's cherished photos on the mantle and was struck by the thought that these people, whom he'd known for such a brief time, had somehow shown a generosity of spirit to him and his wife that is rarely seen, even in a family. He said simply, "Thank you."

"You're most welcome," Edward said.

"One more thing we thought you would like. Come," Roberta said as she led them into the bedroom. Placed prominently on the wall opposite the bed and lit by a recessed halogen was "Bordando." "We thought this might make it feel a bit more like home."

Leonardo and Esmeralda were hypnotized by the painting and overwhelmed by feelings that were difficult to express without bursting into tears. Thank you, seemed such a pallid phrase. Finally Leonardo said, "You have made us feel like family."

Edward and Roberta were beaming broadly, satisfied that they had successfully accomplished what they had planned.

Lance and Claudia stood off to the side and watched all of this play out like a movie's happy ending. Lance was vaguely aware that he had slipped into that feeling of bliss that was accompanied by an intense concentration and an echoey buzz in his ears. This usually happened in dreams or while he was making love to Claudia. He had a dim understanding that it was connected to the intense expression of love pervading the room. When he realized that Leonardo and Esmeralda were staring at him with puzzled looks he realized he had his arm around Claudia who'd been mesmerized by his pleasant visage.

They all sampled the delicacies, drank the sparkling cider, talked, laughed and mused about how it felt like they had known each other for years, as Edward said. Forever, as Leonardo said.

Edward and Leonardo sat at the game table next to the window overlooking the rose garden. "You play?" Leonardo asked pointing to the ebony and ivory chess set.

"A little," Edward said with a wicked smile that also said formidably. "Do you?"

"A little." Leonardo returned a wicked smile. "Do you want to find out?"

"Maybe tomorrow?"

"You're on."

At one point everyone sensed that Leonardo had faded a bit and needed to rest.

Esmeralda, needing to show proper gratitude for the extraordinary hospitality, insisted on making *carne asada* and a big pot of *menudo* for Sunday dinner. Her grandmother had taken her in when her parents died and taught her many things, one of which was that when you want to show your appreciation you prepare a feast.

Esmeralda would make a shopping list for Claudia and Lance that included various organs that the Van Ardens wouldn't need to know about. Nonetheless, Esmeralda knew they would find the combination of tastes in her pot to be addictive. If she and Leonardo could sell steaming bowls of it to *gringos* in Michigan and leave them wanting more, it would work here.

Edward and Leonardo agreed that tomorrow would be a California versus Michigan chess match along with Esmeralda's feast and said their goodnights. Lance took Claudia to the supermarket with Esmeralda's list.

Chapter 29

While navigating the aisles and filling the shopping cart, neither of them could stop talking about the events of this remarkable week. They stopped in the Ethnic Foods aisle for spices, picked up three kinds of chili peppers in the produce section, and when they got to the meat department Claudia scurried ahead to make sure they wouldn't have to find a Mexican market for the tripe. She knew he would love her mom's *menudo* but wasn't sure his Beverly Hills sensibilities could get past seeing what was going to be in it. She spotted some, slipped it into a plastic bag when he was distracted, and hid it under the steak. *What he doesn't know won't hurt him*, she thought.

They were bubbling over with affectionate excitement as they rehashed the Thanksgiving dinner and all of the things that had happened since.

"Your cousin is a trip," Claudia said.

"Biddy?"

"What kind of name is that?"

"Her real name is Dutch—Betje."

"Biddy's better. If looks could kill, she'd be dead after that look your mom gave her when she whined about my dad spoiling Thanksgiving."

"It was pretty amazing when my mom said if it had to happen she's glad it happened at our house."

"She wasn't just taking a shot at Biddy was she?"

"She really meant it. She's a pain when she's on a tear, but she's got a good heart."

"I really like her, Lance." She leaned against him as they sauntered down the last aisle and said, "This has all been like a fairy tale. I hope it doesn't blow up in our faces."

He put his arm around her as they rounded a corner and nearly bumped into Principal Adashek who looked like he'd just seen a priest fondling an altar boy.

"This is inappropriate, Miss de la Rosa. We will discuss it on Monday. Please be in my office at 7:30."

"No she won't!" Lance said.

Principal Adashek was stunned into speechlessness.

"Mr. Adashek, you just saw me comforting a family friend whose father just had a heart attack while he was having Thanksgiving dinner with my whole family at our house and you jumped to some horrible conclusion. For God's sake, Miss de la Rosa's mom and dad are staying in my parents' guest house until he's well enough to go home. My parents are not going to take your *insinuations* kindly!"

Adashek remained speechless, his mouth agape.

Lance didn't let up. "I very strongly suggest, sir, that you apologize to Miss de la Rosa!"

Adashek blinked nervously.

"Now, sir."

Adashek finally saw a way to escape. "I... I misunderstood," he said.

"And?"

"And... I'm sorry. Excuse me." He left his unchecked-out basket and fled the store.

This had, of course, attracted the attention of a couple dozen customers not to mention the checkers and baggers, all of whom were now applauding. Feeling both rescued and vulnerable, Claudia pushed Lance toward the checkout counter so they could escape this much-too-public display.

Adashek, once safely behind the wheel of his vintage Volvo, careened out of the parking lot. Not a man to easily bear public humiliation, he pounded on the steering wheel. "Damn them! Damn them! Family friends? Bullshit! This will not stand!"

Chapter 30

Leonardo had stretched out on the sofa near the fireplace as Esmeralda browsed the cupboards to make sure she had everything she needed. No *menudo* pot. She called Claudia's cell phone to ask her to buy one.

Before Claudia snapped the phone shut at the end of their conversation, Esmeralda heard her giggle and say, "Lance! Stop!

Esmeralda hung up and said to Leonardo, "Leo, Claudia is in trouble."

"*Que?*"

"That boy. They are more than *maestra y estudiante.*"

"I don't think so," Leonardo said without enthusiasm.

"You saw what I saw," she said leaving it hang until he had to admit to himself that seeing his daughter's face earlier as she gazed at Lance whose arm was around her shoulder was, in fact something more than teacher and student. "Hmmmm," he said.

"Maybe we should not be staying here," she said.

"Hmmm," he said again.

"Hmmm, what? These Van Ardens, do we really know them? What will they do if they find out? They are very powerful people. Think, Leo. What do we do?"

"I will speak to her," he said.

Esmeralda did not hesitate. "No, I will speak to her. You will speak to him."

Claudia and Lance wound their way upward through the hills toward the Van Arden estate. They'd resolved that they would quickly drop off the supplies and rush back to Claudia's apartment to satisfy the impulses of forbidden love that had risen to the fore after their encounter with Principal Adashek.

As the darkness of the back roads through the hills enveloped them, Claudia reached over to unzip Lance, brushing her soft fingertips against his instantly attentive flesh.

She let up after he almost missed a turn that would have sent them sailing through what used to be Cary Grant's house. He made her stop so he'd be presentable when they arrived in the motor court. Still, they had to sit in the car for awhile trying to keep their minds chaste until the protuberance was no longer noticeable.

Laden with supermarket bags, they were still holding back naughty smiles when Esmeralda held the door open for them.

"Claudia, put those on the counter and come talk to me," Esmeralda said sternly as she headed toward the bedroom. "Mr. Lance, please sit with Mr. de la Rosa for a few minutes, ok?"

Claudia sobered, directed a puzzled glance at Lance, set the bags on the counter and went into the bedroom. Esmeralda closed the door behind them, sat down on the bed and motioned Claudia toward the chair.

"Mama, what is it? Is it papa?"

"No, *mija*. It's you. You and the boy." Esmeralda measured Claudia's reaction which confirmed her suspicions.

"What do you mean?"

"You are more than teacher to him, aren't you?"

"Mama! Why do you say that?"

"I am your mother. I know what I see. The way you look at him."

"He's a nice kid and I like him."

"Kid. You call him kid to me, but you are angry at the ambulance man when he called him kid."

Claudia was anguished. She'd never lied to her mother about anything important and this felt just awful. She stared at the floor.

"This is wrong, *mija*."

Claudia thought for a moment, looked her mother straight in the eyes and said, "No, mama. It's not. It's not wrong."

"*Dios mio!*"

"Mama, I know it seems wrong. I don't know how to explain it to you. To anyone."

"He's too young. And you are his teacher! You make us come to Thanksgiving dinner with his family and you keep this secret? Now we stay in the house of his mama and papa and they treat us like *familia,* and you are doing this behind the back of everyone! Why?"

"I don't know, Mama. I don't know. When we're together it seems so right."

"How old is he?"

"Eighteen. It's legal, Mama."

Legal, but you are his teacher. They will fire you from your job if they find out. Roberta and Edward—what will they do?"

"But this week we really all became like one big family, didn't we?"

"Yes," said Esmeralda. "But based on a lie."

Claudia burst into tears. "It's only a lie because no one would understand, Mama. I love him. We know we're soul mates and that we have some purpose for being together. I know it doesn't seem logical from the outside. He's wonderful. Mama, he saved Papa's life."

That stopped Esmeralda for a moment. After Lance engineered the aspirin, the ambulance, and sat attentively with his parents in the E.R. she'd been impressed by his strength of character. "Your papa likes him. We both like him, but even if he saved your papa's life this is wrong. Papa is having a talk with him now."

"Oh, my God," Claudia said, wondering if Lance could handle a bulldog of a man like her father when he was in protective mode. She started to move toward the door to save him.

"Claudia, wait," Esmeralda said. "Have you slept together?"

Claudia dropped her eyes to the floor once again.

"Then you must stop. You are 26 years old and I can't tell you how to live anymore. You always go your own way, but while your papa and me we are staying in the house of his *familia* you cannot be sleeping with the son. *Comprende?*"

"Yes, Mama. *Sí.*"

Leonardo and Lance had spent the time talking about football, basketball, soccer and everything but what a concerned father who suspected a boy of sleeping with his daughter should have been quizzing him about. Leonardo had even turned up the volume on the TV to drown out the conversation that had begun to drift from the bedroom. This quick-thinking young man had quite possibly saved his life and he just didn't know how to embark upon this conversation. He liked him and his family a great deal. So what if he had a crush on his daughter. Youthful indiscretion. He'd get over it. No harm done.

The bedroom door opened and with somber faces, Claudia and her mother joined Lance and Leonardo. Lance was searching Claudia's face for a hint of what had transpired. Leonardo was merely hoping to avoid a difficult conversation. *What's the point of getting myself all upset*, he thought. *I just had a heart attack. No point in making myself sick again.* It was a great excuse but also probably true.

"Lance," Claudia said a bit formally, "you should probably run me home so my mom can get started cooking and my dad can get some rest."

"Sure," he replied.

Esmeralda assumed Leonardo had his chat with Lance so as she walked them to the door she said, "Mr. Lance, you are a very nice boy. I know you will do the right thing."

"Well...sure," said Lance.

As Lance pulled his car up to the guest house door Esmeralda was wagging her finger at Claudia who was nodding her head in reassurance.

As they drove away, Lance said, "What was that all about?"

"Us."

"Us?"

"I told my mom, Lance."

"About us?"

"I couldn't help it. I've never lied to her about anything really important and she asked me directly. I thought I could make her understand."

"Did she?"

"No.'

"How much did you tell her?"

"She asked if we were more than student and teacher. I'm sorry, Lance. I just couldn't tell her a bare-faced lie. She made me promise as long as they're staying in your parents' guest house that we won't have sex."

"You told her we have sex!?"

"She guessed and I couldn't deny it."

"No wonder you dad was acting so strange. He turned up the TV so I couldn't hear you guys in the other room."

"He was supposed to have a talk with you."

"He was? He didn't." The realization hit him. "Oh! That's why your mom said she knew I'd do the right thing. She thought he did."

When they reached Claudia's apartment, she unlocked the door, turned to him and said, "I did make her a promise. It seemed the right thing to do at the time."

"Actually," Lance said, "it was. And I admire it." His face clouded. "Sometimes I feel like I'm too comfortable lying to my parents, not just about us, but in general. It bothers me. You didn't lie to your parents when you were my age?"

Claudia cocked her head to ponder. "Maybe when I was little, but later I don't think I ever lied about anything important. I'm not sure if that's because I was a good girl or because my mom always knew when I was lying. I guess that says I did lie and then sort of gave it up—outgrew it."

The thought impressed Lance. "Time I grew up then," he said.

"What do you mean?"

"If we go on like this it's all going to come crashing down around our heads isn't it?"

"It could."

"What exactly did you tell your mom?"

"That I loved you and that we're soul mates. I tried to explain that we have a purpose being together, but even as I said it I knew how it must sound to her."

"Did she understand at all?"

"How could we possibly make anyone understand? Our story is just another lurid tabloid headline. *Evil, immoral teacher seduces student.* How do we make the world see this is different if we can't even make our parents understand?"

"Maybe we have to just start with them no matter what. If your mom made you promise we wouldn't have sex while she and your dad are staying at our place, she kind of left the door open didn't she? And my mom and dad didn't totally melt down when they saw me with my arm around you at the hospital."

"It does seem like our only chance, doesn't it?" she replied.

"Tomorrow?"

"Let's just see how the day goes." Claudia had a twinkle in her eye. "Maybe everyone will be in such a satisfied stupor after they finish my mom's dinner that we can drop a bomb."

Chapter 31

On the drive home Lance dialed Marco's cell phone.

Marco smiled as he scoped out the caller ID. He'd been expecting the call. "Yo."

"Can you talk? I'm kinda desperate."

"I can talk but I can't listen." Disco music was blasting and the room was full of men trying to shout over it. "Hold on a minute. Let me go outside."

"Where are you?" Lance shouted.

"Hold on. Hold on. I'm almost on the street. What did you say?"

"Where are you?"

"It's tea dance at Rage, sweet cheeks. Want to come over?"

"The gay disco?"

"Of course. Do you know any other Rage?"

"How did you get in there? You're only 16."

"You ever hear of a fake ID?"

"Oh."

"So, come on over and we'll talk. I have a message for you."

"Great! I need a message. But I don't have a fake ID."

"Oh, please. Everyone has a fake ID."

"Well, I don't!" Lance never felt the need to score one. It was kind of a kid thing to do.

"OK. Don't get your panties in a bunch. Meet me down the block at Starbucks in 10 minutes. I'll buy you a cappuccino, then I can get back to shake my pretty butt at a horny dentist who's hot for it."

Lance shook his head and smiled. "You're too much."

"For you, maybe, but not for the dentist. Ten minutes."

Marco ordered two cappuccinos from the counter and commandeered an outdoor table with a perfect view of the steady stream of cruisy hunks out bar-hopping. As Lance approached he noticed the prime seating and smiled.

Marco pushed Lance's cappuccino toward the chair opposite him and said, "Sit, drink and listen."

"I'm listening," Lance said.

"So, you think you're ready to come out of the closet."

"I'm not gay," Lance said, perplexed.

"Dummy. To your parents. And hers."

"Oh, yeah. Maybe. That's what I wanted to find out from you."

"I told you before, I can't tell you what to do. But I got a message. You'll be tempted to lie about something, but don't. Remember what they told you before. Be a man of honor."

"This is frustrating. Did they tell you what our purpose is yet?"

"No." He cocked his head in listening mode, questioning an unseen source. "What? Boll weevils?" He gave Lance a puzzled smile and said, "When you're looking for an answer think about boll weevils."

"Boll weevils?"

"Don't shoot the messenger, dude. Boll weevils. I don't even know what a boll weevil is. Do you?"

"Yes," said Lance. "It's a bug or worm or something."

"So remember the bug. And it would help to find the boys. Sounds like me in West Hollywood, but it's not."

"Marco, what the fuck is all that supposed to mean?"

Marco leaned forward, looked him straight in the eye and said, "Be a man of honor, remember boll weevils and find the boys. There's a battle ahead and you need tools to win it. You're the general. Don't worry about it. Just be open to it and it will come."

Marco was so very certain about the words he chose that the images evoked in Lance's mind formed something of a fine and noble cause that he couldn't imagine comprehending much less commanding. He shook his head and said, "Every time I see you I don't get answers, I just get more questions."

154

"Welcome to my world," Marco responded.

"You said that in the dream, didn't you?"

Marco smiled. "Did I? Love to stay and talk but there's a dentist down the block who's wanting to do some drilling and I think I have a toothache. Call me tomorrow night and let me know how it went."

Lance laughed, thanked Marco, and gave him a go-have-fun gesture toward Rage and the waiting dentist. As Marco stopped to discard his empty cup he looked back and noticed Lance's troubled look. Marco returned to the table. "Lance, really, just trust yourself. I don't know what's coming exactly, but it looks good. Remember the clues they gave you, and trust. *Ciao*."

Lance sipped, his cappuccino burning the words into his memory. Honor, boll weevils and the boys. It occurred to him that if he told any rational person about his English teacher soul mate and his friend Marco's boll weevil advice he'd be judged a lunatic and sent to the funny farm.

He remembered something one of his friends who had done a mind-bending, be-in-the-moment seminar had told him was one of the secrets of life: ride the horse in the direction it's going. It made sense to him now.

Chapter 32

Edward sat at the easel in his study absentmindedly sketching a gown. Roberta brought in a tray of tea and cookies. Seeing her husband engrossed in his work and knowing you don't interrupt genius, she quietly poured for him and sat down in the reading chair with this week's *The Nation*. Edward ripped up the sketch and started another. Roberta chuckled at a Calvin Trilling poem, but couldn't concentrate on the article about electronic voting machines. When Edward ripped up another false start and began again Roberta said, "You're thinking about them too aren't you?"

"Lance and Claudia? Yes, I am. I don't think we've been taking this as seriously as we should. At least I haven't."

"I was on a mission to stop whatever was going on, but I've lost my drive."

"I think we got too fond of Leonardo and Esmeralda," he said with some sadness.

Roberta sighed. "I absolutely hate to say this, but I got too fond of Claudia. I really like her. She's spunky and sweet and there's a charming innocence about her. But she's 26 years old and I know she's having sex with our 18-year-old son. I feel it in my bones."

"I'm really torn. Lance is happier and more mature than I've ever seen him," Edward said.

"Truth be told, I like them together. That's supposed to be horrible, but I do. They remind me of us when we were young."

"We're still young," he said.

"You know what I mean." Tears welled up in her eyes. "I only knew you about a month when Mom had her first cancer surgery, remember?"

"Of course I remember."

"You sat on the arm of my chair in the hospital waiting room, put your arm around me and I put my head against you. I've never forgotten that moment. Seems odd, but it was then I knew you loved me. Just think about what we saw when we walked into the E.R. today. Our son sat on the arm of Claudia's chair with his arm around her and she leaned her head against him. *Déjà vu?*" Roberta turned to Edward and saw that his eyes were glistening and said, "I think he really loves her. That's what makes it hard. That and moving her parents into our guest house. What were we thinking?! What do we do?" she asked.

"Honest to God, I don't know."

Ever the pragmatist, Roberta said, "And, if this ever gets out in this town, it will be scandalous."

"If that happened it would devastate our family and theirs."

"Do you think they know?"

"How could they not?"

Edward threw another sketch into the wastebasket, got up from his easel and settled on the arm of Roberta's chair with his arm around her. She leaned her head against him and said, "We have to talk to them."

"Yes." he said. "Tomorrow."

Claudia had rung Monica's doorbell three times already and there was no answer. She was hoping Monica might dissuade her from taking the awesome tell-the-parents step tomorrow. She went back into her apartment, poured herself the last of the Pinot Grigio, plopped down in the wicker chair on the terrace and wondered, *what the hell have I gone and done?* When she was with Lance, everything seemed so clear and right. How in God's name could they possibly think this would all work out? *But,* she thought, *there's no stopping this now.*

Lance threw his jacket on his bed, booted up his laptop and googled boll weevil. In no time he had more information than anyone would ever want about the cotton-ruining beetle named *anthonomus grandis* that crossed the Rio Grande from Mexico in the 1890s. There were blogs with experts arguing whether any pest can be completely eradicated, and organic farmers in Texas complaining that their businesses would be ruined if the state government made them spray their fields with Malathion. All of this information seemed pointless to his dilemma, but he couldn't stop hopping from site to site just in case there was something that clicked.

Chapter 33

Sunday afternoon Claudia picked up a case of Corona and a half dozen limes on the way to the Van Ardens—a last minute request from Esmeralda to complement the *carne asada* and *menudo*. Actually Esmeralda had asked for two six packs. The full case was an impulse buy. She thought there might be a need for ample lubrication today.

Edward and Leonardo were watching college football in the living room. Roberta had volunteered to help Esmeralda and had been conscripted to brown the tortillas. Roberta wondered if this was the time to bring up Lance and Claudia. Esmeralda had clearly worked well into the night to give the best gift she could manage to thank Edward and Roberta for their kindness and hospitality. The kitchen smelled of appreciation and affection. This was not the time, Roberta concluded.

Lance came in to stack more logs for the fireplace which was burning cozily.

When Claudia arrived Lance went out to the car to bring in the beer. Seeing the full case he grinned and said, "Getting them in a receptive mood are you?"

"Did cross my mind."

"We really going to do this?"

"Let's see how it goes," she replied.

Their hands touched as they both reached for the beer. Fingers entwined, they turned toward each other, their lips inches apart. They both whispered I love you simultaneously and kissed gently; a kiss that was harshly interrupted by screams and shouts from Edward and Leonardo. Touchdown for the University of Michigan. Claudia glanced up at the kitchen window and saw an incredulous look on her mother's face. Claudia gave her an *I'm sorry* shrug and Esmeralda turned quickly away.

Edward and Leonardo were still whooping and high-fiving in testosterone heaven when they carried the beer in. Roberta was delivering chips and salsa to the living room with a boys-will-be-boys roll of the eyes. She grinned at Lance and Claudia and said, "Your fathers have just had a major attack of male bonding that your mothers are totally at a loss to understand."

Edward said, "Oh, c'mon. You enjoy a good football game as much as I do."

"Yes, but we've never engaged in a spasm of high-fives now, have we?"

They all laughed and the mood for the afternoon was set.

Maria came over from the main house, picked up a full garbage bag sitting by the door and said, "Just call me if you need me to bring anything over."

Edward stopped her. "Maria, stay. Join us."

Glancing down at her uniform she said, "Oh, no, Mr. Edward. I have things to do."

Lance jumped in. "Nana, please. Go put on that red dress my dad gave you that you never wear and come right back." Maria looked at him oddly. "Please," he said. Lance was being kindly inclusive, but in his look to Maria there was also a plea that said, *I need you here.*

"Yes, Mr. Lance," she said.

When she returned she was wearing the red dress which had been perfectly fitted by America's master designer. It beautifully emphasized her ample but shapely figure. She had hurriedly but accurately remembered the makeup lesson she had gotten from the Dior counter at Macy's. As she made her grand entrance, everyone oohed, aahed and applauded.

"Maria," Edward exclaimed, "I've never been prouder of a dress than I am of that one. You look stunning."

"I think," she said, "that is a compliment but it is, how you say, making a silk *bolsa* from a pig's ear?"

They all laughed and began to settle in at the table. Claudia brought in a tray with six bottles of beer and set one at the places of the four parents, Maria and herself. (Esmeralda had made it clear that Leonardo's heart-conscious ration was to be one bottle for the entire day.) It was odd to put a Coke at Lance's place. Nothing said under-age more than an 18-year-old without a beer.

The *menudo* was a hit, the *carne asada* was devoured in its entirety and the conversation turned to favorite foods. Maria bragged about her *pipian*, the secret of success being how long—how very long—you grind the chocolate, sunflower seeds, sesame seeds and other ingredients, not in a blender as the recipe books tell you, but stone on stone by hand.

Leonardo and Esmeralda told stories of finding the right combination of spices and uniquely Mexican ingredients to satisfy the Midwestern gringo tastes of their largely blue collar clientele.

Esmeralda explained how it took awhile to realize that spicy, in Michiganese, meant add a little black pepper.

Leonardo's face clouded. "Not that any new taste is going to save us now. I figure we can last about six more months, then we close for good."

"Papa, no."

"*Sí, mija.* We had over 25 great years, but with the factory closings, and more coming, so many customers are out of work. What can we do?"

"There must be something," said Claudia, not really knowing what that could be.

"I've been looking," continued Leonardo. "I just read this book, the one about how the middle class is being screwed by the politicians and corporations. Depressing. And not a single practical thing in it that I was looking for to find what I can do about it. He says we need new leaders who know what the hell is happening and can do something about it. Not soon enough for me. Meanwhile, nobody in Harbor Point can figure out what to do."

Edward said, "I should have tried a little harder to help Tom and Jack keep the mill open."

"You did what you could, Mr. Edward," Esmeralda said.

"I could always count on them to get it right. I don't think I ever had to send an order back in 20 years. Best fabric in the world in my book."

Cotton, thought Lance. It drove him crazy that two and two seemed to be there to be put together, but he couldn't make it equal four yet.

After Principal Adashek had come home from the humiliating experience last evening in the supermarket, he played the circumstances over and over in his mind. Was he mistaken or were his instincts correct? Lance Van Arden seemed genuinely and passionately disturbed about the incident. So much so that he'd made Adashek doubt what his eyes were seeing.

But there was something that didn't fit. Claudia had told him about her diary project and her pledge of confidentiality with the students. If there was something indecent going on between them it could be discerned by reading Lance's diary. Even if Adashek had to read between the lines he was certain he might find something that would reveal the truth he expected to find. If there was a scandal in his school he must be the one to uncover and expose it. That would show everyone that he was vigilant and in control.

His mind wouldn't stop turning. He took an Ambien around 1 a.m. to stop the mind-rehearsals of how he would terminate Claudia's employment if he found incriminating evidence.

Claudia and Lance offered to clean up after dinner while Maria and the parents retired to the living room. Edward and Leonardo had settled *mano-a-mano* at the chess table. Maria stoked up the fire and sat down in the reading chair next to it to savor the warmth of the ripe embers. Roberta had been nagging Esmeralda for the soup recipe ever since the first bite. Esmeralda hadn't quite figured out how to avoid explaining the primary ingredients and made up some story about her grandmother making her promise solemnly never to betray the family recipe.

Finally, Roberta said good-naturedly, "Oh, well. I swore I would never, ever cook tripe like my grandmother used to make it. Hideous! But if I could cook it like your grandmother, I would try it. So I guess I'll never cook tripe again."

Esmeralda grinned. "You knew what it was?"

"Of course," Roberta replied. "When I saw it floating in my bowl I thought 'oh, Lord, this is going to be a difficult afternoon', but it was fabulous. When Edward and I got married, we had no money and a new baby and I used to try to make magic with the cheapest ingredients I could buy. I was pretty good at it but I tried tripe once and it was worse than my grandma's."

"How long did you cook it?" asked Esmeralda.

"Oh, I don't know. Maybe half an hour."

"Next time try six."

"Six hours?!"

"And with three kinds of chilies and a calf's foot."

Across the room Leonardo proudly bellowed, "Checkmate!"

"Damn!" exclaimed Edward. "How the hell did you do that in six moves?"

Claudia carefully rinsed and handed the dishes to Lance who loaded the dishwasher.

"If you're going to wash each one," Lance teased, "why am I putting them in the dishwasher?"

"You asked for it," she responded, swiftly swishing each dish through the faucet and handing it off to him as he struggled like Lucy and Ethel in the candy factory. Their spontaneous and joyous peals of laughter spilled over into the living room where the undeniable song of it struck Maria, the Van Ardens, and the de la Rosas simultaneously with an infectious happiness that, in each of them, just as suddenly turned to discomfort.

Esmeralda noticed that Roberta and Edward had shared a quick look. Roberta noticed that Leonardo and Esmeralda had noticed that look and said, "We all know, don't we?"

Esmeralda was paralyzed with distress. She looked at Leonardo who turned to the Van Ardens and sighed deeply. "We weren't sure until last night but, yes, we know."

Esmeralda jumped into the abyss, "We are so sorry. We know this isn't right and you've been so kind to us. We understand if you want us to leave."

"Leave? Nonsense," said Edward.

Lance and Claudia had become aware that their horseplay was getting a little out of hand and had stopped it just in time to overhear Esmeralda's offer to leave and Edward's response.

"God, what's happening?" asked Claudia.

With anxious faces they entered the living room.

"I think we need to have a little chat," Edward said.

Roberta nodded. "We all know that the two of you are having an affair."

"Mom!!"

Edward jumped in. "Then tell us it's not the truth."

Lance's mind started to turn with escape clauses. Then he remembered Marco's admonition. He looked at Claudia who was both frozen with fear and certain that they must move forward or risk losing the rightness of being who they were. "Yes. We are."

Esmeralda burst into tears, turned to Edward and Roberta. "I am so sorry."

Roberta reacted to the anguish she saw in Esmeralda's face. "Esmeralda, please don't apologize." She turned to Lance and Claudia. "Come over here, sit down and let's talk about this calmly, ok?"

Lance and Claudia looked at the loveseat and a chair across the room. They were both considering whether sitting across the room from each other might be a good idea, but their exchanged look solidified that if they were to make a case for their oneness, the loveseat was the only answer. They sat and Lance took Claudia's hand.

Their words spilled out effortlessly and with great intensity as they described their surprise at discovering how much they liked just talking with each other the night of the rain forest party; how they were both drawn by an intensity of feelings that neither had ever experienced. Lance made it clear that it was he who took the initiative. Finishing each other's sentences, they seamlessly wove the images and experiences back and forth to tell a story that spellbound everyone in the room. They described how they had decided after that first night together that it wasn't right and should never happen again. They spoke of how they were both anguished about doing what, in ending it, seemed right but felt so wrong; how they had both been committed to going their separate ways.

"We had both decided it was over," Lance said, "and it would have been but then something really awesome happened. I had this amazing dream."

"So did I," Claudia said. "The exact same dream."

By this time the atmosphere in the living room of the Van Arden guest house was charged.

"It's true. By accident we found out we both had the exact same dream."

Claudia continued. "We were both in this lofty room. It was like a cathedral but with tall, tall bookcases like a library. Big, iron chandeliers with candles and torches along the walls. Lance was sitting at a table and I was sitting across from him with a group of other people."

"I didn't know Claudia was there at first. I was like signing a scroll with one of those quill-type pens."

"Then I signed it too," Claudia said. "We were sitting on cushions by a triangular table. Lance was here," she said pointing, "I was here and there was a..." She turned to Lance. "How do we describe him?"

"Some sort of teacher. He had on a white robe and was like transparent."

"Luminous," Claudia corrected.

"Luminous," Lance continued. "He was kneeling at the third side of the table."

"And there was this extraordinary music."

"Like a choir. "And the awesome sound of it was..." He paused. "It gives me goose bumps just to think about it."

"Then," said Claudia, "the luminous man took out a sharp stone..."

Lance interrupted. "He called it lapis lazuli."

"He turned our arms over and made a cut on Lance's wrist and on mine and put our hands together like this." They demonstrated.

"A blood covenant," Lance said. "Then the whole roof opened up and we floated up and out into the light together."

"I know this all sounds strange to you," Claudia said, "but the next day we both had cuts on our arms. See?" she extended her arm, "You can still see a mark there."

Lance held out his arm and said, "Mine too." He took Claudia's hand. The marks touched when they brought their arms together.

"After all this," Lance said, "how can we not believe it's our destiny to be together?"

Their story told, they paused and searched the faces in the room. Esmeralda's eyes glistened. She crossed herself. Roberta wiped away tears. Leonardo sat with his hand over his mouth to mask his emotions. Edward stared at his son as if he'd never really known him. Lance glanced at Maria. She too was crying.

Edward finally spoke. "I don't know what to think. In any other circumstances involving anyone but my 18-year-old son, I'd say that is probably the most romantic story I've ever heard. But it's also scary as hell. This is way beyond my comprehension. Claudia, forgive me. I don't mean to be insulting, but there's a lot to digest here and we need some answers." He turned to Lance, gave him a *don't bullshit me* look and asked, "Son, you're sure this is not some kind of cult thing you've gotten yourself involved in? One of these things I read about with kids slashing themselves?"

"Dad, no!"

"Your father and I have been very conflicted with what we thought was going on between you. We had no idea it was this…deep. If you want us to understand this we need to know more about the circumstances. Were the two of you together when you had the dream? I mean sleeping in the same bed? The truth."

Lance was confused. "No, Mom. I was here at home."

"And I was at home too," Claudia said. "We didn't even know we'd had the same dream until days later. We'd already decided we couldn't continue on with anything between us and we had said goodbye to each other. I went over to cry on my neighbor Monica's shoulder. She's the one who noticed the cut on my wrist and then I remembered that it happened in a dream and that Lance was in the dream too. I just thought it was wishful thinking."

Lance said, "Me too. I wrote about it in my diary. I turned it in to Claudia the next day."

"And when I read it, things started coming back. At first I was horrified. I called him in a panic."

"Dad, remember I got a call while we were playing tennis and I rushed off? She was panicked."

"He came over and we went through the dream moment by moment and that's when we knew this was something way beyond physical attraction."

"I don't understand," Edward said. "How can two people have the same dream?"

"*La Bruja.*" Esmeralda crossed herself again. They all looked at her. "*La madre de Leonardo*—his mother had the same dreams as his father…" She looked at Leonardo. "I don't know how to explain in English."

Leonardo responded. "My mother was a *bruja*. She made magic and cures for sick people. My father told me he and my mother had the same dreams." He turned to Claudia. "I never told you this, *mija*, but God help us, one was like yours. The man of light, the *pacto de sangre*—blood…what did you call it?"

"Covenant. Blood covenant."

"They married 21 days after the dream."

"I've got goose bumps," Roberta said.

"Twenty one years after they married, they both had another dream that a terrible earthquake would destroy our village on the 21st day of the seventh month. They warned everyone in the village. Most people laughed at them. But a lot of people knew she made good predictions and those people left the village with us before July 21st. Many people died in the earthquake. We survived. But my father died 21 days later."

"Now," Edward said, "I've got goose bumps."

Leonardo continued. "The night my father died he told my mother he loved her and that their work was done."

Claudia took Lance's hand. "Something has happened to us that we don't understand. We have to find out why."

"Last night we decided that we can't do it alone," Lance said. "We can't do it in secret."

"And we decided to tell you because we can't do it without all of you."

"This is going to take some digesting," Edward said.

Roberta shook her head with a resigned smile. "I feel like I'm in a movie on the SyFy channel. Dreams, witches, miracles, and things that go bump in the dark are one thing, but let's look at the real world, here. Whether or not we support this, your 26-year-old daughter and our 18-year-old son cannot continue as teacher and student."

Edward nodded. "*Mija*, they could send you to prison for this!"

"I don't think so," Edward said. "Lance is 18 so he's legal. But, we're a very high profile family and if the tabloids ever got hold of this it would be dreadful for all of us. At the very least the school would be forced to fire you," he said to Claudia. "Do you think anyone there suspects?"

Lance and Claudia looked at each other sheepishly. "When we were in the supermarket last night the principal saw us together."

"And Lance had put his arm around me to make me feel better."

"Good Lord," said Roberta.

"I think I handled it though," Lance said. "I made him feel guilty about getting the wrong idea about what he saw."

"He even made him apologize to me."

Edward was smiling. "I have to admit, I'm enjoying the image."

Roberta was less caught up in the humor of Principal Adashek's humiliation. "Nonetheless, whatever you did with him, or to him, it was still based on a lie. This is a man you don't trifle with. You both have put yourselves and all of us in a very untenable situation."

Leonardo said, "*Mija*, you must resign from your job."

"You can come back home with us," Esmeralda said.

Lance said, "No! That would make them right!"

"Them, who?" Roberta asked.

"Them. Adashek and…and everyone who can't understand that what's happening to us is good."

Edward shook his head. "Even if we give you our blessing— and I admit it would be hard not to after what you've told us tonight—out there it's a scandal if you are having an affair with your student. You can't ignore this. Even if you ended it now, which I'm not sure either of you could do or should do under the circumstances, the risk is still there. I'm afraid I have to agree with your father, Claudia. You have to resign."

"You made the right choice to tell us," Roberta said. "And you're very right that you can't do this without us. Now we have to figure out how to proceed."

Lance and Claudia had finally allowed the real world into their private bubble and it had burst. Their romantic little world where nothing could touch what they had was gone forever.

Edward turned to Maria. "Maria, what do you think?"

Maria had listened raptly to the momentous unfolding of the story. She stifled a sob and covered her face with her hands.

Lance rushed to her side. "Nana, what's wrong?"

Maria threw her arms around Lance and hugged him as if he were being led to the gallows. She released him and looked into his eyes. "You are not my *niño* any more, Mr. Lance. You grew up." He smiled at her as she wiped her tears away. "You both have heads in a hole in the ground like ostrich." She turned to Claudia. "Miss Claudia, Mr. Edward is right. You cannot be teacher to Mr. Lance and be also his *alma gemela*."

Lance looked confused. Claudia translated. "Soul mate. Gracias, Señora. You are right. You are all right. I'm sorry we've had our head in the sand. I don't know what to do. If I quit my job…"

"Come home with us until Christmas," Leonardo said. "I have to figure out what to do with the restaurant and I could use your help for awhile."

"Claudia," Roberta said, "maybe your father is right. It might help us all get a little distance on this so we can think straight. I'm not saying this to keep you apart." She looked around the room to include Edward, Maria and the de la Rosas. "I think we're all convinced that conventional wisdom doesn't work here."

Everyone nodded.

"Son, I think I can speak for all of us in saying that we all want to do what's right for you both. I have no idea what that is right now. You've got high school to finish, then college…"

"I know, Dad. We've talked about it and we don't know what to do either. But we do know I have to go to college and we also know we need to be together. We'll figure it out."

"This has been quite a shock to all of us," Edward said. "Leonardo and Esmeralda are planning on going back to Michigan in another week. Then there are three more weeks before your Christmas break. Claudia can resign and take care of things here this week and go back with them. Then we can figure out where to go from there. Maybe Claudia needs to stay there awhile to help out. If this relationship is as important to you both as it seems right now, it'll all sort out." He turned to Leonardo and Esmeralda. "What do you both think?"

"*Sí*. Yes," said Leonardo."

Esmeralda said, "God gives us what we need. He gave you something we don't understand. If you and Lance are really *almas gemelas*, then he will show you the way."

Claudia turned to Lance with tears in her eyes. "I think somewhere deep down we both knew it might come to this, didn't we?" Lance nodded as she continued. "I do have to resign and I'll go back home with you for awhile at least." She looked at Lance. "Mama is right too. I know we're meant to be together and we'll find a way."

Claudia's resignation letter got written and the families settled into the overstuffed furniture staring silently into the gentle flames of the dying fire. Maria served some mud pies and Kahlúa—comfort food to take the edge off of a stressful but somehow wonderful day. Roberta mused to herself that in spite of her previously vengeful quest to get to the bottom of something that seemed so very wrong, she was now enjoying the feeling of an extended family with people who were brought together in the most unlikely of circumstances. Norman Rockwell couldn't have painted a more genuine family tableau.

Chapter 34

After the tumultuous revelations of the day, Roberta found that sleep would not come, even after two Tylenol PM. How could she and Edward even consider approving their firstborn's dalliance with his teacher? It flew against every fiber of her responsible parenting instincts. It defied the first and foremost rule of secondary school education that you don't, under any circumstances, have sexual relations with a student. What was keeping her from absolutely forbidding Lance from continuing this thing? Was she afraid that they might run off together? Would Lance give up the golden future they had planned for him for a piece of ass? Was she afraid of the scandal that would swallow their family if word got out? Had they gotten much too fond of Claudia's parents? Had Claudia charmed them all into believing this was a good thing?

There was all of that, but bottom line, she concluded, it all hung on that damned identical dream. Was there really something bigger going on here? Had they really been brought together on some mystical journey?

She finally went downstairs to the study, fired up the computer and Googled mutual dreams. Kipling, she found, had written "Brushwood Boy" about shared dreaming and finding a soul mate. *Fiction*, she thought. *What's real?* The number of hits on dreaming and mutual dreams was staggering. Blogs, books, clubs of people training themselves to dream together, etheric, shamanic dreaming and on and on. Roberta found it confusing and not answering her fundamental question: *Was Lance and Claudia's experience a good thing?* After two exhausting hours of this she finally got to sleep, vowing that tomorrow she would continue the sleuthing.

As Roberta frowned into the dregs of her morning coffee, she brooded about what to do next. In the mid-'70s she'd been charmed by a coalminer's wife from Pittsburgh who claimed to channel an entity who imparted grand wisdom and personal advice. She wished she had someone like that who could give her some other-worldly advice about Lance and Claudia since the problem seemed to be an other-worldly problem. As she thought about identical dreams and worried if what was happening was good for Lance, the phone rang. Caller ID said "Cerasuolo." She sighed and answered.

"Umm, could I talk to Lance, please?"

"I don't know if he's up yet."

"I tried his cell and he didn't pick up."

"Who's calling?"

"Is this Mrs. Van Arden?"

"Yes it is, but you didn't answer my question."

"I'm Marco."

"The psychic friend."

"Yes."

"Did Lance tell you he told us about the dream?"

"No, but I knew."

"Did you, now?" She laughed. "I'll have him call you when he gets up."

"Actually, I really called to ask him if I could talk to you."

"Oh?"

"But, here we are talking."

"*You* are. I'm not so sure *we* are."

"Mrs. Van Arden, do you believe in spirit guides?"

"Yes and no."

"Your mother has asked do you remember the *castello*, the castle?"

Roberta could feel herself blanch. The castle was her secret hiding place in the attic behind the stack of old mattresses where her father could not find her when he was in one of his moods. No one ever knew about the castle except her mother, whom she told many years later.

Marco responded to the silence. "I'm sorry, *signora*, but they tell me things sometimes so people will listen."

"I'm listening. What's the message?"

"Just that it *is* good."

"What?"

"They say it's your question. You asked if it was good and it is."

Chapter 35

Adashek drove into the school parking lot an hour earlier than usual, rushing to his office to drop off his briefcase before heading for Claudia's classroom to search for Lance's diary. On his desk he found a sealed envelope that said, "To Principal Adashek, From Claudia de la Rosa". He opened it and read:

> *Sunday Evening*
> *Dear Mr. Adashek:*
> *I am sorry to inform you that as a result of my father's heart attack on Thanksgiving, it is necessary for me to accompany my parents back to Michigan and assist them in running our family business until my father has fully recovered. I'm, therefore, sadly tendering my resignation.*
> *I have truly enjoyed my brief time here. This is a wonderful school and I've enjoyed my association with it. Our family friends, the Van Ardens, whose son Lance, as you recall, recounted our plight to you on Saturday evening, have been very kind to my parents during this difficult period. My parents have been staying at their home since the heart attack. Mr. and Mrs. Van Arden have asked me to let you know that, if my immediate departure causes any additional costs in finding a replacement for me, they would be happy to make a contribution to the school to cover such costs. Whether that's the case or not, they have asked me to let you know that their endowment contribution this year should more than make up for any difficulty my leaving should cause the school.*
> *I plan to come in early this morning to drop this letter off before you get in so you have sufficient time to get a substitute*

teacher. By the time you get in I'm sure I will be in my
classroom. If you need to speak with me please let me know.
   Yours truly,
   Claudia de la Rosa

Even though Adashek felt that a potential problem had likely been averted for now, he concluded that if there was something going on between Claudia de la Rosa and Lance Van Arden he would be seen as remiss in his duties if it came out later and he had no knowledge of it. He would have to find a way to see Lance's diary.

Lance's class had assembled noisily as usual, but when Claudia stood up from her desk and rapped her pointer on it they sensed something that quieted them immediately. They had developed a respect for her and were stunned when she announced her departure.

"Why?" wailed Dutch who had come to trust a teacher for the first time in his life.

"My dad had a heart attack on Thanksgiving and I need to go back to Michigan to help out in their restaurant until he gets better."

"Will you come back?" Dutch asked.

"I don't know," she replied. "Probably not." She looked at Lance. "At times life gets complicated and you just have to follow your heart. Last night I was feeling sorry for myself. Then I remembered something Winston Churchill once said." She smiled. "You know me, I can't get through a class without my literary quotes."

They laughed. Quotes were gifts she gave them to make them understand an obscure idea. They had grown to love them.

"Churchill said, 'For myself I am an optimist—it does not seem to be much use being anything else.' So I decided to be optimistic even though leaving all of you is very hard. I've really loved being your teacher. When I moved out here from Michigan I thought I was embarked upon a whole new adventure. And I was. I am." Again a fleeting look toward Lance. "It's been more of an adventure than I could possibly explain. I'm really going to miss you guys."

The girls had gotten misty-eyed. The guys were doing their best not to.

"I'm going to pass out everything from my files on your diaries. I hope you found the project useful and maybe even fun."

Dutch piped up, "Even I did." Everyone applauded Dutch's unlikely pronouncement. They gave her a standing ovation.

As she reached for the stack on her desk, Principal Adashek's secretary, Mrs. Travertine, breezed in with three Bloomingdales' Big Brown Bags folded under her arm. "Mr. Adashek needs to see you in his office right away. I'll mind your class."

"Thank you, Nadine. Just tell him I'll stop by in a few minutes. I'm in the middle of something right now."

Mrs. Travertine assumed her most commanding posture. "Immediately, please. Mr. Adashek was very insistent."

Dutch jumped to Claudia's defense. "She's busy. Tell the old dork she's busy." The class erupted in whistles and cheers.

Claudia held up her hands. "Class, class, please!" They settled down instantly. "It's alright. I'll be right back." She turned to Travertine. "Maybe you could just read something to them. Try this." Travertine opened the book Claudia handed to her and stared at it until Claudia closed the door behind her. She tossed the book on the desk, turned and shook her finger at the class. "You will read silently at your desks." She unfolded one of the Big Brown Bags and began to load the contents of Claudia's desk into it.

Lance restrained himself from rushing to liberate his diary. "Miss de la Rosa was just giving those back to us."

Travertine brushed him off. "Mr. Adashek wants to look them over before returning them to you."

Dutch was on his feet. "The hell he will!" He bulldozed down the aisle, grabbed the bag from Travertine, and dumped its contents on the desk. "Miss de la Rosa promised us nobody would ever look at these except her."

Travertine stepped away from the hot tempered quarterback. "Sit down, Dutch! These papers are school property and I'm taking them to Mr. Adashek."

That did it. Everyone was now on their feet with cries of protest, rushing forward to block her. Dutch called out names and distributed the work. Josh...Mickey...Lance..." Lance retrieved his with great relief.

Janie Roberts stomped her four-foot-six frame up to Nadine Travertine and hissed in her face, "Lady, you just made the biggest mistake you ever made." There was a chorus of *right on Janie, amen, awesome, busted.* Janie turned to the class and shouted, "Are we gonna take this shit?"

The class screamed "No!"

Janie raised her arm like a general leading a charge. "Then let's get the fuck out of here!!"

Claudia de la Rosa's first period English class found mob rule to be a liberating experience—a wildly expressive way to honor Miss de la Rosa.

Principal Adashek was telling Claudia about how very sorry he was to hear of her father's heart attack. Claudia was puzzled as he rambled on and on saying nothing of substance. He was interrupted by distant whistling and cheering and the crackle of the public address system. "All security personnel please report to room 312. I repeat, all security personnel report to room 312 immediately!"

They both hurried down the hall in time to meet the rush of students pouring down the stairs and out the main entrance. Claudia caught up with them. "What happened?"

Dutch shouted, "Adashek made her take our diaries."

Lance waved his manila envelope and grinned. "But she didn't get them."

Claudia looked up to see Mrs. Travertine at the top of the stairs, empty Big Brown Bag in one hand and the other two bags still folded and clutched protectively against her chest.

As the last of the group swept down the stairs and gathered around her, Claudia reached in her bag, pulled out her ring of school keys, handed them to Adashek, and turned to follow the exodus.

"Class dismissed," she said as she strode out the door like a rock star exiting the building with a swarm of devoted groupies.

Upon the mass evacuation of room 312, Mrs. Travertine had summoned security and security had called the police who were now swarming the building. Adashek was livid that something that should have been as simple as collecting a few notebooks had resulted in the school being full of cops. Students were calling parents on cell phones and the situation had escalated beyond all reason. He had never felt more humiliated and he was determined that Claudia's resignation was not going to be the end of his investigation.

Adashek tried to reach the school's computer technician, Clyde Hampton, to disable Claudia's e-mail account and give him the password. He was certain he'd find something incriminating there.

Clyde had gone golfing so Adashek summoned "Doogie" Demirjian from his sophomore chemistry class. Doogie was well known as the school's foremost computer geek. If you needed a term paper or if you wanted to know the likely questions on the next algebra test, Doogie was your go-to guy. With Doogie's reputation, Adashek would, of course, not permit him to be alone with his personal office computer so he assigned Mrs. Travertine to monitor his activities with a warning that she'd better not screw this one up.

Unfortunately, Mrs. Travertine got the weekly phone call from her daughter and her daughter's therapist to talk through this week's emotional crisis. She kept an eye on Doogie, but from behind the glass separating her cubicle from Adashek's office. Doogie, of course, needed less than a minute to handle the e-mail matter and after that he couldn't help himself. He was legally inside the school's system. Every so often he would look up to see Travertine, distracted by her heated phone conversation, looking in his direction. He would hold up a hand with an I'm almost done gesture, then keep digging at the innards of the treasure trove at his fingertips.

Doogie noticed a PC Anywhere icon. He clicked through to Mr. Adashek's home computer. Surprisingly it was not password protected. A quick scroll led to folders called *School Administration*, *Mom*, *Indian head pennies* and *love*. He clicked on *love*.

Like many teenagers in the internet age, Doogie had seen pornography. But this! Dozens of photos. Doogie had gotten so mesmerized by the train wreck of Principal Adashek's lurid fantasy life that he hadn't noticed that Mrs. Travertine had finished her call and had quietly entered Adashek's office. She was standing behind him as stunned and horrified as he was. She grabbed him by the collar, lifted him bodily from the chair and dragged him out of the office as Principal Adashek and two uniformed officers came in.

Travertine was hyperventilating and shaking Doogie as if he was a rag doll. "I caught him! I caught him red handed!"

The look on Principal Adashek's face said what the hell more can happen today? "What did he do?"

"I caught him watching pornography on your computer! Go look."

The officers sprang into action. Adashek followed them into his office. There on the screen was Rosie, age 12, posing in a calf-length, Scotch plaid school uniform split-screened with another shot of Rosie spread-eagled with the plaid skirt hiked up to expose things that no 12-year-old should be exposing. Adashek pushed past the officer in an effort to turn it off.

"Whoa," said the officer closest to the screen who had reached out to stop Adashek. "This is evidence." He turned to Doogie. "You're in deep trouble, son."

Doogie pointed to Adashek. "It's his! Just look where it's coming from. This computer is connected to his home computer and he's got loads of these fucking pictures on it. And they're all little girls. What the fuck is the matter with you, man?"

Needless to say, any suspicions anyone might have had about Lance Van Arden and Claudia de la Rosa were copiously overshadowed by Oliver Adashek's difficulties.

It mattered not that Adashek insisted he was just innocently curious and had never actually done anything with a pre-pubescent girl. No one ever came forward to charge molestation. It came out at the trial that he had never done anything but look at mesmerizing computer images of innocence corrupted. He would stare at these children imprisoned in the screen on his desk and wonder why they caused such desperately powerful feelings that both exhilarated and sickened him. He had read books to try to understand what was wrong with him, but he got no answers that would take away the need to look. Maybe the looking, he thought, might help him understand. If he let the temptation rise in him and satisfied it with pictures secretly compiled in a folder called "love", he reasoned it might keep him from needing to come in contact with real flesh. Only God knew, he thought, how hard it was to keep from looking at the real flesh that he faced in hallways and classrooms every day. It pleased him that his efforts had protected the precious girls entrusted to his stewardship from such as himself.

What he did not see, and what devastated him when he was honest enough to understand it many months later, was that someone had made all those pictures of little girls whose lives would be forever marked by the experience. Oliver Adashek had to admit to himself that, by witnessing the product of the photographer's acts, he had been blindly complicit in them. His looking was not as innocent as he had wanted to believe.

He had gotten a suspended sentence for possession of child pornography. His life, too, was forever marked.

Although Lance and Claudia had initially felt vindicated by Principal Adashek's predicament, they ultimately recognized their own part as the catalyst in his drama.

When they watched the TV coverage of this broken man whose life and career were in shambles, they speculated that, if they had continued as teacher and student, Claudia might have had to face a similar humiliation. In the minds of most people, there were no degrees of sexual indiscretions. A sex offender was a sex offender no matter whether love or lust got him or her there.

It did not seem odd to Lance and Claudia to feel compassion for Principal Adashek's suffering.

Chapter 36

Claudia's last week in L.A. flew by. The Van Ardens and the de la Rosas gathered on Friday evening for a final dinner together. Roberta and Edward hosted, this time with Waterford crystal and Limoges dinnerware certified to have once belonged to French royalty. The rack of lamb was delectable, the scalloped potatoes and julienned carrots superb. But something was amiss. Lance and Claudia sat next to each other holding hands under the table through much of the dinner conversation. They said little and their sadness was apparent.

Edward finally said, "It's not the end of the world you know."

Sarcasm was not one of Lance's usual attributes, but it got the best of him. "To you, maybe. You're not losing the most important person in your life. We're all sitting here like everything's normal talking about war, talking about the president, talking about the trade deficit. It's *not* normal. We're miserable. I know everything is supposed to work out for the best, but it's sure as hell not the best right now. You're leaving."

Claudia squeezed his hand. "Yes, but it's not the end, it's the beginning."

With the week's busy schedule, Lance and Claudia had spent most of their evenings with the de la Rosas in the guest house. Now and then they had sat by themselves in the garden. There had been a sweet and tender intimacy between them in those moments, but they hadn't made love since they'd announced their relationship. Lance said, "This seems really odd to ask this, but we've hardly had a moment to ourselves—alone. We need to be alone to…" He was surprised at the sudden surge of emotion that broke his voice and brought tears to his eyes. "…say goodbye." Could we use the beach house tomorrow night by ourselves?"

There was dead silence for a moment while the parents checked out one another's reactions. Lance's plea and Claudia's welling tears affected them all.

"This is going to seem a little strange coming from the father of and 18-year-old who's in love with his teacher, but I'm ok with it."

Chapter 37

Lance stopped by Marco's house the next morning. Marco had left a text message that said, "Congratulations. Let's talk."

Marco's mother met him at the door, her manner businesslike and severe. No unctuous greetings, no offer of refreshments. She tied a red sash around Lance's waist and said, "Come, please. Marco is making an exercise and you are allowed to watch."

She led him to Marco's work space in the guest apartment above the garage. They had to step around three candles and a glass of water at the door. A low triangular table dominated the center of the room very much like the one he and Claudia knelt at in their shared dream. Marco looked up and motioned him to a chair. Propped up on the bed was a nine-year-old girl, pale as death, her features drawn, eyes chili-red, body twitching, as if someone was shocking her with electrodes.

Lance was clear this was not, as Marco's mother had explained in misguided English, an *exercise*. It was an *exorcism*. Marco spoke some names and other words of power and commanded a foreign spirit to depart. And depart it did. No insane growling, vomiting or revolving heads. Just a troubled spirit looking to not leave the earth who was ultimately convinced it was a good idea to move on.

The girl's father who had watched the whole thing with doubt and trepidation strode forward and pumped Marco's hand.

"I gotta tell you, son, I don't understand what happened here and it scared the shit out of me. But, thank you! Thank you!"

Marco said his goodbyes and led Lance down to the pool. He collapsed into a lounger, closed his eyes and took several deep breaths. Lance sat in silence, realizing that Marco needed time to come back.

At last he opened his eyes, grinned and spoke. "Well?"

Lance shook his head and grinned back. "My life is feeling like I'm in some long, strange dream."

"Life *is* one long, strange dream."

"Mine feels out of control."

Marco measured his friend for a moment. "It's not. So far it's on schedule. My guides told you to be careful leading someone up a mountain, that it would not always be like it was in the beginning, that you needed to tell the truth and be a man of honor. So far so good."

"Yeah, but Claudia resigned her job and she's going back to Michigan with her parents."

"And?"

"What do you mean, and? What am I supposed to do now?"

"You figured everything out so far on your own, didn't you?"

"Everything except boll weevils."

Marco cocked his head in the listening mode. "What does a boll weevil do?"

"Eats cotton"

"What's cotton?"

"What??"

"What's cotton?"

"A plant."

"Which becomes?"

"Thread. Fabric."

"Exactly. Who uses fabric?"

Lance felt like there was something staring him in the face and he couldn't quite see it. "People. People use it."

"For what?"

"Clothes."

Marco raised an eyebrow and smiled. "I wonder who makes clothes."

"Van Arden?" Lance laughed. "Damn. What do I do with that? You always make this so frustrating. Always something to figure out."

Marco laughed. "Ain't life a bitch?"

Chapter 38

Lance and Claudia arrived at the Malibu compound as the clouds were beginning to build in advance of a storm that would hit tomorrow. That always made the sunsets spectacular.

Carlos was on the gate and waved them down. "Good evening, Mr. Van Arden. The lifeguard station asked us to let everyone know to stay off the jetties tonight. Tide's super high and the surf is way up."

"Thanks, Carlos. We'll be careful."

Claudia had imagined that the Van Arden beach house was not one of those narrow little houses crammed on a lot jammed against the Pacific Coast Highway that made up much of the Malibu coast. She was right, and once again overwhelmed. A manicured lawn led up to a modernist gem on its own little peninsula jutting into the Pacific. Its architect had a spread in *Architectural Digest* at least twice a year. The contemporary furniture was Eames and Roche Bobois, the artwork Ellsworth Kelly, Robert Rauschenberg and Andy Warhol, and the kitchen Sub Zero and Miehle. From the moment you stepped through the front door the expanse of glass overlooking the Pacific drew you in and worked its magic.

Before she left, the housekeeper had lit the fire pit on the deck and left a pile of beach towels and blankets inside a custom-designed, towel-warming chest. They walked outside and even with jackets zipped, the Plexiglas shield at deck's edge, and the blazing fire pit, the wind made it bone-chilling cold. The sound of the storm-stoked surf was overpowering. Lance had wanted to make this last night together memorable. As he put his arm around her, Claudia looked up at him and said, "It's perfect. You're perfect." She shivered.

Lance opened the warming chest, quickly threw the toasty towels over the double chaise next to the fire pit, flipped the heated blankets over them and invited Claudia to crawl in with him. Two thermos cups sat on the side table. Lance handed one to her. "Yes, I've thought of everything. Mulled cider. Cheers. No better way to watch the sunset."

Claudia smiled. "Cheers. If I didn't know you were a romantic at heart by now, this clinches it."

"Being here with you clinches it." A huge wave hit the rocks. "Carlos was right. Look at that."

They sat snuggled beneath heated blankets hand in hand, heads nestled against each other, sipping the cider, listening to the awesome power of nature and watching the eons-old beauty of a day's death. As the sun descended below the horizon they watched the swells begin to form in the distance and strain against the shore until they burst against the rocks protecting the house. Each roaring crash hurled a thrill of power at them. They could soon tell when a particularly large swell would be born on the horizon, overwhelm all the others and crash against the rocks like a mighty god's orgasm, sending a foamy spray 20 feet in the air.

"I've never seen it like this," Lance said.

"Really? Do you think we're safe?"

"I've never felt safer."

They kissed—gently at first. The next wave crash drove them into a deeper kiss. The chill made it impossible to even think about taking off clothes. But a zipper down here and some buttons undone there let their hands discover the places of ecstasy they had learned from their hours of practice. The energy of the tide was expanding their sensual boundaries.

"You counting orgasms again?"

"How'd you guess?"

"Kind of figured you're out to set a record."

She laughed.

Lance looked out at the horizon. "Look at the awesome size of that one. Let's go for it."

Their mouths devoured each other's, their hands accelerated the exquisite tension. As they approached climax they backed off slightly, waiting for the monster wave's eruption to push them over. And it did. As the towering spray reached them, the shock of icy water mixed with spent passion prompted joyous laughter.

Showered and wrapped in lush terrycloth robes, they attacked the chicken and rice casserole that had been left for them by the housekeeper.

"I can't believe I'm leaving tomorrow."

"Are you scared?"

"Strangely, no. It just seems like another chapter." She smiled, leaned over and kissed him on the forehead. "I'll be right back."

She returned with Monica's Venetian bag, reached in and handed Lance a wrapped gift. From the shape and size he guessed it was a book. "I brought you something so you won't forget me."

"Very funny." He opened it to find an antiquarian edition of *Songs and Sonnets of William Shakespeare*.

"It's the 1924 McMillan edition bound by Baynton of Bath, England."

He ran his hand over the raised bands and gilt lettering. "That's so cool."

"Check out where I put the bookmark."

She had written Forever on the bookmark which opened the book to Sonnet CXVI. "Let me read it." With moist eyes she read,

> Let me not to the marriage of true minds
> Admit impediments. Love is not love
> Which alters when it alteration finds,
> Or bends with the remover to remove:
> O no! it is an ever-fixed mark
> That looks on tempests and is never shaken;
> It is the star to every wandering bark,
> Whose worth's unknown, although his height be taken.
> Love's not Time's fool, though rosy lips and cheeks

Within his bending sickle's compass come:
Love alters not with his brief hours and weeks,
But bears it out even to the edge of doom.
If this be error and upon me proved,
I never writ, nor no man ever loved.

Lance said simply, "Our love is that ever-fixed mark. I have something for you that proves it."

She guessed from the size and shape that it was a CD case, confirmed as she unwrapped it finding a hand-written title on the CD that said "They Say It's Wrong."

Lance's band had been blown away by his intense performance when they recorded it. Jason had said, "Dude, that's deep."

"I wrote it for you." He put it in the CD player and pressed *play*.

They say it's wrong
To love you.
They say it's wrong that
You love me.
They say it's wrong,
But you and I know
Two souls in one
Are meant to be.

Not just the brush of your lips,
Not just my hand on your face, no.
When awesome passion's done,
What's left and what's to come?
We know,
We will show them.

We dream our dreams
Not their dreams.
Wild trip beyond,
We dream as one.
Take a step off
The cliff together.
Wherever we go
Our quest be done.

189

Not just the brush of your lips,
Not just my hand on your face, no.
When awesome passion's done,
What's left and what's to come?
We know,
We will show them.

I know I know
I need you.
I know I know that
You need me.
No stopping us now,
Forever.
Wherever you are
I'll be.

Only one way to start.
Going down on one knee.
Only thing you can do.
Marry me.

Lance reached into the pocket of his robe and retrieved a blue Tiffany box.

Claudia opened it and found a modest but exquisite diamond in a classic Tiffany setting. Her heart was racing as he took her hand and slid the ring on

"I don't know when or how, but whether it's soon or whether it's later, I know I want to marry you." He knelt in the classic way. "Will you marry me?"

There was no hesitation. "Yes, darling Lance. I will marry you." With that they adjourned to the master bedroom.

They snuggled quietly for awhile and Lance could sense that Claudia was far away in worried thought. "What are you thinking?"

"That everything seems so perfect and I'm waiting for the other shoe to drop. Life isn't supposed to be this good is it?"

"Who said? It'll only get better."

"Promise?"

"Promise. Starting now."

He led her into the marbled bathroom past the his-and-hers sinks, spa-tub and fireplace, and opened a door to the exercise room filled with the latest machines to trim you up.

She teased. "What, I'm too fat? You're putting me on a treadmill?"

"Over here." He removed her robe and his own and guided her onto the massage table. "I know you're the one who went to massage school so tell me if I've got the touch."

From the rack of unguents and oils he selected Kama Sutra Oil of Love and massaged it in finding all the spots that needed finding.

She moaned. "You know me so well!"

He worked her back like a pro but his hands strayed quite often to places no pro would ever dare to go. When she rolled over onto her back he worked slowly around the curves of her breasts until he could sense the desire mounting in the nipples he'd purposely ignored. There is, of course, something about the texture of Kama Sutra oil that quite accurately defines it as an oil of love. He poured some in her palm -as she reached to tease an erection that was as eager as her nipples. As he leaned in to kiss her navel, she arched her back, he mounted the table and she guided him home.

They were sitting in the darkened sitting area—an alcove off the master bedroom with bay windows permitting a 180 degree view of the curving coastline on both sides. To the left the twinkling masses of Santa Monica's high-rises; to the right the blackness of cliffs topped by mansions with a handful of lighted windows. Beneath them at the shore, clusters of cottages were dimly marked by the lights in a few of their windows. In summer the cottage clusters would be filled with sun worshipers and ablaze with lights. Winter brought only those who loved a December surf, storm-inspired sunsets and quiet walks on deserted beaches.

Claudia stared at the dim whitecaps of the breaking waves. "I wonder how many years it will be before all this is under water."

Lance looked at her oddly. "Where did that come from?"

"Global warming. I read somewhere that the sea level here will be at least three feet higher by 2100. We probably won't be around, but our kids will."

Lance sighed. "That makes you stop and think, doesn't it? People are really stupid. I don't think it's gonna change until we can't breathe, then it's too late. Damn politicians. They don't want to do a fuckin' thing about it because the big corporations own the government. Nuke 'em all!"

"What?!"

"I'm kidding. Makes you want to punch 'em out though. What can anybody do to make a difference anyway?"

"Do you recycle?"

"Me?"

"Of course, you. You're the only one who can make a difference you know. And if enough yous do their part the big yous will maybe follow along. So, do you recycle?"

"Maria does."

"Maria does. What do you do?"

Lance a bit defensive: "What do you do?"

"Are we starting to have our first fight?"

He smiled. "I hope so. If it's about saving the world it's ok.

"I'm serious. When we get married we recycle, we don't use aerosol cans, we use energy efficient bulbs…every single person makes a difference. We buy food not grown with pesticides, we buy organic t-shirts and clothes."

"Do you have organic t-shirts?"

She smiled sheepishly. "One."

"Well…?"

"Well, it's a start. If that robe you're wearing isn't organic cotton, then you're wearing pesticides on your back."

"You too."

"I know me too. So let's do things to change it." She slid her robe off. "What does the label say?"

"I don't know what the label says, but I say you look fully organic."

Her face brightened as she read the label. "Look at this. It is. *This product is handmade from organic cotton and dyes.*"

Lance laughed. "See, I am doing something to save the world. I'm wearing an organic bathrobe."

"Yeah, thank you, Mom and Dad," she chided.

192

"They're into green. You came to the rain forest party, remember?"

"How could I forget?"

"My dad's thinking about using organic fabric too."

One night a month or so ago Lance had gotten up in the middle of the night to grab a snack and found his dad in his study sitting with a lapful of organic fabric samples—fingering them, holding them up to the light, looking at them with the same intense concentration he used on the Sunday Times crossword. During times of extreme creativity Edward often woke up at precisely 3 a.m. and started thinking through a design concept or figuring out a marketing campaign. This night he told Lance he couldn't sleep because he had this idea about incorporating organic fabric into the Van Arden line but didn't know how to market it. Green was becoming fashionable, he knew, but you'd have to make some kind of spectacular marketing blitz to make people want to buy more than organic t-shirts, towels and bathrobes. Edward liked the feel of the organic bathrobes Roberta had bought to stock their houses. He liked the heavenly softness but more importantly, he liked his brain knowing there was not a speck of chemical corruption against his skin. It made him feel clean and good. How could he make people feel that way about an organic gown or suit or blouse?

"I have to find a way to make them want to save the world and look like a million dollars," he said, hoping that his son might make some observation or ask some question that might trigger an impression—something that would click in his mind and give him one of those flashes that held an inspired kernel of certainty. Edward had learned to ponder then wait for those kernels that would always present themselves if he was patient. It didn't come that night but Edward knew it would eventually. There was something about letting an idea and a feeling incubate in his mind that always seemed to bring beauty and reward. Edward had tried to impart this way of thinking in his eldest son and liked to think that it would help Lance find inspiration as he approached the life challenges he would face. Edward had done a good job.

Lance and Claudia sat looking at the black Pacific and its flickering shore line when the inspiration struck. "Holy shit!"

"What?"

"Marco. Holy shit. Marco told me to pay attention to boll weevils. He made me think about what cotton is used for and who uses it. It's us. Van Arden."

"What on earth are you talking about?"

"Our purpose. I was asking him about our purpose together and we got into boll weevils and cotton and…my God!" Lance had leaped to his feet and was pacing the floor as fast as his mind was racing. "I know what we have to do."

"About what?"

"About you. Your family. Your town. I know what to do." He looked at the clock. "Damn! 3:30. My mom'll kill me if I wake them up in the middle of the night."

"Whoa! Slow down. Tell me what you're talking about."

"Your hometown is dying, right?" He didn't wait for an answer. "The fabric mill—the one my dad used to buy cotton from—closed, right? Cotton!! Boll weevils eat cotton. That's why they use insecticides. It's harder for farmers to grow organic because they can't use chemicals. Factories have to clean their machinery when they change between organic and non-organic so it's more expensive and they don't have a big market for it."

Claudia interrupted. "How do you know all this?"

"I googled everything I could find on cotton after Marco told me I had to know about boll weevils. Did the guys in your town sell the mill and equipment?"

"I don't know. I don't think so. Who would buy it?"

"I gotta talk to my dad. I know I'm on to something big. Trust me."

His mind was firing on all cylinders. "My dad told me that to sell organic clothes he needed something to *make people want to save the world AND look like a million dollars.* There's a factory sitting in your town full of equipment and a bunch of people who know how to use it. And there are people who will pay more for organic clothes because they're from Van Arden. They can look like a million bucks and—the big AND—they can save your town."

Claudia saw it.

Chapter 39

Edward, Roberta, Leonardo and Esmeralda sat on the terrace overlooking the city. Maria had prepared a departure brunch of *enchiladas suizas* with *salsa verde*. She'd made the long trip to the Guatemalteca Bakery near downtown L.A. to get the *pan dulce*. They were enjoying the sweets and sipping their coffee when Lance and Claudia burst upon the scene. Esmeralda and Roberta, at the same moment, caught the sun's glint on the diamond.

Roberta seized Claudia's hand, looking at her son. "You didn't!"

"We did," said Lance.

Claudia looked at her mother. Her eyes said, please be happy for me. "I said yes."

None of the parents seemed quite ready to embrace the idea with kisses and hugs. Lance reassured them. "We haven't set a date. We know Claudia's going home for awhile, I still have to finish high school and I've got to figure out college plans. We don't really know how we're going to make that all work, but it will and sometime we're going to get married. We know that. We all know that." He looked from his parents to her parents. "Don't we?"

At last Edward said what he sensed they were all feeling. Yes. I think we all do. Congratulations."

Maria came out with plates of hot enchiladas and joined the celebration. Lance and Claudia told them of watching the massive swells and pounding surf and how they started talking about global warming and living green.

"And then I had this flash," said Lance. "Dad, you remember that time when you were up in the middle of the night when I came down for cookies and you were trying to figure out how to market organic clothes?"

"I do."

"Do you remember what you told me you'd need to make it work?"

"I remember that too. I said I'd need to find something to make them want to save the world and look like a million dollars."

Lance gave Claudia a see, I told you so glance. "Would saving a town from going bust work?"

Edward asked, "What town?"

Claudia jumped in. "Ours. Harbor Point, Michigan!"

Edward was already putting two and two together and Roberta wasn't far behind. "There's a dead mill there and your future in-laws restaurant isn't far behind."

Lance launched into explaining Marco's predictions about finding their purpose and his advice about boll weevils. He turned to Leonardo. "Have Jack and Tom sold the mill and the equipment?"

"No. It's all just sitting there like it was the day they closed it down. There was some talk about making a brewery out of it, but nothing happened."

"Dad, we need to find some way to get them to open it up and put people back to work to manufacture organic fabric. We could buy enough of it from them so they wouldn't have the extra cost of cleaning the machinery between regular cotton and organic runs. Even if we had to pay more for the fabric, we can sell it for more money with our name on it and people will lap it up because..." He stopped to let his dad process the thought. Edward finished the sentence: "...because they can save a dying Midwestern town and look like a million dollars."

Esmeralda was afraid to hope. "Is this possible?"

Roberta had been taking it all in. "Let's not get too far ahead of ourselves. But it is possible, I suppose, We'd have to sell an awful lot of it to support a factory. It would have to be part of our ready-to-wear lines, maybe using the marketing glitz of our couture line to launch it."

Edward took Roberta's hand. "Sweetheart, I've been struggling for months to find something new. I like this." He turned to Lance and Claudia. "And I like how it happened. It feels right." He reached for his Blackberry. "If Tom and Jack are at their lake house, I have the number." He dialed.

Tom and Jack had been together for 42 years and had concluded it was time to retire and enjoy their success. When Edward called they had been sitting in rocking chairs on the porch of the cedar-shingled beach house they had built on a Lake Michigan bluff. Tom had fallen asleep with a magazine spread across his chest. Jack was staring blankly at the sunset as the phone rang.

"Jack here."

"Hey, buddy. Edward Van Arden."

"Jeez, good to hear your voice."

"Same here. How's retirement?"

"Hate it. I'm so friggin' bored you can't imagine."

"Who's that?" asked Tom.

"Edward Van Arden. Wants to know how's retirement?"

"Tell him crappy."

"Tom says he hates it too."

"Good."

"Good?"

"You still have the factory?"

"We've been trying to sell it, but who the heck wants an old building in the middle of nowhere when they can get as good and cheaper in China."

"You still have all the equipment?"

"Everything. All but the 15 sewing machines we had in the annex. They never got used much and I sold them to this guy in Guangzhou."

Edward didn't lose a beat. "Hot damn! I've got 150 sewing machines in a warehouse in Nevada from when I scaled back the cutting and sewing rooms three years ago."

Edward explained Lance's idea. In 10 minutes they had decided to see if they could reopen the mill to not only make organic fabric but to train the workers to finish the garments too. Jack and Tom were not sure whether they could manage the overhead and pay the workers enough to make it work for the union.

"Maybe we can make them all owners, said Edward. I read this thing about co-ops in *Apparel* a couple of months ago."

Enough seeds had been planted to raise the hopes of everyone. Tom and Jack might be able to play again, Leonardo and Esmeralda might be able to save their restaurant and Edward might be able to realize his next big assault on the fickle fashion market. Roberta had always found Edward's ferocious creative spurts like this to be a turn-on. She was likely to share the sauna with him tonight—and the shower was likely to be hot.

When the Van Ardens and the de la Rosas made the trip to the airport you would have thought this family had been a unit for years.

Chapter 40

During Lance and Claudia's first week apart they used several hundred mobile minutes trying to quell their separation anxiety. Finding that unsatisfying, they decided to buy webcams. Lance talked Claudia through the setup and suddenly they were fuzzily together.

When the images first popped up on screen, Lance saw Claudia in a cut-off University of Michigan t-shirt and bikini bottom. "Wow. I hope you got the security software installed right."

Claudia pointed the camera around the room showing him the team pennants on the wall over the bed flanked by pom poms. On a high shelf she pointed out a row of collectible Barbies including a Ferrari Barbie, a Queen Elizabeth I Barbie, and a Badgely Mischka Barbie Fashion Doll in pink charmeuse and Swarovski crystals. "If I'm ever in desperate need of a couple of grand I can always raid the shelf for an eBay sale."

They discovered that the idea of webcam sex was more intriguing than the reality of it. As tantalizing as a cheerleader uniform looked on Claudia and as hot as Lance looked shirtless carrying grocery bags with *Where would you like me to put these, miss?* lines, they missed each other's touch.

*

Edward, Tom, Jack, and Leonardo were all working on their individual agendas. Edward had gotten the marketing team planning the SAVE A TOWN AND LOOK LIKE A MILLION BUCKS campaign. He spent many hours in the laboratory inspiring the chemists to develop organic dyes that wouldn't run and organic cottons, wools, and silks that would drape beautifully.

Tom and Jack met with union leaders to give them the good news. Good news that the former employees could be co-owners of the plant. Good news that was met with skepticism and negativity. They couldn't get their collective bargaining heads out of the box long enough to look around and see opportunity staring them in the face.

Selling the union on it might have been easier if Tom and Jack could have told them the essential ingredient of the idea. But it had been a strategic decision not to reveal the SAVE A TOWN AND LOOK LIKE A MILLION BUCKS slogan because it needed to be a blockbuster surprise when they were ready to launch.

Tom called Edward to report on the lack of progress. Edward, Roberta and Lance were on the speakerphone in the study.

"I don't understand what the hell these people want," said Tom. "We tried to explain employee ownership to them and everything you folks are doing to help. The workers we called seemed real excited, then these union schmucks scare the shit out of them with stories of co-ops that go belly-up and all this anti-capitalist crap. I just don't know what to do, Edward."

"Would it help if I talked to them?"

"Is there any way you and Roberta could come out for the meeting we got them to set up with us and the employees for right after Christmas?"

Edward saw Lance brighten, caught his eye and winked. "We'll be there, Tom. School's out so we'll bring the whole family. You gotta promise us some snow, though. If the kids are giving up our Aspen holiday they'll need some winter fun."

"I'll work on it. Maybe there'll be ice on our pond by then. Do they skate?"

"Michael's thinking about hockey if he can pry himself away from the Xbox long enough to tie his skates on. He'll love it. So will Jenny." He gave Lance a teasing look. "Lance can't wait to see the de la Rosas again. Tom, we'll make this work. All my teams are hugely excited about it and I'm excited about it."

Roberta said, "When he's on a roll like this he's never been wrong, Tom. Ever."

Edward gave Lance a wry smile. "And we've got a really interesting story about how Lance came up with the idea that was the catalyst for this whole thing." Lance gave him a *be careful* look. "We'll tell you all about it when the time is right."

They were eager to break the news of their impending visit to the de la Rosas.

Once Lance made the webcam connection and Claudia had called Leonardo and Esmeralda to her room, he wasted no time in preliminaries. "Guess what, we're coming to visit you right after Christmas."

They were delighted. Edward explained why and what they needed to accomplish, then the subject changed to Christmas festivities.

The de la Rosas had settled quite an extended family of relatives and sundry hangers-on in Harbor Point. Over the years Christmas had become a major event. They painted a compelling picture of a de la Rosa Christmas Eve. Leonardo and Esmeralda had a big family room and half the furniture had to disappear to make room for a giant tree surrounded by mounds of wrapped and ribboned gifts. At midnight everyone would exchange a hug and heartfelt *Feliz Navidad* with everyone else, moving from one to the next until everyone had made the connection. Then the gifts were opened in an act of good-natured consumerism, plates of tamales were passed around and the feasting and drinking lasted until dawn.

"It's too bad you can't be here for Christmas," said Esmeralda.

On the Van Arden end of the line Lance, Edward and Roberta gave each other puzzled looks.

"Is it possible you could come for Christmas?" Leonardo asked.

Without hesitation, Roberta and Lance nodded in the affirmative with a questioning look at Edward. He smiled, and as a chorus, all three said, "Yes!"

Chapter 41

The de la Rosas were both joyful and anxious about the Van Arden visit. Esmeralda worried that they had too little to offer in creature comforts if they invited them to stay at their home. The Van Ardens were, after all, used to luxury and a staff to satisfy their every need.

Claudia called Lance. "My mom would love to invite you all to stay at our house, but she's afraid it's not big enough or luxurious enough. What do you think? Would your folks be more comfortable at a hotel?"

"Where would everybody sleep?" There was a wry double meaning to his question.

"Well," she teased. "You and your brother will sleep on the sofa bed in my dad's study, your mom and dad will have the guest room and Jenny can sleep in my room. I have twin beds."

"Damn," he said.

"Don't worry. Somehow we'll find a way. But really, do you think your parents would rather stay at the Lakeside Inn? It's a nice resort not too far from here."

"Maybe. I don't know. Let me go ask and I'll call you back."

Edward and Roberta were on the terrace waiting for the sunset with their evening aperitifs. Lance relayed the question and figured they'd probably go for the Lakeside Inn.

Roberta asked, "Do they have room for all of us?"

Lance explained the sleeping arrangements.

"You know, we've gotten terribly spoiled with all of this," Roberta said as she gestured around them at the splendor they had created. "I think we have a need for something we don't have enough of here. We've drifted away from our Midwestern roots and the regular kind of folks we used to be."

Edward had been feeling the same thing. "I can think of nothing I'd like better than to hang out with Leonardo and Esmeralda at their house. We don't need more than a bed and a bathroom."

"I think a shared bathroom," Lance said.

"So what?"

Roberta hit a speed dial number on her cell phone. "Esmeralda. Roberta. How are you?"

Esmeralda and Roberta had talked often since they left Los Angeles, but Esmeralda was sure this call was about the housing arrangements and she didn't quite know what to expect. "I'm just fine."

Roberta sensed her hesitation and jumped right in to the matter at hand. "Lance just told us about your very gracious invitation to stay at your home when we visit and we'd be absolutely delighted to accept."

"We wondered if you'd rather be at the resort if you're on vacation."

"My dear, we're not coming for a vacation. We're coming to be with you and Leonardo and Claudia. That you want to share your home and your Christmas with us is far more important than any fancy resort. We would be honored to stay with you."

It was settled. The Van Arden family experienced a rejuvenated holiday spirit. Roberta had insisted that Esmeralda send her a list of names, ages, and relationships of everyone in the family, along with their pictures if she had them. With pictures Roberta could read enough about their personalities to pick a simple but personal gift for each. Since they would be flying by private jet, getting them all there would be no problem.

*

During one family webcam conference the subject of the engagement came up and how to let friends, neighbors and eventually the world know about it. They'd decided it would still be regarded as a scandal and that they should at least wait until Lance had graduated from high school before going public. Lance and Claudia had already decided that she would wear the engagement ring on a gold chain around her neck until they were ready to make the announcement.

Chapter 42

On Christmas Eve afternoon, the Van Ardens were greeted by a small army of de la Rosas who showed up to witness their Gulfstream arrival at the Harbor Point airport. Esmeralda lectured the assembled aunts, uncles, cousins, nephews and nieces that they were not to embarrass the family by asking to go out on the tarmac to see the private jet. Uncle Javier was the first to break any rule and did not disappoint. While Lance, Claudia, and Roberta went into the terminal to organize bags and get them stowed in the collection of vans the de la Rosas had brought, Edward invited the rest of the clan aboard the Gulfstream.

The younger children bounced on the bed in the back, the older ones crowded into the cockpit to marvel at what looked like a giant-sized video game, the men sank into the leather armchairs and the ladies oohed and aahed over the sheer extravagance of it all. Edward was enjoying the collective glee that was mortifying Esmeralda who had come aboard to police the mayhem. He said playfully, "Shall we take them all for a ride?" She didn't know what to say. Was he serious?

Edward shouted over the din to the pilot who was standing in the cockpit door also enjoying the family's delight while keeping a casual but sharp eye on the boys who had plopped into the pilot and co-pilot seats. "Paul, can you call the tower and see if we can take her up for a quick spin out over the lake and back?" The kids cheered. Paul did just that.

Edward dialed Roberta's cell phone. "Hi. Just wanted to let you know Paul wants to take us all for a ride."

Roberta laughed. "Yeah, I'm sure it was Paul's idea."

"Maybe we'll pop over and buzz Chicago."

"Spontaneity has always been one of your strong points."

The kids all had a great story to tell when school started in January. Edward became an instant hero to the de la Rosa clan.

Lance and Claudia had greeted each other with a chaste hug since they had decided not to reveal their secret yet. Claudia had been thinking about where the two of them could escape to have some private time. They were both volcanoes ready to blow.

With the Gulfstream joyride over, they divided up into several vehicles for the drive to the house. Claudia's 20-year-old cousin, Barbara, jumped at the chance to drive Lance. She'd been drooling over the photos of him she'd dredged up online from celebrity websites. Lance was nowhere near flirting with Barbara, but Claudia's guard went up instinctively. Barbara had opened the passenger side door for him. Claudia deftly grabbed 12-year-old Luisa and hoisted her in, steering Lance into the back seat. As they chatted casually with Barbara and Luisa, they rested their hands on the seat between them with fingers touching.

After 10 years of hard work at Cocina de la Rosa, Leonardo and Esmeralda had built a modest but charming brick house on a lot that sloped down to the St. Joseph River. Over time they had furnished their home with a combination of comfortable, overstuffed chairs and sofas mixed with flea market antique tables and chests. Walls were covered with reproductions of well-known Latin American artists. "Bordando" stood out as a singular masterpiece and was now illuminated by a halogen spot. Casa de la Rosa was cozy and inviting.

Snow had fallen yesterday and there was a light dusting on the lawn. Thin layers of ice lay along the shoreline of the river. As the vans approached the house silhouetted against the dusky sky, the windows glowed warmly. A wisp of smoke rose from the chimney and moonlight fell coolly on the snow.

Barbara took a shivering Luisa inside the house along with the rest of the clan who were coming down from the excitement of their jet-set adventure. Lance and Claudia walked to a little knoll overlooking the house and the river and listened to the snow-deadened silence. Lance shook his head in wonder. "It looks like one of those old fashioned pictures you'd see in an antique shop."

Claudia smiled. "Currier and Ives-like."

"Wow, I didn't expect this. It's beautiful."

She teased him. "What? You were expecting the Mexicans to have a shack with goats and chickens?"

He laughed and looked up to make sure everyone was inside the house. "God, I've missed you." They kissed gently and melted into each other. He pulled her behind the giant oak which had survived on this spot for a century or more. Its five foot trunk shielded them from all eyes. At 15 degrees it was too cold to remove a single piece of clothing, but it didn't matter. It was all about the kisses—kisses that said everything that needed to be said about the intensity of their pent-up distance from love.

The Van Arden gifts were added to the gargantuan pile around the tree. It had become a Christmas tradition that everyone gave Esmeralda a tree ornament every year. She'd saved every one, from the handmade ones Claudia had proudly brought home from grade school, to the franchised collectibles, to the ones happened upon by relatives at a flea market or souvenir shop. By now there were so many that the overflow was hung on pine garlands that wound around every naked railing, pillar and post in the house and at the restaurant. Roberta's first reaction was that it was a bit much, but once she looked at them and realized the emotional significance and the overwhelming love they represented she, once again, remembered why this family had become so important to her.

Barbara kept looking from room to room for Lance, and Uncle Javier wondered aloud, "Where is Claudia?" Lance and Claudia finally stumbled in laughing and shivering with faces reddened from the cold.

Barbara swooped in behind them. "You're freezing," she said as she gave Lance's arms and shoulders a brisk rub. "Let me warm you up."

Claudia took Lance's hand and drew him away. "Let's sit by the fire."

As Claudia dragged Lance away from her, Barbara caught a glimpse of a grin between them. "Damn," she said to herself. "That's ridiculous."

The welcoming party dispersed to go home and get ready for the festive evening ahead. The Van Ardens were shown their respective sleeping quarters. Esmeralda had insisted that Edward and Roberta should take the master bedroom and wouldn't take no for an answer. She and Leonardo would be just fine in the guest room. Michael dumped his duffel bag in the study he would share with Lance. Jennifer had brought along only four of her American Girl dolls and asked Claudia where they could sleep. Claudia took her up to the perfectly preserved girlhood bedroom they would share and found a place for them to nestle in the pink beanbag chair. Jennifer looked up at Claudia's doll collection on the high shelves ringing the room and resolved she would absolutely have to find a Barbie store when she got back to L.A.

Another de la Rosa holiday tradition was to wear new clothes on Christmas Eve. Claudia had told Lance who had told his parents and they brought along Van Arden's best for themselves and for Leonardo, Esmeralda, and Claudia.

Christmas Eve unfolded as promised. Edward gave Lance permission to have one glass of hot Christmas ponche loaded with apples, guavas, pineapple, sugar cane, and cinnamon, spiked with an ample supply of rum. Uncle Javier had amped it up a bit more with some Southern Comfort.

Aunt Guillermina, after a couple of glasses, was conscripted to take center stage to tell her famous jokes. They were in Spanish and off color, with double meanings that even the best translator couldn't make English-speakers comprehend. The Van Ardens found themselves laughing as hard as everyone else, carried along by an unexplainable infectious contagion. Edward and Roberta grinned at each other and shrugged. Roberta remembered a seminar she'd gone to in her Me Generation days where a Tibetan monk was being questioned on-stage by the latest New Age American Guru and all 3,000 people in the audience were laughing simultaneously at the monk's witty responses before they were translated. Something in the air.

There was certainly something in the air this Christmas Eve that swept everyone along toward midnight magic, and the tone was set by Leonardo and Esmeralda. These two had made a happy life for themselves and their extended family in one of the most unlikely bastions of white bread America. By their goodness, hard work and determination they had offered hope when there seemed to be none, given work when a living wage was impossible to find, and every Christmas Eve this family rewarded them with laughter and love.

Edward leaned over to Roberta and said, "I think we've found something we lost a long time ago."

Roberta smiled and nodded her agreement with misty eyes.

Leonardo counted down that last 15 seconds to midnight and the hugging ritual began in earnest. Single files formed in opposite directions. Young and old moved along them with smiles, hugs, kisses and heartfelt *Feliz Navidads* and Merry Christmases. Edward hugged Leonardo. "Leo, you are a true friend. Thank you."

Leonardo replied simply. "It is good, yes?"

"Yes."

Lance had hugged several cousins, nieces and nephews and was headed toward Barbara when she turned abruptly and hugged an aunt. What was that about?

Claudia put her hand on his shoulder and when he turned, she winked. "She'll get over it. *Feliz Navidad.*" They hugged for a good bit longer than a *Feliz Navidad* should take. She gave him a quick kiss on the lips when she knew Barbara was looking, spun him around and sent him on to hug Aunt Julia.

Leonardo rapped on his glass. "Our family has nagged us for weeks about what to get the Van Ardens for Christmas and we finally came up with something. We all chipped in and before you all go home we got you something you can do together—actually that most of us are going to do with you." He flipped open a poster with a single-masted vessel on a sea of white surrounded by people in parkas. "We're going to take you ice boating."

Everyone cheered and Michael shouted, "Cool! This is better than Xbox."

Roberta's gift choices made from Esmeralda's personality descriptions and photos were right on. Uncle Javier loved the contraband Cuban cigars. Aunt Julia loved the antique Portuguese lace scarf. Cousin Alex was the hardest one to buy for since his hair style in the photo Esmeralda had sent looked like a crown roast with alternating pink and green ribs. Jewelry he didn't seem to need since every available digit and protrusion seemed to be covered with silver rings and studs. Lance's band-mate, Plunger, recommended some appropriately noisy CDs and that did the trick. Cousin Barbara really did like the big box of Van Arden separates but her thank yous were muted by a constitutional peevishness triggered by Lance's apparent unavailability.

Barbara was only two years older than her niece, Lorena, and both their parents were reluctant to verbalize their worries that they had become the family's unholy alliance. Barbara was the ringleader. The two were generally bra-less in low-rise jeans with bare midriffs, drooping a bit more flesh over the waists than you'd find in *Cosmogirl*. They seemed to attract the local bad-boys. Barbara leaned into Lorena and said, "She's fucking him."

Lorena, the wide-eyed one, reacted. "Who?"

"Claudia. She's fucking Lance. Every time I put the moves on him she jumps in."

"Nooo!"

"Lorena, are you blind? Didn't you see the kiss she just gave him?"

"Everybody kisses everybody at Christmas midnight."

"Wake up and smell the coffee. They're doin' it." She uttered a theatrical retch. "He's 18 and she's old." She looked determined. "If I can get his pants off, Claudia's history."

Chapter 43

Familial warmth pervaded the de la Rosa household for the next few days leading up to the big meeting with Tom and Jack's former employees and the union reps. Between family events, visits to the mill and planning meetings, Lance and Claudia had not yet found a way to properly consummate the holiday week. Stolen kisses had become frustrating. Claudia managed to be present any time Barbara showed up with an invasion of Lance's pants in mind.

∗

The meeting was set for December 28th. Tom and Jack had rented the Elks Lodge's Woodland Room for it. They and the families gathered next door in the Heritage Room for a last minute pep talk while the crowd assembled.

Every stacking chair in the building had been set up and began to fill quickly. Like the bride's and groom's sides of the aisle, this group had intuitively divided itself between the supporters of the idea on one side and the union doubters on the other. When Tom and Jack entered the room, the supporter side cheered. The doubters applauded politely. The group acted very like a combative joint session of Congress during a presidential address.

Jack introduced the Van Ardens and explained the plan in the simplest terms he could think of without revealing the still secret slogan. The Van Ardens needed large quantities of organic fabrics and would also train employees to do the finishing. He and Tom would sell the plant for a song to a co-op in which all of the employees would have an ownership stake and they would manage it until they could train others to take over.

At that point Harold Hackson, the union rep, got to his feet, commandeered a microphone and began haranguing the crowd. "You hear that?" he shouted. "They want you to borrow money so you can buy their worthless factory. Believe me, I've seen this before. They can't dump the place and they want to cash out on your backs."

He rattled on and on about greedy capitalists until a shouting match started between the two sides of the room.

Edward took a mike and tried to calm them. But the mob mentality had taken over.

Claudia caught Lance's eye. She was crying. Esmeralda had buried her head in her hands. Leonardo looked beaten. Roberta looked like she could machine gun the whole bunch.

When Lance and Claudia compared notes later, they realized that they were both feeling that the "purpose" they believed they had found was evaporating along with the confidence in their reason for being together. Claudia questioned if they had been wrong about this, could they have been wrong about everything else? Lance wondered if his inspiration was misplaced. Was this a message? Had he done something wrong—not followed the path Marco had so carefully made clear? It was that momentary doubt that prompted a rush of fury in Lance, but gave way to a calm certainty that his vision was destined to work. It compelled him to take a microphone and shout, "Stop! Quiet!" The teenage voice that could spill out an awesome falsetto with his band had become resonant with power inspired by this challenge to a destiny he could not abandon. The room was reduced to awed silence. *Who is this kid and what is he so passionate about saying to us?*

He spoke calmly but with a focused intensity. "I'm Lance Van Arden. Half of this room understands that your town is dying and are looking for a way to save it. The other half of this room wants that too, but they're scared shitless of being taken advantage of. Both halves are right from the way they're each looking at it. But what neither half really understands is how this all happened or what it means to you and to my family, our friends the de la Rosas, and Tom and Jack. When you do understand you'll see how it makes sense because everybody wins."

Lance paused briefly. They were listening.

"My father had a great idea awhile back that he wanted to use organic fabrics to make a new Van Arden clothing line. But he couldn't figure out how to market it because it costs more to make the fabric and it would need a marketing idea that would make it possible to sell millions of garments at high enough prices to make it pay. He was up nights trying to figure it out and couldn't. I got up one night for a snack and he was sitting downstairs just staring at organic swatches. He said to me that he was looking for a way to make people feel they could save the world *and* look like a million dollars."

Lance took a deep breath. "I know you're going to think what I'm going to tell you now is really, really bizarre but hang with me. I have a psychic friend who told me I had to find…" He was looking at Claudia. "…that *we* had to find a purpose in our life and that the purpose had to do with boll weevils."

Someone laughed. Lance smiled. "Weird, huh? I laughed too and he told me I had to figure out on my own what that meant. I didn't know what to make of it. Maybe a bunch of bull, I thought. But he had said things to me other times that were right on. I mean, really right on. So, I thought give it a shot. I logged onto the web and found out about boll weevils and cotton and the problems with pests and chemicals and a bunch of stuff like that. I couldn't figure out what I was supposed to do with it though. Then later we found out from the de la Rosas about the mill here shutting down and all the jobs going to China and how Harbor Point was going downhill and their restaurant being in trouble because of it. Somehow I put two and two together and remembered what my dad said about finding something that would make people want to save the world and look like a million dollars."

A couple of people in the crowd on both sides of the aisle were smiling and whispering to each other. Lance relaxed. "I can see some of you have figured it out, right? We decided if we could get you all on board we could get the factory opened up and market the clothes from the fabric you guys make and finish. See? Your town is the key to the whole marketing campaign. We can get millions of people to buy my dad's great looking clothes made with organic fabrics because they can save your town AND look like a million bucks."

The room was buzzing. "My dad's got the marketing and design teams revved up. Our whole company in L.A. is ready to move. All we need is a place to make the fabric and finish the stuff. We need you guys. And you need jobs and a future."

Lance's impassioned rush through the story had more than kept their attention. They wanted to hear more.

"See how all the pieces fit? Tom and Jack still had the factory and were just going to retire and let it all go. They said they'd give the building and the equipment to a co-op that you could all own and train people to manage it. You can get government loans for setting up a co-op and get the business started up again. We want to help you get your jobs back so you can help us make my dad's dream of mass marketing organic clothes come true. It will work. We all know that. Tom and Jack can't even sell the factory as a brewery, for God's sake. Let them turn it into a co-op for you. Make something of it. We'll all be winners from this."

Lance's intensity had silenced the room and most of the audience was with him. Harold Hackson still had a mike in his hand. "That's a good story, son, but this could make your family rich at our workers' expense."

Lance tried not to show his irritation. "Sir, my family is also taking a risk. No one has ever mass marketed anything made of organic fabrics other than with stuff like t-shirts, sweatshirts and towels. My dad knows it will work, but we can't do it without all of you."

Hackson wouldn't give up. "Yeah, but what's in it for you? Why this town? Why not farm it out to China like everybody else? The fabric would be cheaper and you could still make your millions."

Someone on the supporter side of the aisle piped up. "Didn't you hear what he just said? We got a factory here. Save Harbor Point and look like a million bucks. That's the whole point! Let's go back to work!"

Hackson shouted over the applause. "That's just marketing. If they want the factory opened up, let them do it and pay a living wage. Don't let 'em sell you on this co-op idea. When it goes down the tubes you go with it." He turned to Edward. "Due respect, sir, but you are rich and famous and you're just looking for a marketing gimmick on the backs of my workers. I don't see any reason you picked this town other than we got a factory you can cannibalize and say you're saving a town. I think that's what's in it for you. What other reason could there be?"

Another couple of doubters chimed in. "Yeah, what other reason? Why us?"

The angry shouting across the aisle started up again. Lance took a deep breath. He beckoned Claudia to his side and took the mike. "Stop! Quiet!" It worked again.

"You want a reason why we're here to help this town? I'll show you." He turned to Claudia, glanced down at her neck where the gold chain and engagement ring were concealed behind her sweater and said, "Shall we?"

Claudia understood what he meant to do and why. She slipped the chain over her head and put it in his outstretched hand. With an intense look between them, he slipped the ring on her finger. The moment could have passed as a proposal. Turning to the crowd he said, "What's in it for me? Claudia de la Rosa is my fiancée. That's what's in it for me. I'm doing it—my family is doing it—for our in-laws-to-be. We are family."

After a beat of stunned silence Lance asked with a wry smile, "How's that for a reason? Good enough for you?"

As the room erupted around them he put his arm around Claudia and said, "I don't know if that was the wisest thing to do."

"It was. Look at them. And more importantly, you've set us free."

The Van Ardens and de la Rosas were elated that they had won the argument but worried that the unexpected announcement might mushroom into a gossipy scandal when people started looking at the age difference and found out that Lance and Claudia had been student and teacher.

Since the Van Arden publicity department had sent press releases to the wire services and newspapers to generate a pre-buzz about a new secret formula to bring manufacturing jobs back to the U.S., there were reporters at the meeting not only from the local gazettes and tribunes but from the Detroit and Chicago dailies as well.

It was soon up on the A.P. wire. Next week the tabloids ran ugly headlines like "VAN ARDEN STUDENT/TEACHER SEX ROMP SPAWNS CLOTHING LINE."

The Van Arden publicity department, believing the adage that any publicity is good publicity, jumped at a chance to book Lance and Claudia on a Detroit talk show.

"Do we have to?" she asked Lance.

"Not if you don't want to."

"It would be good for the cause though, wouldn't it?" she said.

"So far so good."

"Doesn't it scare you?"

"Shitless!"

She grinned. "Then let's do it."

Eva Gregg, the Van Arden publicity director, coached them to expect the inevitable questions about when they first had sex and if a teacher/student relationship wasn't wrong. She advised them to steer the conversation away and focus on the Van Arden Organics talking points listed on the paper she handed each of them.

The morning show had bubbly co-hosts named Rick and Terri. They greeted Lance and Claudia in the green room with charming smiles. They were flattering and supportive, or so it seemed.

Once the red camera light went on Terri introduced them. "Last night in Harbor Point, 18-year-old Lance Van Arden of the famous fashion family announced his controversial engagement to Claudia de la Rosa, his former high school English teacher, at a mill workers union meeting. It's caused quite a splash and we have them both with us this morning." Turning to them she said, "Good morning. And thanks for joining us. I have to ask you the question that's on everyone's lips this morning: Were you sleeping together while you were still teaching and isn't that wrong?"

There it was. Talking points flew out the window.

Claudia laughed. "Shame on you, Terri. You're looking for a scandal and there is no scandal if you have incontrovertible proof that destiny has intervened in your life and presented you with your soul mate."

"Well, that's unprovable isn't it?" said Rick.

"We have proof," said Lance as he pulled back his sleeve to show the scar on his wrist.

Claudia did the same and said, "Ever hear of a blood covenant?"

They launched into their story with certainty and charismatic believability. Rick and Terri got goosebumps at all the right moments as did thousands of their viewers, and more thousands as the interview was satellite-fed to affiliated stations nationwide. It became a most-watched YouTube video.

Over the next few weeks Lance and Claudia appeared on *Today*, were grilled by Larry King, charmed Oprah, and found themselves beaming with joyful smiles on the cover of *Time*, billed as "The Miracle Couple with a Purpose." Theirs became a fairy-tale relationship in the minds of America and the *SAVE A TOWN AND LOOK LIKE A MILLION BUCKS* campaign generated so much heat in such a short time that getting the factory up and running to meet the staggering demand for Van Arden Organics seemed nearly impossible.

Somehow Tom and Jack got everything working even before the co-op ownership plan was finished. The former employees decided to put their trust in them and the Van Ardens and threw out Harold Hackson. They dubbed the new mill and sewing factory *Spankin' Clean Clothes*.

The employee management committee voted to turn the factory's vintage cafeteria over to the de la Rosas. Vintage cafeteria was the real estate description used in the former sales brochure for the factory that really meant throw this ancient junk out and start from scratch. Leonardo, Esmeralda and their clan did just that, creating a multi-cultural ambience and adding pizza, burgers, and other customary American staples to their Mexican specialties. To keep the green theme consistent, they bought only organic fruits and vegetables, grass-fed beef, and non-antibiotic'd free range chickens. Their customers raved about how much better everything tasted—which prompted many of them to start buying organic foods for their homes, and prompted the de la Rosas to build a street entrance to welcome the general public to their successful new restaurant that they named the Boll Weevil.

Chapter 44

Lance and Claudia were together nearly non-stop. They had become instant celebrities and the primary marketing hook for Van Arden Organics. Lance and his famous family were used to media attention, but he'd never experienced the spotlight so intensely.

Claudia's prior dreams of fame had centered on her expected aspirations as a novelist. Their overnight recognition by everyone on the street in whatever city they visited on the promotional tour was overwhelming.

She countered vicious talk show questions and tabloid attacks with grace and humility. Her penchant for quoting famous writers about life, love, dreams, destiny and purpose delighted interviewers who knew their audiences wanted her to charm and inspire them. Amazon.com had a surge in sales for the writers she quoted.

Their popularity eclipsed Paris' jail time, Britney's latest arrest and whether Tom or Brad's marriages were in trouble. Lance's "They Say It's Wrong" became a Billboard hit.

They were invited to opening night of "Lucia di Lammermoor" at the Met. They found it beyond stunning to step into a box at the Metropolitan Opera and see people pointing up at them. A small group of twenty-somethings in the orchestra section began cheering and applauding. A few of the older, tuxedoed and gowned patrons in the Orchestra and Dress Circle clucked and shook their heads at the perceived threat to the Met's decorum. But it was clear that Lance and Claudia had captured the hearts and minds of a cross section of Americans who were looking for something to believe in. Pundits had opined that by being themselves and standing for what they believed in they had given a divided America, embroiled in useless wars and just waking up to the fact that protecting the environment does matter, a hopeful message of integrity and tolerance. They had inspired a new generation to not only think green, but, thanks to the teacher in Claudia, to think for themselves. As an engaged couple, they found legitimacy in sharing a hotel room each night, but they usually collapsed into bed after a non-stop day of interviews and public appearances. It was beginning to seem odd to them that they hadn't made love in the last two weeks.

Lance broke the ice. "Am I still your sexy stud?"

Claudia had wanted to break the ice too. "More than ever, but..."

"But, what?"

"I don't know. I'm afraid of something."

"Me too. But why are we afraid of something we're so good at?"

"Before, when it was just us, sex was the most important part of being together. Now the most important part of our being together seems to be what we're accomplishing for our parents. I started thinking maybe sex was what was meant to keep us together until we found our purpose."

"Me too. I can't believe we're so in synch even when we're both wrong. That logic is totally bogus."

"In my language," Claudia said, "I believe that means completely false!"

They laughed as light was shed on the absurdity of their fears.

"We have a lot of catching up to do," said Lance. Wanna take a hot shower with me?"

"Thought you'd never ask."

He docked his iPod in the travel speaker. Ever since that first night on the bench with "Casta Diva" playing softly as they sat shoulder-to-shoulder overlooking the city lights, that aria always provided an ardent stoking of the fires between them. Claudia dimmed the lights in the bathroom and turned on the shower. Lance found a rose in the complimentary bouquet the hotel had delivered and scattered the petals from the bathroom to the bed before joining her in the shower. Their hands lathered with fragrant bath gel found each other once again. With one hand on the small of her back, he held her tight against him. With the other hand he stroked her face and whispered, "I never want to stop making love to you."

"Don't. Ever."

Chapter 45

Van Arden Organics became so successful that other fashion behemoths like Lauren and Karan jumped on the bandwagon. Spankin' Clean Clothes was hard-pressed to keep up.

Lance had finally graduated and, with nothing to hide any longer, he and Claudia moved into the Van Arden guest house two weeks before Leonardo and Esmeralda came to L.A. for the Labor Day weekend. As they all sat by the pool enjoying Edward's perfectly grilled Kansas City Steaks, the conversation turned to where the wedding would take place.

Edward suggested their Beverly Hills church for the ceremony with the reception at the Beverly Hills Hotel. Roberta said that was too staid, given the uniqueness of Lance and Claudia's relationship. Leonardo was concerned that it should be somewhere the whole de la Rosa tribe could get to without too much expense. Esmeralda only cared whether it was in a nice Catholic church.

Claudia had been quiet during the wedding banter and Roberta picked up on it. "Claudia, we're barging ahead planning your wedding and haven't even asked you what you want. If you could have a wedding anywhere, where would it be? What's your wildest fantasy?"

For a moment Claudia's face brightened. She did have a fantasy but didn't want to say it. "No. It's outrageous."

Edward was intrigued. "Come on. Say it."

"It's not possible. I'd be embarrassed."

Edward continued. "What's not possible? Look around you, sweetheart, we're perched on the edge of a cliff overlooking Los

Angeles, surrounded by our outrageous castle-in-the-sky. Your fantasy can't be any more grand than ours. Money's no object. What's your dream wedding?"

Claudia looked at Lance whose smile was encouraging her.

"Ok. Don't laugh. St. Mark's Basilica."

Roberta laughed. "Venice! I'm not laughing at the idea. It's wonderful. Edward, my dear, you should know why."

Edward did know why. "After our first showing in Milan we took a side trip to Venice. It's the most magical city on earth. When we went into St. Mark's Roberta wished we could come back there some day to renew our vows."

"We still haven't made it back. But Claudia, if you and Lance want St. Mark's, St. Mark's you shall have!"

Lance put his arm around Claudia and said, "It's Venice then."

Esmeralda was overcome with emotion. "She came home from her senior trip saying she wanted to get married at St. Mark's. Can this be?"

Claudia pulled herself together to tell the story. "We got off the train and took a boat down the Grand Canal. It was just at that sunset hour, you know, where everything was golden and I felt like I was passing back in time through centuries." She looked at Edward who had used the word she had always used to try to describe that moment. "It really *was* magical. We got to Piazza San Marco and there was this wedding party coming out of the church. It was so beautiful. I thought…" She had to stop a moment to collect herself. "…I thought this is where I'm going to be married."

Leonardo had witnessed this with great feeling for his daughter, but with a bittersweet sadness that he would never be able to afford it. It would only work if the groom's father footed the bill and, traditionalist that he was, something didn't feel right about that.

Edward noticed and said, "Leonardo, I know it's customary for the bride's folks to pay for the wedding, but Roberta and I are rich as Croesus and it would be our great pleasure to do something grand if you'll let us."

"But we should take care of our family," Esmeralda said. "If we book tickets now, maybe we can get bargains."

Edward wished he could find a way for them not to worry about money. "Tell you what. I pay a huge amount of money to a charter jet service every year whether I use the planes or not, so if I reserve one of the jets to get us all there with our families, it's actually helping me get my money's worth." That was a white lie because just having access to the jets cost $15,000 a month, a membership fee with no flights included. Flights were extra—a lot extra. *Let them think it's free*, he thought. "I've also got a good friend who owns the Hotel Bauer there and I'm sure she'll just give us the rooms we need. So I'll take care of the transportation and the hotel rooms." Another stretch of the truth. He'd get a decent group rate but Leonardo would never need to know that. "There's this great restaurant, Quadri, with an orchestra playing outside on the Piazza. We could have the rehearsal dinner there. If you'd like, you can cover that."

Leonardo's ego finally salved, he smiled and said, "Yes, that's good. We will cover that."

Chapter 46

Van Arden dressed everyone who traveled to Venice for Claudia and Lance's magical wedding. The reception was held in a candle-lit 12th century villa on the Grand Canal. Guests had changed into period costumes that Edward had rented from Atelier Tiepolo. He chose to be a Venetian doge and Roberta was a French queen. Maria sat at the head table with the family, dressed as a Spanish contessa.

The gala garnered a centerfold spread in *Italian Vogue*.

Monica, delighted to have been invited to this happy ending, sang at the reception with a voice that could still touch hearts in this magical city as she had done decades before.

Sally was Claudia's maid of honor. In the bride's dressing room before the ceremony she laughed and said, "I was just thinking about that phone call."

"With the hippo enema?"

"I asked you, very bluntly, I think, if you were thinking of doing Lance?"

"Very bluntly! I think my exact words were that I couldn't possibly do something *that* stupid."

"Congratulations, Stupid."

Lance and Claudia adjusted to living in a fish bowl as best as any celebrity couple could. Lance was accepted at three top universities—Harvard, The University of Iowa, and Columbia. Claudia was offered a publishing job as an editor in New York so, of course, Columbia was the choice.

Life continued to unfold as life usually does, with unanticipated tribulations, tragedies, and triumphs.

Claudia sometimes wondered if helping with Lance's homework was what a wife should be doing. Lance sometimes wondered if dancing until dawn at a hot disco might be more fun than watching classic movies on DVD. They soon learned that Claudia couldn't stand Damien Rice and Paolo Nutini, and that Lance was not too fond of Maroon 5 and Madonna.

But despite the generation gap issues, they always seemed to find surprising middle grounds. He got her to appreciate John Mayer and James Morrison. She got him to appreciate Gwen Stefani and Arctic Monkey.

They enjoyed Sunday morning walks down Broadway to pick up bagels and lox at Zabars, early morning sprints around the reservoir, and Woody Allen moments of crisp autumn sunsets over Central Park. They suffered inside out umbrellas in sudden thunderstorms and steamy rush hours on the M104.

They were devastated by Claudia's miscarriage and her recurring bouts of fear-stoked rage that rose from panic at her loss of control. Lance's sheer determination to reach her in those dark moments brought her back from the brink.

Claudia's first published novel was about two characters transcending the surprise of bi-polar depression. She called it a comedy of terrors.

Lance loved Claudia's literary success, even if it somehow kept him from writing anything of substance for several years.

In the roughest of times, merely looking at the tiny scars on their wrists reminded them of a larger picture in which the moments of their lives played out against the background of a solemn and joyful ceremony they could never prove really happened, but whose reality existed for them as their truth. That dream was the truth that served them in good times and bad, the truth that led Lance to nurture Claudia's healing from the agonies of a lost child through the birth of a son and daughter. It was the truth that led Claudia to keep encouraging Lance to write. *What if I have nothing important to say?* he had thought through years of staring at a blank screen. Finally he remembered something Claudia had said in class on the first day of school. "If you know you have a talent and don't use it, you are cheating yourself and the world." She had pulled out her day-planner and showed the class a quote taped on the inside front cover.

> *Hide not your talents, they for use were made.*
> *What's a sun-dial in the shade?*
> *Benjamin Franklin—1706-1790*

Lance started thinking that he wanted his first novel to be about visionary dreams and the mysteries of life and love. He closed his eyes and took a deep breath. The hair stood up on the back of his neck and he got goosebumps. He realized what his story would be about and who his hero was. He saved the blank page as a new file entitled *SOUL MATE* and began to write.

www.ingramcontent.com/pod-product-compliance
Lightning Source LLC
Chambersburg PA
CBHW031953240626
47153CB00003B/966